That part was easy.

"She's a brunette with a ponytail. Olive complexion. Dark brown eyes. Black lashes and eyebrows. Five-four, five-five. Slender." He sucked in his breath. "Very well built." Great legs, but he didn't add that.

"She was wearing white shorts, a sleeveless yellow blouse and leather sandals. The heel strap on the right sandal is broken. Said it got caught on the accelerator." If he sounded a bit sarcastic, it was because he didn't swallow the story about her broken shoe strap causing the accident.

"Coral polish on her fingers and toes." He liked those touches on a woman.

"If that's the brief description, I wonder what the long one sounds like," Gideon said dryly.

Max frowned. The woman was too attractive by far. *His enemy?*

Checking his watch, he said, "It's time to phone Nikolai and pretend I don't know someone tried to wipe me out a little while ago."

"Max, this woman *could* be an innocent party who has nothing to do with the scam. But if she ran into you on purpose, I'd wager it's Nikolai's doing. You know he's gunning for you."

"If he sent her to do his dirty work, I sure as hell am going to find out."

Dear Reader,

I don't suppose anyone would fully understand the pain of losing a spouse except the person who's been through such a difficult and heartbreaking experience. In *Accidentally Yours*, Gaby Peris has lost her husband after two and a half years of marriage. Her family wants her to leave Florida and move back home to New Jersey, where they can love and support her. But Gaby fears that returning to the safety of her childhood home might cause her to live in the past for the rest of her life. When she's offered the opportunity to set up a new law firm in San Diego, Gaby rises to the challenge.

It is there, in San Diego, that she runs into a situation that brings a new man into her life. Someone different, exciting, dangerous. Someone who takes her out of her comfort zone and forces her to really live again. I know you'll applaud her courage. And I hope you'll thrill to the tension that crackles between her and the man who brings her heart to life.

I always love to hear from readers. You're the reason I write! Please visit me at my new Web site. The address is http://www.rebeccawinters-author.com. You can e-mail me from there. I'll be delighted to e-mail you back.

Happy reading!

Rebecca Winters

Accidentally Yours
Rebecca Winters

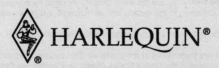

HARLEQUIN®

TORONTO • NEW YORK • LONDON
AMSTERDAM • PARIS • SYDNEY • HAMBURG
STOCKHOLM • ATHENS • TOKYO • MILAN • MADRID
PRAGUE • WARSAW • BUDAPEST • AUCKLAND

ISBN 0-373-70981-1

ACCIDENTALLY YOURS

Accidentally Yours

CHAPTER ONE

MAX CALDER DIDN'T SEE the white car through the left side-view mirror until a split second before impact. What happened next was out of his control.

The black Audi he was driving did a forty-five-degree spin. Its right back end butted up against a parked Buick. The white Sentra that caused the accident jammed the Audi's left back end. The three vehicles were now locked together.

A cacophony of curses in three languages—Russian, Japanese and Korean—came from Max's passengers. Trapped in an accident that wasn't supposed to have happened until they'd reached Palm Avenue two blocks away, they forgot to speak English.

Known in FBI jargon as ''stuffers,'' the occupants of his car had been recruited by a designated member of the Russian mafia called a ''capper'' to ride in the vehicle involved in the staged accident.

After it had taken place, the stuffers would file fraudulent insurance claims with the assistance of corrupt doctors and lawyers for bogus injuries. When the doctors received insurance payments, they'd send a portion to the cappers who kept their share before paying off the stuffers.

Though Max didn't believe any of his stuffers were seriously injured, no one was going anywhere.

"Khue'vye den'ki nastali!"

Sofia, the nervous Pole sitting in front, took the words out of Max's mouth. This was a bad omen all right, but not for the reasons worrying her or the others in the back seat.

Though it might have been a freak accident, Max couldn't discount the possibility that an undercover police officer had caused the collision for reasons that would come to light later.

Then again, someone in the mafia might have become suspicious of Max and had decided to get rid of him using one of their more blatant methods of elimination. If that was the case, they'd bungled this job and would come after him until they got it right.

A blown cover meant he'd be forced to kiss goodbye any more arrests carried out by a specially trained team of his colleagues in the bureau.

For the past year the FBI, along with a large team of undercover police officers, had been working successfully on an investigation code-named "Tangled Steel" with the U.S. Attorney for the Southern District of California and the California Department of Insurance.

For something to go wrong now when he was so close to breaking into the top echelons of the mob....

By this time a crowd of pedestrians had gathered. San Diego's El Cajon Boulevard was a busy street at any time. Noon was a nightmare. With his window rolled down, he could hear people shouting for someone to call 911.

He felt a tap on his shoulder from behind. "Anatoly?" the other man addressed Max in Russian. "What are we going to do now?"

Paranoia was the constant companion of the stuffer. "Relax, Sergey," he answered back in the same language. "Let things happen naturally. With so many witnesses, the person driving the Sentra will receive the citation. If nobody loses their cool, we'll be able to pull this off to our advantage and keep Nikolai happy."

Except that Nikolai Gromyko, a driver who'd been made a capper in the San Diego region a couple of months earlier, was never happy.

Though it had been a big promotion for him, he despised Max, who'd moved up in the ranks three times as fast and had been notified by Boris, the cappers' boss, that he was going to be made a capper over the beach cities next month.

Nikolai had wanted, coveted, the beach cities' position. The ambitious Russian immigrant had a personal vendetta against Max for being singled out for the plum capper job. It you did well there, you were moved up in the mafia hierarchy.

Since being made a capper, Nikolai had held all the business meetings for the drivers at his latest girlfriend's apartment. From what Max could tell, Galena Pedrova and her daughter, Irina, lived in fear of Nikolai.

After drinking too much, he would start to bait Max over trivial matters like the colored T-shirts he wore, the French brand of cigarettes he smoked. He continually looked for ways to embarrass him. His jealousy was apparent to all. When he couldn't get a rise out of Max, he'd go to the bedroom and turn all that venom on Galena.

The combination of various nationalities and mass paranoia among the ring members made personality conflicts inevitable, if not flammable and dangerous. Max couldn't help wondering if Nikolai's hatred had escalated to the point that he'd decided to take matters into his own hands and get rid of Max for purely personal reasons.

"Choi Jin's hand is smashed!" Hebi cried, unleashing another string of Japanese profanity.

Through the rearview window Max could see the Korean holding up his right hand at the wrist with his left. Getting hurt was one of the hazards of the business. They knew the risks.

But this was Choi Jin's first time. Like all stuffers who operated under multiple identities, he was frightened because something had gone wrong. Depending on the amount of police involvement, he might decide the outcome wasn't worth the physical pain or the kickback, especially when cash didn't change hands until the capper got his fee from the doctors and lawyers in on the scam before paying the stuffers.

It had taken Max nine months to work his way into the ring here in San Diego. Little by little he'd gained their trust. As driver of the "nail" car, the vehicle destined to be crashed into, part of his job entailed doing damage control among the stuffers. One change in plans and they turned into hysterical children.

"It's okay, Choi Jin," he said slowly in English.

The Korean knew about twenty English words. That was it. "Don't talk. Let me." Choi Jin nodded.

Max turned to Hebi, who spoke fairly good English and knew a little Korean. The two stuffers lived in the same apartment building.

"Tell Choi Jin it doesn't matter if we didn't stage this accident. He's to follow through exactly as he was trained to do and there will be no problem."

Hebi did his bidding.

Too bad Max couldn't use his cell phone in front of the others to alert Gideon that today's mission had hit a snag. Gideon Poletti, his best friend from their earliest days working together for the New York Police Department, was his major contact. By now he'd be wondering why Max hadn't shown up at the staged accident site.

As Max opened the door of the Audi and climbed out, a new gold Passat cruised by in the opposite direction. It was the "hammer" car, the bureau's name for the at-fault car. But for this unexpected accident, the Passat would have crashed into Max's car on Palm Avenue, the way they'd rehearsed it at the last meeting.

Oleg, the driver, made eye contact with Max before speeding off. It was his duty to get on the cell phone to Nikolai and report that their carefully formulated accident on paper hadn't gone off as planned.

If Nikolai was behind this crash by the Sentra, he would report to Boris that it was a major failure on Max's part to carry out a simple job. Anything to diminish him, and hopefully get him demoted.

Max could hear sirens blaring in the distance. Before police and paramedics arrived, he intended to check out the driver of the white car—who might or might not be the assassin hired to take him down.

"YOU'RE SURE you're both all right?" Gaby Peris asked, frantic because she'd been the cause of an accident that might have hurt a lot of people, not just the two pregnant teens in her car.

Instead of enjoying a warm September afternoon at the beach, it looked as if they'd be spending their time in the E.R. getting examined.

"Sí," Juanita assured her.

Gaby looked over her shoulder. "How about you, Sandra?"

"It scared the heck out of me, but I'm okay now."

Those were Gaby's exact sentiments. She could only pray the jolt hadn't done something that would cause them to lose their babies.

At three months, Juanita wasn't showing yet. But Sandra was another matter. Her baby was due in six weeks.

Gaby took several deep calming breaths. Thank heaven she'd told them they would have to fasten their seat belts or there'd be no outing. Otherwise there might have been serious injuries.

On the surface they seemed all right, just shaken up. Still, Gaby refused to take any chances where their well-being was concerned. Her fear now was for the people in the other car.

Several sirens wailed. "The paramedics are almost here."

"I'm not going to any hospital."

"Sandra, if they decide that's where you and Juanita need to be, I'll take care of the expenses, so don't worry."

Those were brave words considering Gaby was saving money for the future and lived on a tight budget. But she was the one who, however accidentally, had precipitated this crisis. It was up to her to pay any doctor bills. She couldn't expect Girls' Village to pick up the tab.

Like other similar volunteer programs she'd worked with in New York and Miami, the nonprofit organization, funded and managed by a group of wealthy San Diego citizens, had been in existence long before Gaby had moved from Florida to the West Coast. Any teenage girl who'd been abused, abandoned, kicked out of her home or had run away from home could have a temporary haven there.

Pregnant teens received medical treatment. Also housing and assistance during their pregnancies and afterward, until they could find work and decent day care for their babies.

When Gaby's job as a lawyer allowed the time, she volunteered at the Village. Three days and nights out of every month she was on call in case a trained dispatcher from the Village phoned her to pick up a girl in trouble.

Unfortunately these two girls were in trouble now *because* of Gaby. If it turned out there were medical costs, the insurance company covering her car would have to pay the bill. She could plan on her policy being canceled after that, but right now she had more

serious things to worry about than the outrageous cost
of another premium with a new insurance company.

"Aieee, Gaby! The driver of the other car is coming this way. He's very handsome—*muy guapo*—but
I think he's very angry, too. *Madre de Dios*." Juanita
crossed herself.

Gaby turned her head. Juanita was right on both
counts.

The tall, muscular man approaching her open window was breathtaking, if you went for the black-
haired, olive-skinned type.

If she didn't miss her guess, this one had Russian
roots. And possibly a little Irish thrown in, judging
from his eyes, which glittered a dangerous green. In
her line of work as an immigration and naturalization
attorney, she'd learned to be ninety-five percent ac-
curate in summing up a person's ethnicity.

Of course it took no brains to figure out the man
was furious that she'd plowed into his sleek new
Audi. It looked as if he'd just driven it off the showroom floor. She wasn't too happy about the situation
herself. To add to the misery of knowing she'd caused
the accident, she was now minus a drivable car.

The Sentra she'd bought used upon her arrival in
San Diego would be in the body shop for a while.
Too late to kick herself for not paying a little more
insurance money for a rental car to be provided in
case of accident.

He lowered his head to look inside. "Good afternoon, ladies. Is anyone in your car hurt?"

His deep voice possessed a sensuous quality.
Maybe it was because he spoke fluent English with a

noticeable Russian accent. The combination had a certain allure.

Up close in the tight black T-shirt he was wearing, he was even more breathtaking. She averted her eyes, surprised at her reaction. Nothing like this had happened since long before her husband's death fifteen months ago.

"I think we're all right. How about the people in your car?"

"Except for one hand injury, everyone seems to be okay."

"I can't tell you how sorry I am." Good heavens, he was attractive! "Here—I've written down my name and phone number, and the name and phone number of my insurance company. Please, if there's anything I can do, don't hesitate to get in touch with me."

He eyed her for a brief moment before taking the paper from her. "Thank you." After feeling in his back pocket, he handed her what looked like a business card. "I can be reached at that number during the day."

Gaby nodded and put it in her purse without looking at it. Her eyes quickly darted to the chaos she'd created. "I had no idea I was going fast enough to do so much damage."

"It was the angle of your approach as much as the speed. I am afraid it will require a wrecker to separate our cars so everyone can get out of their prisons."

Like many immigrants, he wasn't yet in the habit of forming English contractions. That, along with the way he rolled the ''r'' in *wrecker,* made her want to smile. It was a crazy impulse, considering the fact that she was mortified by what she'd done. There was nothing remotely amusing about the situation.

"Thank you for not yelling that the accident was my fault. I take full responsibility for it."

After a brief pause, "Your honesty is refreshing."

She could still hear anger behind his words, but who could blame him. She cast another glance at the smashed-up Audi.

An exquisite car. Unusual for an immigrant to afford one. Maybe he'd borrowed it from someone he worked for. Maybe without permission.

America. The land of wealth and opportunity. Unfortunately no one ever told the desperate souls pouring in over the borders, legally or otherwise, that their problems were just beginning.

Feeling guilty because she was one of those problems, Gaby darted him another curious glance. But he'd turned his head to talk to the investigating officer. Soon paramedics were huddled around the cars, figuring out the best and fastest way to get everyone extricated.

Another officer approached her.

"How are you feeling, ma'am?"

"I'm still trying to calm down, but there's nothing wrong with me."

"You're sure about that?"

"Yes. We all wore our seat belts, so we were protected. But both girls are pregnant and need to be examined."

"The paramedics will see to that right now. Want

to tell me what happened here?'' He opened the door to help her out.

The second her right foot met the hot pavement, she let out a moan. "Just a minute, Officer." She reached inside the car for her broken sandal, then slid her bare foot into it.

Though the Russian was half turned from her, Gaby got the distinct impression he was listening to her conversation with the patrolman.

"The girls and I were on our way to the beach. While I was making a left hand turn into the left lane of the boulevard—" she gestured behind her "—the heel strap of this sandal caught on the accelerator."

Indicating her right leg, she said, "I tried to brake, but my foot was trapped. In the process, the car veered to the right. The force my foot exerted snapped the strap in two, but it was freed too late to prevent the car from crashing into the Audi. I was the one at fault, Officer. No one else."

He shook his head. "I thought I'd heard them all, but a caught sandal strap is a new one on me."

"Me, too. It was a pretty terrifying moment."

"I can imagine."

"Needless to say, I won't be driving in sandals again." In fact, it was going to be a while before she would be driving again, period.

The officer didn't respond to her comment. He probably investigated so many accidents every day, he didn't have time for chitchat. That suited her fine.

"I need some information from you, ma'am. Let's see your driver's license first."

She reached in her purse for her wallet. Just last

month she'd gotten her California driver's license. Gaby swore that moving to a different state involved more paperwork than relocating to a foreign country.

While he studied her license and wrote down the particulars in his incident report, she looked beyond his shoulder. One of the firefighters had managed to back up her car enough to separate the others without requiring a wrecker. But just as she'd feared, the girls were being loaded into an ambulance.

It looked as if one of the passengers in the other car also needed to be taken to the hospital. As far as she could tell, all its occupants were foreign.

"Officer? Do you think I could ride with the girls? They're under my care away from Girls' Village. I'm sure they're frightened."

"You work there?"

"I'm a trained volunteer."

He nodded. "Go ahead. Someone from the department will catch up with you at the hospital to finish the paperwork. Your car will be towed to one of the body shops listed on this card I'm going to give you. You can call the number I've circled after nine tomorrow morning for the particulars."

Oh, joy.

"Thank you, Officer."

"You bet."

The passengers of the other car seemed to be in a great discussion about something. As Gaby walked over to them, the Russian broke off talking to watch her approach.

"Excuse me for interrupting," she told him. "I just wanted to say once again that I'm very sorry. If there's anything I can do to help you or any of your friends, please let me know.''

He stared at her through shuttered eyes. ''Everyone is fine.''

She knew they weren't fine at all, but for the moment there was nothing more she could do. The ambulance was waiting.

As she climbed into the back, she noticed that the blond woman and Japanese man she'd glimpsed in the Russian's car had started walking down the street as fast as possible. The door closed before Gaby had an opportunity to find out what the attractive driver and his other friends were going to do.

She felt so badly about what she'd done. But at least she could be grateful that everyone was still alive and in one piece, no thanks to her.

AWARE THAT the first ambulance had just left, Max needed to act fast. ''Take off now,'' he muttered to Sergey. ''I'll ride to the hospital with Choi Jin and phone you later.''

Like the others, Sergey's nerves were on edge and he didn't hesitate to leave when given his freedom. As soon as he melted into the crowd, Max walked to the door of the ambulance. One of the attendants was already assisting Choi Jin, who looked ready to pass out from panic.

''Which hospital are you taking my friend to?''

''The Bay Shore.''

''What about the other ambulance?''

''I have no idea. Maybe the driver knows.''

Max walked around the front to ask the man at the

wheel. St. Anne's, he was told. Then he climbed into the back of the ambulance with Choi Jin. The sooner the Korean could be seen by a doctor, the sooner Max would find himself alone long enough to make a vital phone call outside anyone else's hearing.

In order not to seem anxious to leave, Max stayed with Choi Jin throughout the long ordeal of getting him checked in to emergency. As soon as the nurse told him to go on back to the farthest cubicle, Max whispered he'd join him after he'd reported to Nikolai.

If Choi Jin didn't like the idea that Max would be out of his sight, there wasn't a damn thing he could do about it. Not with a swollen hand and wrist needing attention.

In case Nikolai had paid one of his cronies to follow him, Max didn't venture outside. Instead, he stole down a hallway beyond the E.R. that led to the pharmacy. There were a couple of doors on either side of the corridor. He looked through the glass of the first one. It was a tiny, unoccupied office.

After a quick glance to make sure no one saw him, he slipped inside and stood in a corner where he couldn't be seen from the hallway. Whipping out his cell phone, he punched the digit programmed to reach Gideon. He didn't have to wait long.

"Max—at last! All our guys were in place on Palm Street with the camcorders. The next thing we heard, you were in a three-car crash on El Cajon. What in hell happened?"

With that question, Max could cross out one of the

possibilities. The driver of the Sentra was *not* working for the police.

"I wish I knew," he muttered into the phone. For the next few minutes he explained the sequence of events. Gideon whistled.

"It might have been a bona fide accident. If it wasn't, then either Nikolai has decided to get rid of me on his own, or else my cover has been blown and there's a contract out on me. But I'm not planning to do anything until I find out all there is to know about the woman driving the Sentra."

"What information do you have on her?"

Max pulled out the paper she'd given him. "Her name is Gaby Peris, and she's insured with Auto-Trust. I've got a phone number and her license-plate number." He dictated them to Gideon. "I'll wait while you search for a home address."

"Hold on."

While Max stood there, he heard voices in the hall. There were people right outside the door. At first he thought they were going to come in, then they moved on.

Gideon came back on the line. "She lives at 1291 West Oak, apartment four. That's in Little Italy."

Max knew the area well. Little Italy had a great deli that reminded him of a favorite deli in New York.

"When I get a copy of the information she gave the officer for his incident report, we'll know more."

"Gideon? Do me a favor and send someone over to St. Anne's pronto. She went there with the girls— both of them pregnant—who were in her car. Knowing how slow the process is, I imagine they could be there a while. That would give me time to search her apartment.''

''As soon as we hang up, I'll put Crandall on it.''

''Good. Tell him to call me on my cell the second he has an idea of how much time I'll have.''

''Give me a brief description of her for him.''

That part was easy.

''She's a brunette with a ponytail, olive complexion. Dark brown eyes. Black lashes and eyebrows. Probably of Italian ancestry. Five-four, five-five. Slender.'' He sucked in his breath. ''Very well built.'' Great legs, he didn't add.

''She was wearing modest white shorts, a sleeveless yellow blouse and leather sandals. The heel strap on the right sandal is broken.''

Max didn't swallow the story about the broken shoe strap any more than the officer did.

''Coral polish on her finger- and toenails.'' He liked those touches on a woman.

''If that's the brief description, I wonder what the long one sounds like,'' his friend said dryly.

Max frowned. The woman was too attractive by far. *His enemy?*

''She's not from around here, Gideon. In fact, I have a gut feeling the mafia brought her in from the East Coast. Her accent is Jersey shore. If you heard her talk, you'd agree with me.''

''Shades of home.''

''You got it.'' He checked his watch. ''It's time to phone Nikolai and pretend I don't know someone tried to wipe me out a little while ago.''

''Max, you wouldn't still be alive if they meant to

get rid of you. This woman is probably an innocent party who has nothing to do with the ring. Freak accidents like this happen to millions of people every day.''

"I don't know. Someone higher up could be suspicious of me, so they planned this minor accident as a clever way to set that female in my path. It's the oldest trick in the book. Send an interesting woman to give me the come-on, then make me vulnerable. Pretty soon I've let my guard down and revealed the information she was after.''

"If she ran into you on purpose, then I'd wager this is all Nikolai's doing. Max, you know he's gunning for you. If he could find a way to cause you to screw up, it'd make his day.''

Max's jaw hardened. "If he sent her to do his dirty work, I'm sure as hell going to find out.''

"Plan on Crandall checking in with you right away.''

"Thanks.''

"Be careful.''

"Don't worry.''

"And, Max, don't forget—she could be a perfectly innocent woman who happened to run into you. I'll call you later.'' They disconnected.

If the woman *was* innocent, then the way she'd looked at him, her dark eyes soft and appraising, was flattering to say the least. The hell of it was, he'd felt an instantaneous attraction to her, too. Things like that just didn't happen, did they?

Max called Nikolai on his private cell phone. The other man answered.

"Da?"

Reverting to Russian, Max muttered, "It's Anatoly."

"Well, well. I've been expecting a call. What took you so long to report in, Kuzmina?"

"I figured Oleg had already informed you."

"He said you met with an unexpected accident." One *you* planned using the good-looking brunette for bait, Gromyko? Nikolai sounded euphoric about it.

"That's right. A woman driver crashed into me. She went to a different hospital with her passengers. I'm at the Bay Shore Hospital with Choi Jin."

"What happened to him?"

"His hand could be broken."

"What about the other occupants of your car?" There was nothing Nikolai enjoyed more than playing inquisitor.

"As soon as the police finished asking questions, my passengers left on foot. As for the Audi, the body is pretty much of a write-off. Though it was an unexpected accident," Max said, steeling himself to give nothing away, "we should still come out ahead, all things considered."

"Let us hope my supervisor, Boris, sees things that way. To allow a crazy woman driver to cause that much damage to the merchandise won't look good on your record."

Listening to the other man, Max was pretty well convinced Nikolai had masterminded today's accident. He couldn't hide his cocky, near-ecstatic state. Relief swept over Max that his cover hadn't been blown, but he'd have to watch his back from here on out.

Nikolai was an arrogant bastard, known for cruelty to his enemies and girlfriends. Every driver and capper in the mob recognized that Nikolai, the Russian from the Buryat Republic, was waiting for the day when he ran the whole ring for the Southern California area.

The man was a borderline psychopath and intimidated a lot of the members. Max figured it was only a matter of time until Nikolai became so power hungry he led an internal coup in order to put himself in command. He'd love nothing better than to get rid of Max.

"When I turn in the papers, you'll see that the accident was unavoidable and the woman was given the citation," Max explained in a calm voice. "How soon do you want to set up another incident?"

"I cannot say with any certainty. Possibly two weeks. As of now, your driving privileges are suspended. Because of your unfortunate accident, my hands are tied. If I were you, Kuzmina, I would sign up for a defensive-driving course while you wait things out. The bosses might look more favorably on you."

You bastard.

At this point Max was convinced Nikolai had set this whole thing up. Telling him to take a defensive-driving course was simply another form of harassment. It was all part of his master plan to prevent Max from being given that capper's job next month.

Unfortunately Max needed that promotion to reach

the top echelons and gather names to bring down the ring.

"How did you know I was just thinking I could use some time off? Two weeks sounds perfect. Thanks, Nikolai."

Judging from the silence on the other end, Nikolai didn't like Max's flippant comeback. To rub it in further Max said, "It will give me time to make a little extra money on the side at my other job. Have a nice day. *Dosvidanya.*"

Clicking off his phone, Max left the room to rejoin Choi Jin. He found the frightened man still sitting on the edge of the examination table wearing a sling. The X ray hadn't come back yet.

Max pulled twenty dollars from his wallet and handed it to him. "When the doctor says okay, you take a taxi home. Do you know your address?"

The other man nodded, but he still didn't look happy about being left alone.

Max pointed to his cell phone. "I'll call you at your apartment later. Okay?"

"Okay."

Not for the first time did a situation like this twist something unpleasant inside Max's gut. Too many foreigners came to America in dire straits. A few were hardened criminals like Nikolai and his ilk. But most of the stuffers, like those in his car today, had turned to a life of crime in a desperate attempt to survive.

To some degree Choi Jin's paranoia sprang from a guilty conscience. If given half a chance, he could probably become a contributing member of society.

"I have to go to work now," Max said in an effort

to make the other man understand. *"Work!"* he emphasized before leaving Choi Jin in the cubicle.

He approached the triage nurse and asked if someone would call a taxi for Choi Jin after he was released.

When that was accomplished, he went through a set of doors in search of the hospital cafeteria. A few minutes later, while he was eating a sandwich, his cell phone rang. He checked the caller ID before picking up to say hello to Karin Vriend, his employer for his part-time job doing deliveries for a flower shop. Neither she nor her husband had any idea he was an undercover FBI agent.

"Anatoly? I'm glad I got you."

"I am eating my lunch," he responded, using his heavy Russian accent. "Is there something I can do for you, Karin?"

"I'm calling because a woman just phoned the shop wanting to talk to you. She told me her name was Gaby Peris." Max felt a jolt. "She said you were in a car accident. Are you all right?"

"I am fine."

"Thank goodness! She said the accident was her fault, and she feels terrible about it. I have to tell you, Anatoly, because she sounded so nice. You know what I mean?" Karin said in that motherly voice of hers. "All her concern was for you and your friends. When I asked her if she had been hurt, she said no."

"The accident was not serious."

"But wasn't it thoughtful of her to phone you? I think you should call her back. Better yet, take her some flowers."

Karin had just given him an idea.

"I will think about it. Now, if you will forgive me, I have another call." He could hear a click on the line. Someone was trying to reach him.

"Of course. See you later."

He clicked the flash button. It was Detective Crandall.

"What have you got? Is Ms. Peris still at the hospital?"

"Yes. I told her the department sent me to follow up on the accident. The doctor said the two pregnant teens are going to be kept under observation for a while—an hour or so. Ms. Peris is going to stay with them until they're released. From there she'll accompany them to the Girls' Village by taxi."

Max breathed a sigh of satisfaction. If he hurried, he would have plenty of time to search her apartment. "It's exactly what I wanted to hear."

"What do you need done next?"

"I'm at the Bay Shore Hospital. As soon as you can, meet me in the back at the loading dock in a phone-company van. Bring me a uniform."

"I'll be there in half an hour."

"Thanks, Crandall." He clicked off.

Now that Nikolai seemed satisfied he was out of commission for a while, Max didn't think he'd have him followed. Even so, Max thought, he'd be wise to take precautions. A slipup could be fatal.

It was vital he get inside that woman's apartment. He had a feeling he'd find answers there....

CHAPTER TWO

THE NURSE CAME into the cubicle where Gaby had been sitting with Sandra and Juanita. She checked their vital signs once more.

"Everything's back to normal. It looks like you girls can go home."

Gaby sighed with relief along with the girls, and asked the nurse if someone at the desk would phone for a taxi.

"You bet. But just remember, ladies. The doctor says you're to come back here if either of you exhibits any post-traumatic symptoms. He wants you to have healthy babies. Understand?"

"Yes, ma'am," they both said at the same time.

"There's a nurse on duty at Girls' Village," Gaby informed her.

"That's good." She smiled. "Now. I'll see about your taxi."

Earlier Gaby had signed as the party paying for the visit. Hopefully the bill wouldn't be too high. The girls appeared to be fine.

On the trip back to Girls' Village, she prayed the taxi wouldn't get in an accident. She breathed a huge sigh of relief when she saw Sandra and Juanita safely inside their temporary home. After she explained the circumstances to the nursing supervisor, the older woman promised to keep a close eye on them.

Turning to the girls, Gaby said, "I feel terrible about what happened today. In a few days I'll come by and we'll go to the park for a picnic." It was only a block from Girls' Village. Close enough that they could walk.

"Thank you for coming to the hospital with us."

"*Sí, gracias,* Gaby."

"Let's just be thankful no one was hurt."

The three of them hugged before she left the building through the main doors.

If it weren't for her sandal, which kept falling off, she would walk to her apartment. But since that might prove difficult at best, she decided to ride the bus home, instead of spending her last ten dollars on a taxi. The bus would let her off on the corner by her apartment building.

Since moving to San Diego, her law clientele had grown a lot, but she was paying off her deceased husband's credit cards and student loans as fast as the money came in so she could start building on the savings she'd already accrued in Florida. With California real estate so expensive she would need a substantial down payment before she could hope to buy her own place. That was her goal. As a result, she was trying hard not to spend extra money.

Paul had been a teacher in Florida. A freak boating accident off the shores of Miami had cut short his life, bringing a tragic end to their two-and-a-half-year marriage.

Husbandless and childless, she'd wallowed in grief

for months. Then came the stage of anger, and finally self-pity. That was when her boss, who'd established firms specializing in immigration law in both New York and Miami, had a serious talk with her.

He suggested that either she go back to New York, where she'd first been hired by his firm so she could be nearer her family, or she should open up a new firm for him in San Diego. A new place, new faces, might be just what she needed.

Gaby was grateful for his offer to let her start fresh in California. As soon as she told him yes, he not only paid for her move, he supplied the funds to help her set up an office.

Before leaving Miami, she sold the car she and Paul just had bought, so she wouldn't have to make monthly payments on it. With the small sum of money from the insurance received at his death, she paid cash for a used car after she arrived in San Diego. The rest she put in savings. As for their household goods, those went into storage until she found a permanent place to live.

Through a stroke of good fortune she met Hallie Townsend, a nun who needed temporary housing. Hallie was actually a lay nun, which meant she'd taken vows but didn't live in a cloister or wear a habit. She was able to mingle freely with people and spread God's message. The two of them hit it off from the very beginning and decided to share a furnished apartment for a while. In time Gaby hoped to move to a condo near the ocean.

She'd never regretted the move to San Diego. Besides Hallie's wonderful company, Gaby loved the beach, and her business had grown to the point where she'd just hired a great woman named Anita Garcia as her secretary.

Anita had worked for a law firm before she'd quit her job to be a stay-at-home mom. Now that she was divorced and her son was in first grade, she was ready to enter the workplace again. Gaby had agreed to give her the month of September to see that her son was settled into the school routine. Then Anita would report for work the first of October.

But as fine as everything seemed to be going, there were still moments when memories of a life filled with love surfaced. Usually it was when something went wrong. Like today's accident.

For the time being she had no car and no roommate to complain to. Hallie had gone on a religious retreat with some other lay nuns and wouldn't be back for another week at least.

WHILE DETECTIVE CRANDALL waited in the phone-company van, Max entered the building through a door where a staircase led to the upper floor. The people at this address in Little Italy lived above the shops.

He spotted mailbox number four. The postman had been by. Max glanced around to make sure he was alone, then searched through the contents.

Amidst the junk mail, he recognized the envelope from the traffic-violations department. It looked like Ms. Peris hadn't paid for a parking ticket yet. He'd had a few of those in his time.

Interesting also to see *American Gun Owner* magazine addressed to her. As for *The New Yorker,* anyone might subscribe to it. But the fact that a copy of it had been mailed to her strengthened his suspicion that she'd been brought out here from the East Coast.

Brill's Content came as a surprise. The consumer guide to information about the journalists in today's media and what made them tick wasn't the average person's favorite reading material. It took a certain sophistication to digest the material with any real appreciation. He always bought a copy when he could find one.

There was another magazine underneath. He pulled it out. The second he saw the title, it sent up a red flag. What would she be doing with *Immigrants USA?* His eyes narrowed as he scanned the table of contents, which included a major article on the recent influx of Russians in the Portland, Oregon, area.

Aware he was lingering too long, he put everything back and took the stairs two at a time. Salsa music came from one apartment, the blare of a TV from another. The smell of tomatoes and garlic permeated the corridor, transporting him back to his youth.

He located her apartment at the end of the hall. Without a buzzer, he had no choice but to knock. If someone answered, he would tell them there'd been a report of a phone problem and he was checking it out.

When he got no response, he used a device to unlock the door, then slipped inside. Crandall would distract the woman if she returned so Max had time to search the place.

The tiny living room cum kitchen wasn't air-conditioned. It was sparsely furnished with an old couch, a Formica-top table with two chairs and an overstuffed chair with an ancient floor lamp. Without paintings or curtains, its stark appearance was depressing.

The fact that there was no television, stereo, radio, phone or computer to connect her to the outside world could be interpreted several ways. Maybe she was too poor. Or maybe she'd done what a lot of people would love to do, and had boycotted the electronic media altogether.

A hallway led to a minuscule bathroom with shower only. In the medicine cabinet he found lip gloss, bandages, Mentholatum, sunscreen lotion and a bottle of pain relievers.

The bedroom was hot and claustrophobic. A fan had been placed on top of the dresser. More surprises awaited him when he discovered a crucifix on the wall above one of the twin beds. Someone lived here with her, it seemed.

On the only nightstand between the beds he discovered a crossword-puzzle book. Three-fourths of the puzzles, which ranked in the most-difficult category range, had been solved. Next to it he found a missal printed in English. If he didn't know better, he would think a nun was in residence.

When he checked the closet, he saw a New York Barrio Gents pennant taped to the inside door.

He'd been looking for evidence that Ms. Peris was a mafia plant. This was the second thing he'd come across that made him wonder....

Stickball had originated in the streets of New York.

Born and raised in the Bronx—he'd lived there until his parents were killed in a subway accident when he was seven—Max had played it almost every day. Even when he and Gideon had worked for the NYPD, they got up a game with the guys on their time off.

He'd always remained a fan of the Bronx Knights, a team that had a healthy rivalry with the Barrio Gents. Now the game had started to become a national sport.

On the weekend coming up, the first Annual Stickball Tournament was going to be held in San Diego. Seven teams would be competing from New York, Florida and California. He and Gideon had been looking forward to it.

Was it a coincidence that she was a Barrio Gents fan? Or had someone in the ring done their homework so she'd be able to find a creative way to use the information to get close to him?

Jerked back to a cognizance of his surroundings, he hurried the inspection. Her clothes were mostly pastel skirts and blouses, a few tailored blazers and dresses. Everything modest, nothing remotely expensive.

He rummaged through the pockets. Found old ticket stubs from the San Diego Zoo, Sea World and a local movie theater. On the floor he saw a pair of running shoes and some high heels in a bone color.

In the drawers he found a couple of extra-large T-shirts, shorts, jeans, a pair of sweats and some underwear. Nothing frilly.

A thorough search of the pillows and beds, both between and underneath the sheets and mattresses, revealed no weapons, no drugs. Not as much as a pack of cigarettes.

Maybe the kitchen would reveal something more. The wastebasket contained newspapers, junk mail, a drugstore sack with a recent receipt for the purchase of deodorant and toothpaste, an empty box of Cracker Jack, a half-gallon orange-juice carton and a dead African violet.

A frying pan and saucepan sat in the drainer at the side of the sink. Except for cookware and a few plates and glasses, the shelves were pretty bare. Alongside a large Ziploc bag of corn flakes and a box of Ritz crackers, he spied soup, macaroni and cheese, a near-empty jar of peanut butter and a tin of Spam. She didn't own a microwave.

In the refrigerator he found a couple of yogurts, milk, a half-full carton of eggs, some apples and two beers. Curious because the shape of the bottles looked familiar, he reached for one. As soon as he saw the label, he blinked. Dreher's imported beer was his favorite!

When there were thousands of different beers sold worldwide, for her to have this particular brand in her fridge…. Without being special-ordered, it was virtually impossible to find on the West Coast.

Another coincidence?

He shut the refrigerator door, then moved to the living room to put a bugging device on the inside of the lamp shade. That was when he spotted a newspaper in the metal magazine rack next to the chair. He pulled the paper out.

To his surprise he found a yellow legal-size pad

full of writing stashed inside. As he started to fold back the pages, two small pocketbooks fell to the floor. He gathered them up. One was an English/Russian dictionary. The other was a phrase book for the serious student of Russian.

As his eyes scanned the notes on her legal pad, he broke out in a cold sweat. She'd written down information about car accidents—times, dates and locations—within the San Diego area. Page after page. Many of them he recognized as being mafia-related. Several were accidents he'd helped stage with Nikolai.

Since he knew she wasn't working for the law, there was only one reason she'd be privy to detailed material of this nature. Though he couldn't account for the religious artifacts, there was no doubt in his mind that *he was this woman's prey.*

Forget Nikolai.

Someone higher up had become suspicious of him and was planning to use this woman to find out if he was a traitor. It explained her phone call to his place of employment.

This apartment had to be a pied-à-terre paid for by the mafia to make Ms. Peris look legitimate. A place to come in between jobs.

He put everything back in the magazine rack as he'd found it, then let himself out of the apartment. Later he would be back to find out if she bothered to sleep here at night. Since he was her target, he wanted the element of surprise on his side by approaching her first.

While Detective Crandall drove him to a point two

blocks from where he worked, Max changed back to his own clothes, then got out to walk the rest of the way.

Every Bloomin' Thing in City Heights West was a small florist shop owned by Karin and Jan Vriend. Max had been their part-time deliveryman since his work with the FBI had brought him here from New York.

A few minutes later he entered the shop and walked through to the back room, where several female employees were finishing up for the day. They greeted him warmly.

Karin was busy wrapping decorator foil around a pot of cyclamen. Her blue eyes lit up when she saw him.

"Oh, good, Anatoly! I'm glad you're here. A few phone orders came in late. I told them we couldn't deliver until tomorrow, but if you're free—"

He stifled a moan because it meant he would have to work faster than usual. "No problem. I will load the van now."

She put a hand over her ample bosom. "What would we do without you?"

He flashed her a smile. "I would not like to find out."

"Nor I." Her happy laughter followed him out the back where he starting loading the half-dozen orders left for him.

"Anatoly? Don't forget this one!" She came running out. "I put it up especially for that nice woman. Just in case."

Though she was always urging him to date, he'd

never seen her go to such lengths before. "You haven't even met her!"

"I don't need to. She sounded very kind. Special. You can tell a lot from a voice. I have a feeling about the two of you."

So do I, Karin. Unfortunately it's not the same feeling you have.

"As I told you on the phone, I will think about it."

He took the flowers, then winked at her before driving away.

Associating with the kindhearted Vriends, who emigrated from Holland some twenty years ago, was one of the bright spots in an otherwise dangerous undercover existence.

They were a caring, industrious family whose generosity reminded him of the delightful people of Little Odessa, the neighborhood in New York where his Russian grandfather had raised him.

Since being in the Vriends' employ, he'd become infected with their love of growing things. Many were the times that a situation got so ugly it took the perfume from the flowers to remind him the world could be a beautiful place.

GABY ENTERED the hallway of her building and reached for the mail. Not only was she still shaken by the accident, she was starving. The bus she'd taken from Girls' Village had broken down en route. This just hadn't been her day.

All the passengers had been forced to wait an hour until another bus arrived to take them the rest of the way. She felt as if she'd been living a nightmare.

Pleased to see a bunch of magazines to enjoy after dinner, she started for the staircase with one shoe off and one shoe on.

Gaby had prided herself on voting in the last state election, and didn't intend to miss the one coming up. Gun legislation was a huge issue.

She didn't own a gun and didn't plan to buy one. But receiving *American Gun Owner* magazine was the best way she knew to keep abreast of the gun lobby's strategies. Like millions of Americans, she was still trying to figure out what the founding fathers of the Constitution meant when they drew up the Second Amendment. It referred to the right to bear arms.

But before she gave any more thought to that, she needed to come up with a plan to get herself to work every day until her car was repaired. Gaby imagined she was looking at two and a half, maybe three, weeks.

Anxious to shower and eat, she dashed up the stairs, then hurried to her door where the paperboy had left the newspaper. Great. She could scan the classifieds for a used bicycle.

Since she'd turned thirty, she'd been meaning to start some kind of exercise program. With her office four miles away, eight miles on a bike each weekday ought to do something for her. After she got her car back, she could take the bike out on weekends for a workout.

Tomorrow she had no alternative but to take the bus to work. On her lunch hour she'd stop at the shoe repair to get her sandal fixed and see about a bike.

As she dug in her purse for the keys, she heard

noise a little farther down the hall. "How are you this evening, Mr. Arnold?" she automatically called over her shoulder before turning to smile at her neighbor. He and his wife had recently celebrated their sixty-second wedding anniversary.

"I do not know how he is, but I am fine. The question is, how are you, Ms. Peris?"

Gaby took a step back. *The Russian.*

Standing in the shadowy corridor, he seemed even taller and more attractive than she'd found him earlier in the day with the hot, early-September sun beating down on them.

"I did not introduce myself properly before. My name is Anatoly Kuzmina."

"How did you know my address?"

"I took the liberty of glancing at the accident report while the officer was talking to us. Naturally I was delighted to learn that you had phoned where I work to find out my condition."

Gaby should never have done it. In fact, she'd regretted the impulse the moment the woman had answered the phone. Now it was too late to undo the damage. Come to think of it, why wasn't he at work now?

"I called because I felt terrible about running into your car. I'm sure it frightened your passengers. If I write them each a note of apology, would you see that they get them? I'd also like to do something extra for the man who was injured."

He studied her for a moment. "Knowing that you cared enough about their welfare to get in touch with me will be compensation enough. I will pass your message along.''

"Thank you, Mr. Kuzmina.''

"You are welcome. I am very pleased to see that you are all right. These are for you.''

From behind his back he thrust a bouquet of long-stemmed pink roses tied with a pink bow at her, forcing her to juggle them with the mail. To her relief the thorns had been removed. She counted a dozen heads at least. Their sweet perfume filled the hallway.

What had she done?

"I don't understand. After crashing into your car, I should be bringing *you* flowers.''

His eyes narrowed on her mouth. If insides could melt, that's what hers were doing. "One day you might surprise me, yes?''

Oh, brother. She should have been ready for that one—she'd worked with all types of immigrants. But this time there was a major difference. She felt a strong physical attraction to him. In fact, it was growing stronger.

And he knew it.

On her last vacation home at Easter, her family, particularly her uncle Frank, who was an incurable romantic, had insisted she wouldn't always remain dead inside.

One day when she least expected it, a man would appear from out of the blue, and *boom*—she wouldn't know what hit her. *That* was when she'd realize her mourning period was over.

Since he'd said that, she supposed she'd been waiting for it to happen. And now who should show up but Anatoly Kuzmina.

After what she'd witnessed at the accident scene, she bet a million bucks some of the things he did were illegal. Look at his sleek, expensive car. Where did an immigrant come up with that kind of money working for a florist?

"How is your friend with the injured hand?"

"He will be fine. What about your young mothers-to-be? One looked very far along. She did not go into premature labor, did she?"

There went that "r" again. "No, thank goodness."

"I think maybe you were the one who suffered the most. When I heard you explain to the officer what happened, I decided you must be an excellent driver to have missed my door. Otherwise I could have been killed. That is why I brought you these flowers. Thank you for saving my life."

What?

Only a man as unique as Anatoly could have come up with an excuse that original.

"If you will permit me, I will be happy to escort you where you need to go until your car is repaired."

Gaby blinked. "But you don't have a car!"

"You are referring to the Audi which belongs to a company I work for. But I have other transportation. Since all three of the cars had to be towed, it is only natural that I offer you my services."

"I appreciate it, Anatoly, but these beautiful roses are enough."

"It is no problem. I have just started my vacation at the place where I do accounting. My other job is part-time doing deliveries, which leaves me free for you.''

He had to be between women at the moment. But knowing how he operated, it wouldn't be for long. If Gaby turned him down tonight, he'd become involved with another woman by no later than tomorrow night.

When she didn't say anything, a concerned look broke out on his face. ''You have work tomorrow?''

''Yes.''

He gave an elegant shrug of his broad shoulders, diverting her attention. ''Then I will drive you.''

From past experience she'd learned that the best way to get rid of someone so eager was to agree with him, otherwise he would pester her to death.

''Fine. I'll be leaving my apartment at seven in the morning.'' Naturally she would be gone by the time he arrived, and that would be the end of it.

She expected to see a satisfied gleam in his eyes. Instead, she glimpsed something she couldn't decipher. It sent an odd shiver down her spine.

''I will be here on time.''

She put her key in the lock. ''If something happens and you can't come after all, I'll make other arrangements.'' Famous last words after the bus breakdown this afternoon.

As she pushed the door open and moved into the apartment, she heard him ask, ''Do you speak to all men like that, or only to me?''

In her experience she found that Russian men took themselves a little too seriously. Exasperated because she knew he was purposely exposing his hurt feelings so she would continue to talk to him, Gaby turned to shut the door. Before it closed on him she said, "Good night, Anatoly."

There was no doubt she'd left an unhappy man standing out in the hall, but he would have to live with his disappointment, just as she would. Because for a minute there, she'd actually been tempted to invite him in.

She locked the door and put on the chain.

To think that only yesterday Gaby had assumed she was one of those widows who would never get that "old feeling" again.

Her eyes feasted on his gift. The roses *were* gorgeous. So was he....

But she couldn't help thinking about the other work he did—the accounting job that allowed him to drive a new Audi and had given him two weeks' vacation.

In her mind's eye she could still see his foreign passengers dispersing from the accident scene as fast as possible. Everything about it set off alarm bells.

Since obtaining her law degree, she'd worked with Russian immigrants in New York and San Diego, though not so much in Florida. For the most part the newcomers were Evangelical Christians who'd flocked to the U.S. to escape religious persecution. Many were outcasts in their homeland, lacking education.

She'd dealt with welders, construction workers, even miners who were looking for the same kind of work here. Gaby found them to be wonderful people, anxious to raise good families and succeed.

Since most of them accepted the black market as a way of life in the former Soviet Union, they had a hard time understanding that the situation was quite different in the U.S.

Unfortunately there was a small percentage who worked on the wrong side of the law. They were members of the so-called Russian mafia, an ever growing cancer perpetrating all types of crime, including organized car theft and staged accidents. Those "accidents" were bilking American insurance companies of millions of dollars and creating havoc up and down the West Coast.

In a recent seminar with other immigration lawyers, she'd learned that besides San Diego, Vancouver and Portland were experiencing a wave of mafia-related car accidents, some ending in violence and death. Gaby had taken notes on several dozen actual police reports. In many cases the latest high-priced model cars were involved. Like a new black Audi, for instance.

The police wanted to hear from any immigration attorney who, after screening a would-be client, suspected he or she might be involved in those kinds of activities.

Gaby wagered that the people who owned the car Anatoly was driving didn't file earnings with the IRS. She had the strongest suspicion the handsome immigrant on fourteen days' leave from his "other job" was part of a mafia car ring clear up to the tips of his ears.

She didn't want to think it, let alone believe it, but the possibility was there. Troubled by her thoughts, she buried her face in the roses to breathe in their delicious fragrance. Suddenly the urgency to shower and eat was superseded by the need to put them in water.

On her way to the kitchen, she tossed her purse and mail on the overstuffed chair. Without a vase she might have to fill the sink and leave the roses there overnight. A quick search of the cupboards didn't turn up any kind of container. The saucepan was too shallow.

Removing the florist tissue from around the stems, she turned to fling it in the wastebasket and saw the orange-juice carton. Glad she hadn't done the weekly cleaning yet, she rinsed it out and filled it with water.

In a minute the roses graced the table. She covered the carton with the tissue and held it all together with the ribbon. A splash of brilliant color had transformed the apartment.

To get a little air moving, she turned on the fan in the bedroom, then took a quick shower. Afterward she went to the kitchen to fix a meal. She was low on groceries and would have to do some shopping tomorrow.

Assessing what was there, she made herself a peanut-butter sandwich and scrambled a couple of eggs. Taking everything into the living room with a bottle of beer, she settled down in the chair to relax and enjoy her magazines.

As she flipped through them, the scent from the flowers was almost overpowering. Anatoly had gotten his way. A part of him had made it inside her door. *Damn, damn, damn.*

To her chagrin, no article held her interest for long. She kept turning the pages and ended up comparing the men in the various ads and photographs to the attractive Russian.

When it became clear there was no contest, she threw down the magazines in disgust and opened the newspaper to the classifieds.

CHAPTER THREE

THE LOUD NOISE came as a surprise. Max removed the earphones for a moment. She'd either dropped or thrown something close to the lamp where he'd planted the bugging device.

From inside the delivery van parked around the corner, he'd been listening to anything he could hear coming from her apartment. So far he'd learned nothing. If she had a cell phone, she hadn't made a call or received one. There'd been no visitors.

He put the earphones back on and waited another twenty minutes. There was the occasional rustle of paper, then silence. Convinced she'd gone to bed, he headed back to City Heights. On the way he phoned Gideon.

"Did Crandall fill you in?"

"Yup. On everything."

"What did you find on her?"

"She obtained a California driver's license a month ago. She's clean except for one parking ticket she received at Chicano Park. It looks like an expired meter."

"I saw it in her mail."

"Anything helpful there?"

"She has a subscription to *AGO*."

"That's interesting. So's this. She held a former driver's license from Florida. Miami Beach, to be precise. No violations. By tomorrow I'll know a lot more so you can make a judgment call."

His jaw hardened. "We've got enough now, and it's not looking good."

"What do you mean?"

"If she was living in Miami, I'm more suspicious of her than ever. She hasn't been in San Diego long. That would explain why she hasn't tried to wipe me out before now. Kind of puts 'license to kill' in a new light, doesn't it?" Max said on an ironic note.

"What are you talking about?"

"Gideon, she has to be a mafia plant." Without wasting words, he explained exactly what he'd found stashed inside the newspaper. "She had notes on a couple of the accidents I helped stage last month."

"Good grief!"

"That's not all. I found a Barrio Gents pennant on her closet door."

After a pregnant pause, "Come on…" Gideon had been raised on stickball as well.

"That's what I said when I saw it," Max muttered. "You want to know something else? She keeps Dreher's Italian beer in her fridge. What are the chances of that happening?" The two of them had always gone for Dreher's back in New York.

While he let his friend digest that he said, "I swear she's been sent to get involved with me. You know, pretend to like the things I like, make me fall in love with her until she learns all my secrets or catches me out in a mistake. Whatever comes first."

"Who would have believed it?' Gideon whispered.

"Did I tell you she phoned where I work to see if my friends and I were all right? She even went so far as to say she would write notes of apology to them. Just now she agreed to let me drive her to work in the morning. The woman didn't even try to give me a hard time."

"You're right, Max. Things are moving too fast."

"Before I searched her apartment, I was willing to give her the benefit of the doubt. Then I got Karin's phone call telling me Ms. Peris had phoned. Coupled with everything I found in her apartment, it's all gone beyond the realm of coincidence."

"It sounds like it. Max, I'm calling an emergency meeting of the guys as soon as we hang up. Don't do anything until I get back to you."

Max groaned. All the groundwork, all the elaborate preparations jeopardized because of a leak that had to have originated in New York.

His infiltration of the Brighton Beach mob over a three-year period had resulted in the FBI making an unprecedented amount of arrests. That was why he'd been sent to San Diego. They were hoping for the same success here.

"Someone at the top wants me free to spend my time with Ms. Peris. They must have ordered Nikolai to give me two weeks off. He probably doesn't have a clue what's really going on, but it's all beginning to make sense."

"Hold on, Max. Karl's on the other line. I want him to know what you've just told me. Where are you headed now?"

"To my apartment."

Though it was only a half mile from the florist shop, Karin insisted Max keep the van overnight when he had to deliver late the day before.

She'd urged him to forget his fiancée back in Russia who'd been separated from him for too long. "Marry some nice California girl and settle down."

The way Karin looked at things, he needed transportation in order to court. Since he didn't have a car, she would help. It wasn't normal for a fine thirty-six-year-old man like himself to be alone.

Bless her heart, she had no idea Max's Russian fiancée was pure fiction. Furthermore, he'd tried marriage to a nice college girl from Vermont when he'd been a rookie on the NYPD.

It was a case of opposites attracting. But after the honeymoon was over, so was their marriage. From that point on she'd made it clear she had a healthy contempt for their lifestyle, the way he earned his living. She asked him to get out of police work altogether.

Her resentment of his buddies, Gideon in particular, drove a bitter wedge between them. When the fire got too hot and he needed her most, she divorced him and went back home. The last he'd heard, she'd married a well-to-do surgeon from Montpelier and they had two children. But that was ancient history.

"Max? Karl's putting a twenty-four-hour backup on you starting now. As soon as I ring off, we're having a meeting. Expect to hear from me within a couple of hours. And, Max, I don't care if our own boys are keeping an eye on you. *You watch your back.*"

The tension in Gideon's voice said it all.

GABY CHECKED her watch. Twenty after six. She finished her last mouthful of corn flakes and put the dish in the sink. One more trip to the bathroom to brush her teeth and apply lipstick. Now she was ready.

Three different outfits completed her working wardrobe. Today it was the matching khaki skirt and jacket with the white linen top. The important thing was to leave the apartment before the Russian showed up. *If* he planned to show up at all.

But when she saw Anatoly in another tight T-shirt, lounging against the wall at the top of the stairs with his strong arms folded across that rock-hard chest, she knew she'd been lying to herself. Part of her had wondered if he might come early.

He straightened. "Good morning, Gabriella."

That was unfair.

Except for her family, no one had ever called her by her full name before. No one had ever made her name sound as if it was something delicious. But then, she wasn't in the habit of being on a first-name basis with her clients.

That was the problem. He wasn't a client. She didn't know what he was....

"Good morning, Anatoly."

His gaze didn't miss a detail. "You look very beautiful."

So do you, she almost said. Unlike her late husband, Paul, this man didn't have a shy, restrained bone in his body.

"Thank you for the compliment."

"You are welcome. Not all women glow this early in the day."

You would know if anyone would.

"My father always said it was the sleep before midnight that counted."

He kept abreast of her as they went down the stairs. His arm and leg brushed against hers several times, increasing her awareness of him. Anatoly had no shame.

"I was thinking that perhaps you have a lover who makes you so alive. Already I am jealous." He opened the door for her, then followed her outside where an overcast sky greeted them.

Before she'd recovered from that outrageous comment, he informed her his van was around the corner. The next thing she knew he'd cupped her elbow to guide her along the pavement.

Talk about a total takeover. The man was like an F-5 tornado, consuming everything in its path.

She wasn't too pleased to hear he had a van. Some immigrants lived in them until they could afford low-cost housing. That meant all the comforts of home, including a bed.

What was she doing allowing him to sweep her toward his handy trysting spot? From experience she'd learned that some foreign men invade the imaginary circle of space a person draws around herself to feel comfortable. It was a cultural thing, but they didn't realize it produced a claustrophobic effect in her. But this was ridiculous!

Just ahead she saw a bunch of people at the corner waiting for the bus. Several of them were her neighbors. As soon as they saw her with Anatoly, they smiled knowing smiles and waved. Mr. Arnold and his wife were among the crowd. They beamed at her. Great. That was all she needed.

"Is the van far?" They'd turned up the block.

"Ah. You must be in pain. I wondered if you hurt your foot in the accident yesterday."

"I'm not in pain," she snapped.

"Do not worry. We have arrived."

Gaby blinked as he opened the front passenger door of a white van with the words *Every Bloomin' Thing* written on the side panel.

"Are you supposed to use this when you're not at work?"

"But I am. My job is to deliver flowers."

"But you're not delivering them right now."

Flashing her a beguiling smile, he said, "My employer gave me express permission to come for you."

He helped her inside and shut the door before going around to the driver's side. She fastened her seat belt, chastising herself once more for calling him at work in the first place.

He revved the engine. "Where is your work, Gabriella?"

"Drive to Fifth Avenue in East Village. Are you familiar with the location?"

"I could not have this job if I did not know San

Diego like the inside of my pocket.'' They pulled
away from the curb and took off.

"That's an idiom I haven't heard before.''

"The Frenchwoman who lives at my apartment
house taught it to me.''

Gaby could imagine....

"I think it makes more sense than the English ver-
sion," he continued. "A pocket reveals many things
you do not see on the back of the hand.''

His mind—she couldn't keep up with it.

"Your English is outstanding.''

He flashed her an oblique glance. "I will believe
you when I have mastered it, not before.''

"I have news for you, Anatoly. No one ever mas-
ters a language. Not even their own.''

A strong hand reached out to clasp hers. "That is
what I think, too. We are even more compatible than
I first suspected." Before she could wriggle out of his
grasp, he let her hand go again to make a right turn.

Gaby flexed her ringless fingers. At Easter Uncle
Frank had urged her to put her wedding band away.
It was time, he'd said with a loving hug. After her
return to San Diego, she'd done his bidding and nothing dramatic had happened, lessening her guilt.

But then, she hadn't met Anatoly.

EAST VILLAGE had a slightly higher percentage of
commercial and residential burglaries than some of
the other neighborhoods that made up San Diego.
Many stuffers lived in this central region. So did Nikolai. Max wasn't surprised Ms. Peris had been
planted in the same area.

"We have reached Fifth Avenue. Which way do I turn?"

"Left. Go to the middle of the next block. You can drop me off in front of Jack's Guitar and Drum Shop."

This early in the morning there were still plenty of parking spaces left. Max pulled into the one nearest the store she'd referred to. He shut off the engine.

"You give lessons?"

"Oh, sure. My specialty is heavy metal."

Sarcasm was one face of anger. She obviously didn't like being questioned.

"Is Jack your current lover?"

"To my knowledge Jack died years ago."

The seatbelt on her side snapped back in place with a loud *zing*. Pleased by that telling display of temper, he climbed out and went around to the other side to help her down.

He noticed she didn't wear hose. With smooth, supple limbs tanned to a fine gold like the rest of her, she didn't need them.

"Thank you for the ride, Anatoly. It was very nice of you to get up this early for me. But now I have a lot to do before my first client arrives."

Client?

"I will see you safely inside. At this hour of the morning, you never know who could be lurking about."

"That won't be necessary. I'll lock the door after me."

Her mouth said one thing. *Her eyes another.* Someone in the mafia had done a superb job of coaching this woman.

"You saved my life yesterday. Perhaps I will have an opportunity to return the favor in some small way today, yes?"

Naturally she didn't argue when he ushered her toward the entrance. Through the glass doors he could see the building was a split level with the drum shop and a women's hair salon occupying either side of the upper level.

She unlocked the outer door and he followed her inside. Just when he'd decided she was posing as a beautician to provide a cover for her nefarious activities, he saw another set of stairs leading to the lower level. A large floor sign with an arrow pointing down caught his attention.

G. Peris, Attorney
United States Immigration and Naturalization Law

She went ahead of him to unlock the door at the bottom.

His jaw hardened.

To front this kind of a setup meant the mafia owned her soul. It wasn't beyond the realm of possibility to assume she'd been raised and groomed by a powerful Russian mafia family. Unlike the past, today's mafia tended to involve their women in active roles. If that was the case with Ms. Peris, the bosses here could be taking their orders from her blood relatives back East.

This could be the break he and his colleagues had

been waiting for to bring down the head of the San Diego ring.

There was no way he was going to pull out of this investigation now. While she played with him, he'd play with her until he got enough names and information to destroy their stranglehold in this part of the state.

Max started down the stairs. There were more signs on the glass at either side of the door.

American Immigration Lawyers Association, American Bar Association, California State Bar, Florida State Bar, New York State Bar Association.

Three states where the mafia had their tightest strongholds....

His gaze swerved to the other glass partition.

This office provides the following: Family-based Immigration and Other Immigration Matters, Labor Certification, National Interest Waivers, Work Authorization, Green Cards, Advance Parole, H1B/B1/B2, Work Visas, L-1, Naturalization and Citizenship, Adjustment of Status, Investor Visas.

She turned on the lights.

When he compared the sparseness of the drab, secondhand furnishings of her apartment to the fabulous state-of-the-art law office he was looking at now, he couldn't believe the difference.

It was here he found all the personality that had been missing from her lifeless apartment. Her office had color and verve.

The conversation area for her clients, with its tables, lamps, a television and VCR, comfortable leather chairs and a couch, drew him in. She'd arranged plants and trees throughout the room with an artistic flair.

He turned around. Two large Thomas McKnight surreal seriographs of Central Park and Palm Beach hung on the off-white walls. A built-in bookcase lined with law books covered the third wall. Legal-size files sat on top of her oak desk, where she'd installed the latest electronic equipment.

By a file cabinet sat a mini fridge and a side table with a coffeemaker and supplies.

Nice. Very nice. Ironic that the place was protected by a sophisticated alarm system connected to the police station.

She shut the door. "You didn't eat breakfast, did you."

"How do you know that?"

"By the longing in your eyes. Sit down and I'll make us both a cup. Then you'll have to leave so I can get my work done."

While she disappeared through another door into what he assumed was a storage area with a bathroom, he planted a bugging device on the underside of the monitor, then reached for the framed picture on her desk.

A dark-blond, blue-eyed Caucasian male with a

mustache, early thirties, stared back at him. When she returned, Max was still holding it.

"This man is someone important to you?"

"Yes." She averted her eyes and started to make their coffee. "Paul was my husband. He died in a boating accident last year."

Ms. Peris was a professional. That meant she mixed in enough truth with the lies to be convincing. Max had no way of knowing if Paul was the fictional part.

He put the picture back on the desk. "I, too, have suffered heartache, though not anything as devastating as what you must have gone through. Now that I see what you do for a living, perhaps you could accomplish what no one else has been able to do for me."

"What's that?" she said over her shoulder.

"Six years ago, after my graduation from university in Moscow, an import company my grandfather did business with before his death filed petition for me to come to the U.S. to work for them as an accountant.

"When I was granted that visa, I was overjoyed because I had hope of becoming an American citizen. To obtain permanent residence, I never went back to Russia and have made application for naturalization. During this time, my fiancée, also from Moscow, has only been able to visit me once."

"On what kind of visa?" Though Ms. Peris gave nothing away, he could tell he had her full attention.

"Student. She is trying hard to learn English."

"I see. Do you want cream or sugar in your coffee?"

"I prefer it black."

In a moment she carried two mugs across the room. After handing him one, she urged him to sit down. "Please. Go on."

Ms. Peris was good. The French described it best. Sangfroid.

"She did not finish college and could not obtain H1B status, so she has tried to get another temporary student visa, but it was denied. I do not understand why."

Ms. Peris eyed him directly. "No one explained it to you?"

"No. Tell me, please."

"It's very simple, Anatoly. She should have applied for the fiancée visa."

"I heard it takes too long."

"Perhaps, but since she has been here once before and wanted to come again on another student visa, that made Immigration suspicious. She probably couldn't convince them that she would depart the U.S. within the prescribed time frame." Ms. Peris paused. "Do you still wish to marry her?"

"I am not sure."

"Is that the real reason you didn't have her apply for a fiancée visa? Are you afraid it will commit you to marriage? You can always back out, you know—*if* the marriage truly isn't working."

"That is my fear."

"Something tells me she is a traditional Russian woman whose priorities are husband and family."

"Yes. It has been a long time, and I have changed a great deal."

"While she has not."

"Exactly. I confess something else. There have been other women. Not as many as you might think. But it is also true that she and I were childhood sweethearts. I have been working two jobs to save as much money as possible for us. But if we are to have a future together, we need more time to find out how we really feel."

"Without the pressure of being forced to marry," she inserted.

"You are the first person who understands. If the feelings are not there, she can go back home on her student visa and save face with her family and friends. Tell me. Do you think I am being a cruel man?"

He'd let Ms. Peris know he was open to a relationship with her. Hopefully it was just enough rope for her to hang herself. But when he felt those velvety brown eyes on him, he wished to hell he didn't want to feel her hands and mouth on him, too.

"No, Anatoly. It's the situation that's cruel. In my opinion, your misgivings make perfect sense," came her quiet comment.

"If that is true, then could you talk to someone who could reopen her case? I do not mean to imply that you should do anything illegal."

"Heaven forbid."

When she smiled at him like that, the effect of her warmth dissolved his bones. His eyes narrowed on her luxuriant ponytail. Without confinement, her hair probably reached past her shoulders. He could imagine his hands tangled in all that rich brown silk. He could imagine too many things.

Except for those early days with Lauren, he couldn't remember the last time he'd experienced such a flat-out physical and emotional response to a woman.

Maybe knowing Ms. Peris had no compunction about being a party to his eventual demise had refined his senses to this degree.

He lounged back in the chair. "If I have presumed too much, you must tell me."

"It isn't a question of presumption."

"Then you are talking about money. I am able to pay your fee. But if you could spend an hour or two on my problem, I will be your taxi service, as well, until your car is repaired."

"My car! I almost forgot."

He checked his watch. "It is not nine o'clock yet. That is the earliest we can call to find out where they took our automobiles."

She finished her coffee. "I'm sorry about the Audi."

"It is all right. Accidents happen."

"I still can't believe how my strap got caught."

"I am very glad it did. Otherwise I would not have met you."

"You're being very nice about it. I tell you what, Anatoly. I'm in the middle of some other cases, but give me time and I'll see what I can do about your problem."

"You are an exceptional woman, Gabriella. I will make deliveries until quarter to five, then come by at five to take you home. We can talk business on the way.'' He got up and took both mugs from the coffee table. ''Allow me to wash these, then I will go.''

''You don't need to do that.'' For the first time he sensed she was uneasy. What was she hiding in the back part of her office?

''It is when I do not *need* to do something that I want to do it.''

As he passed her desk, he noted the framed certificate on the wall behind it. Gabriella Peris had a master's degree from Rutger's Law School in Camden, New Jersey. It appeared he'd been right about her Jersey accent.

The Russian mafia had a strong base up and down the eastern seaboard. Little by little everything was adding up to one inevitable conclusion.

Peris happened to be an old Welsh name. It could be her husband's, but Max had an idea it was her father's name. It would account for those black Celtic eyebrows and lashes that made her coloring so remarkable. Like several married female attorneys he knew, it appeared she'd chosen to practice law using her maiden name.

He'd been right. Beyond the door was a small storage room with a tiny bathroom attached. Other than some supplies for her various machines, he found nothing incriminating. She kept everything neat and clean.

The bathroom revealed even less. He washed out the mugs and used paper towels to dry them. When he returned them to the side table in the other room, he saw her shaking hands with a middle-aged Hispanic man.

Max nodded to the stranger before settling his gaze on her. "I will be back, Ms. Peris. Have a wonderful day."

"Thank you, Anatoly. You, too."

There went those eyes beckoning him again. The woman was an artful predator.

He smiled going up the stairs. Ages ago the FBI had placed phony documentation on him and his bogus fiancée from Russia on the Immigration and Naturalization Service computers. Names, backgrounds, visas, jobs, everything was there to provide an airtight cover for him. While Ms. Peris tapped into those files, Max would go to work on her. When he thought about it, he hadn't had this kind of fun in years. Maybe never.

FOR THE REST OF THE DAY Gaby buried herself in work, stopping only long enough to eat a yogurt and an orange from her mini fridge. Throughout, she tried to pretend she didn't feel a growing excitement that Anatoly would be coming to get her at five.

After what she'd learned, perhaps her initial judgment of him being involved in illegal activities might have been too harsh. Part of her wanted to get into the computer and access his file, if only to find out that everything he'd told her about himself was true. Another part wanted to take him on faith.

Throwing down her pen in disgust, she rummaged in her purse for the card the police officer had given her so she could discover the whereabouts of her car. Another card came out with it. The one Anatoly had given her when they'd exchanged information.

He'd written his full name at the top of a florist card in the Russian way, with that beautiful penmanship you didn't see taught in American schools.

Setting the card aside, she made the phone call about her car and learned that her Sentra was at the H and L Body Shop in Balboa Park. That wasn't too far from her office. They didn't have the estimate worked up yet, and there was a backlog. She should inquire tomorrow.

What the guy in the shop was really saying, she knew, was that her car wouldn't be ready for some time. Her guess of two weeks had been optimistic. A month was more like it. And although she was tempted to let Anatoly be her personal chauffeur, she didn't dare do that. Since her attraction to him wasn't about to go away soon, it would be inviting disaster to allow him one more foot inside the door.

The best thing to do was put her original plan into action and buy a used bike.

As for Anatoly, she would phone where he worked right now and tell him not to come by her office. He could give her the information about his fiancée over the phone. After she'd looked into the matter, she would phone him with any news. End of dilemma.

Without hesitation she called his place of work for the second time. The same cheerful woman she'd talked to before answered the phone.

"Good afternoon! Every Bloomin' Thing. Karin Vriend speaking."

"Hello. Forgive me for bothering you. This is Ms. Peris again. Is Mr. Kuzmina there?"

"Oh, no! He just left to do the afternoon deliveries and will be so sorry he missed you. May I help you?"

"Will he be coming back before you close?"

"Not this evening."

"I see. Well, thank you for your time."

"If he should check in, I'll tell him you called and were anxious to find him."

"That's all right. I'll find another way to get in touch with him. Goodbye."

Gaby put the receiver back on the hook and worked straight through until four, when her last client for the day walked out the door. She was about to do the same thing.

It took a few minutes to straighten her desk and water the plants. When everything was done, she wrote a message on a sticky note and put it on the outside of her office door. The beauty salon didn't lock the outer door of the building until eight-thirty, when they closed.

Dear Anatoly,
Something came up that required my leaving the office early, so I realized I wouldn't be needing a ride home. I called the florist shop to tell you not to come, but it was too late to reach you.

You were very kind to drive me today, and I appreciate your offer to be a taxi service, but since you left this morning, I solved my transportation problem.

When it's convenient, call me at my office and we'll discuss your fiancée's visa. The number is 555-0467. Naturally there will be no charge.

G. Peris.

Glad to have done something positive about an impossible situation, Gaby headed for the bank around the corner to deposit some checks that had come in the mail.

Feeling rich with forty dollars in her purse, she rode the bus straight home, then changed into her navy sweats and running shoes to go grocery shopping. Tonight she'd cook up enough spaghetti sauce to last her for a few days. Garlic bread and salad sounded good too. While she enjoyed a hot meal, she'd look in the classifieds for a bike.

As she started down the hall to leave, Anatoly appeared at the top of the stairs with a plastic bag in his hand, looking terrific in an open-necked blue sport shirt and beige trousers. An adrenaline rush kicked up her pulse rate.

But judging by the expression on Anatoly's face, he was very upset at the moment. She'd forgotten about his fragile Russian-male pride.

When he couldn't find her at her office, he'd chosen to feel injured. Her sincere note of apology had done nothing to mollify him. He walked up to her without hesitation, invading her space once more. "You were leaving to meet someone?"

One of the interesting aspects about Anatoly was that he never minced words, just came out with whatever was on his mind. It was fascinating, but also frustrating. He seemed to play by another set of rules.

"I was on my way to the store," she said.

"I need to do some shopping myself. After we eat dinner—" he held up the bag "—and accomplish our business, I will take you to a place where I have a membership. It is open twenty-four hours, every day of the year.''

Gaby wasn't particularly fond of enormous malls and warehouse shopping. But she could see why it would appeal to Anatoly. Though she might not have been to the former Soviet Union, she didn't think American capitalism had managed to get its stranglehold on their poor unsuspecting culture to quite that degree yet.

''You can buy anything you want for a fifty percent discount.''

She gasped. ''Fifty?'' In a place like that, her forty dollars would go far.

''I know the owner,'' he added. Oh, of course. ''Otherwise I would only get thirty.''

He didn't need to say anything more to seduce her. Besides, at this point she was salivating over the divine smells coming from the bag.

''We can eat here, but my apartment's horrible.''

''You mean it is ugly?'' He asked solemnly.

''Let's just say it's temporary. I've been pouring everything into my office.''

''If you mean you do not have any furniture, that is not a problem. I am no stranger to hardship. When I first came to America, I slept in a bare apartment on the floor with thirteen other immigrants. Together we scraped enough money to live there a month until I received my first paycheck.''

She wasn't surprised.

''I didn't mean to imply that I don't have a chair for you to sit on.''

''Then you do not want me to see the mess.''

He'd been around other women all right.

"The American female worries too much over details that are unimportant." His bold gaze studied her features. "A man is not capable of noticing anything else when it comes to an alluring woman."

In sweats and a ponytail? Gaby stifled the impulse to tell him the Russian male chose to be blind, as well as tragic. She turned to let herself back in to the apartment.

CHAPTER FOUR

"DID YOU CALL about your car?" Anatoly followed her inside. The click of the door reminded her they were alone. Gaby hadn't been this kind of alone with a man since her husband.

"Yes. They couldn't tell me anything yet. What about the Audi?"

"It should be ready in ten days."

To have Anatoly's connections wouldn't be a bad thing. "If you'll put the food on the table, I'll get the plates and cutlery."

"I do not understand why you were worried. Your apartment is uncluttered. No technical toys."

"If I want TV, I can watch it at work," she called from the kitchen.

"I am happy you like these roses." She watched him inhale their perfume. "A genius bred this variety of shocking pink in Germany. By their thick stems, you know they were grown and cut in South America just before their overnight flight to San Diego. You will find they last sixteen days."

Everything he said either exasperated or fascinated her. "They're exquisite, Anatoly." The heat in the apartment had forced the heads open.

As she brought everything to the table, his eyes

captured hers. "Don't you want to know their name?"

"I was just about to ask."

"Royal Dream." The famous "r" was in evidence once more. "The way they stand out from the drabness around them reminds me of you."

She sucked in her breath. "You've picked up a lot of knowledge working at that florist shop."

"I find that I like growing things."

"Did your family farm in Russia?"

"No. We always lived in the city. They died when I was seven, so my grandfather raised me. Until his death, he ran a shop importing gifts from all over the world."

"How old were you when he died?"

"Eighteen."

She swallowed hard. "I'm glad you had him for as long as you did."

"I, too, am glad. Sit down and I will serve you. I hope you like chicken."

"I like most anything."

"As I said before. You are a special woman, Gabriella." He pulled out several cartons of hot food and lifted the lids. Nestled in the wine and mushroom sauce lay tender breasts of chicken wrapped around cheese and spinach.

She stared up at him. "That's chicken rollatini. You went to Salvatori's Deli!"

He smiled down at her. "I see this pleases you."

"It's one of my favorite places."

"Mine, too."

"Even if you're kidding, I'm not complaining."

"I never say what I do not mean," he reminded her in a serious voice. "But I regret that I did not bring any wine for you. There was a long line of people. I wanted to get to you as soon as possible."

Drowning in a surfeit of emotion, she excused herself from the table. "I'm glad you didn't, because I don't care for wine, except in food, of course." She pulled her last beer from the refrigerator, mentally kicking herself for draining the other one last night.

"Now *you* are the person who is kidding," he muttered when she placed the bottle next to his glass.

"What do you mean?" Perhaps he preferred something stronger, like vodka. But she couldn't imagine him wanting it with a meal. In any event, she had nothing else but water or milk to serve him.

He caressed the neck of the bottle as if it were a woman's. "All my life I have preferred beer. More and more I am convinced the crash that brought you into my life yesterday was for a very great reason. Do you believe in destiny, Gabriella?"

Those green eyes shadowed by secrets had settled on her mouth, which was now full of chicken.

She shook her head.

"Kismet is an old Persian term my Turkish friend believes rules our lives. To think I once scoffed at him." He opened the bottle and poured half the contents into her glass.

"We shall drink a toast, yes?"

Gaby raised her glass. "May my car be repaired as fast as yours!"

He held his glass away so they wouldn't touch. "*Nyet.* I refuse to drink to that. May your car be stolen so that I will have the privilege of driving you to work every morning and bringing you home every night.''

After a resounding clink, she choked on her first sip while he drank the contents of his glass in one swallow.

"You are all right?" He reached out to rub her back until the coughing subsided.

No, I'm not all right. Don't touch me like that. Don't talk to me like that. Not ever again.

"The business about the stolen car wasn't funny, Anatoly." She put her glass down hard.

He stopped rubbing her back to reach for her hand. "I think we are having our first miscommunication," he whispered. Like fire, she felt the brush of his lips against her skin. "When you know me much better, you will find out I never try to be funny." He buried a kiss in her palm before letting her hand go.

She felt so weak, she feared she might slide right off the chair onto the floor. "Cars get stolen around here all the time," she snapped to counteract her reaction to the intimate contact. "The parts are either used to repair salvaged vehicles, or else the thugs steal the vehicle identification number and place it on a 'hot' automobile."

Anatoly's eyelids had dropped to half-mast. "I agree it is a serious problem. But your insurance company will replace your car if that happens."

"That's true. However, I've already received a citation for causing the accident. If my car gets stolen on top of it, they'll pay everything, then tell me to look for another insurance company. My rate will be astronomical!''

The room fairly echoed with her diatribe. She felt embarrassed, suddenly, by her display of temper.

''I did not know my comment would upset you so much. Forgive me, Gabriella. Let me make this up to you by having your car towed to the body shop where the Audi is being repaired. It is very safe. I would have suggested it in the first place, but I did not want to seem like I was trying to take over your life.''

He had to be joking.

Except that he said he never joked. Anatoly was one of a kind, and she was beginning to believe him, beginning to… What was happening to her?

Coming out of mourning left her vulnerable in a new way. If she could go back to yesterday before the crash, Anatoly wouldn't be sitting within touching distance of her right now. He wouldn't be saying and doing things that seduced and frightened her at the same time.

She needed her psychiatrist, fast. But Dr. Karsh lived in Florida. A fifty-minute session in his office or over the phone cost two hundred dollars without insurance. Her health insurance paid only a pittance for psychiatric care.

''You are flushed.'' Anatoly put the back of his hand to her cheek. ''I think you should lie down and relax while I do the dishes.'' He rose to his full height and started clearing the plates.

The situation was spiraling out of control.

She jumped up from the table. ''I have a better

idea. I'll find my notepad and we'll get busy on your fiancée's problem.''

He paused in the midst of filling the sink with hot water. ''You work too hard, Gabriella. You have no distractions here.''

I can see a great big huge one right in front of me.

''That's the way I like it.''

MAX CLEANED UP the kitchen, aware he was enjoying the situation a little too much. If Gideon knew what was happening to him, he'd tell him to get out before things got any hotter.

That was the problem. Emotionally, physically, in fact, every damn way a human could be, he was already in too deep.

After all the years of working in law enforcement, this was the first time he could feel himself losing ground with every skirmish. Until he'd met Ms. Peris, he'd always dismissed the notion of bonding to the enemy. But her con was sucking him in.

Watch your back.

Gideon's famous last words.

She'd put on her attorney's hat and sat in the chair by the lamp with one leg tucked under her. On her lap perched the yellow legal-size pad he'd seen before.

With her coloring, she looked good in navy.

His eyes closed. She looked good in every outfit she wore. The thought of her without clothes...

Somewhere in the room he heard a phone ring. She reached into the purse by her chair and pulled out a cell phone. He could hear her voice, but she spoke in such low tones it was impossible to understand the words.

Max stayed where he was, wiping off the counter. Gideon had put her apartment and office under twenty-four-hour surveillance. Whoever was on duty at either site would get any conversations on tape.

Tonight a patrol car would show up at the building where she worked on the pretext of checking out a suspected burglary in progress. One of the guys would get inside her office and put a listening device on her phone wire.

Whenever she left either place to go anywhere else, there'd be a tail on her. That way everything was covered except her cell phone. Max would take care of that at the first opportunity.

Except for the time he spent delivering flowers, the next two weeks he would be in her face, watching every move she made. They would play attack and retreat until she had nowhere to run and he'd learned everything he wanted to know.

To his chagrin he wanted to know things that weren't necessary to the investigation. He had a gut feeling his need was already insatiable.

"Anatoly? Forgive me for being on the phone so long. Come and give me the particulars on your fiancée."

"Her name is Natasha Azarnova, born in Moscow January 19." He sat down on the couch, stretching his arm along the top of it. "She has blond hair, blue eyes, is five feet nine inches tall and weighs a hundred twenty pounds. She came to San Diego four years ago on July 6. She is thirty-two years old and works as a secretary for a photographic company.''

He'd memorized the litany a long time ago.

Gabriella didn't lift her head while she wrote. ''When did she make the second application for a student visa?''

''Six months ago. The first week of February. Last month she found out it had been denied.''

''That must have been a terrible disappointment for both of you.''

''It is life. But we need to see each other one more time to discover if the fire still burns. You have been married, so you know what I am talking about.''

''Yes. Do you have a recent picture of her?''

''I carry one in my wallet.'' He pulled it from his back pocket and removed the picture Karl had given him. ''You can keep it. There are more at my apartment.''

She took it from his fingers. ''She's lovely.''

''I think so, too. The trouble is, she has been gone so long I have trouble visualizing her without the picture. I used to feel guilty about that.''

''I know what you mean.'' Her voice betrayed the hint of a tremor. So far her acting was beyond comprehension. ''Sometimes you need a reminder.''

''Gabriella, do you smoke?''

''No.''

''Do you mind if I do?''

''Not at all.'' She jumped up from the chair and brought him a bread-and-butter plate from the kitchen cupboard. ''Just let me get the fan and bring it in here.'' In a second she was back and had put it on the kitchen table facing them. She turned on the switch.

"That feels good. I have cut down to one a week."

"Do you mean a pack?"

"No. A cigarette."

"That's very admirable."

"I am on the Nicorette plan."

Her chuckle worked its way under his skin. "I wish there was a plan to get off Cracker Jack."

"Is that something you smoke?"

Her lips twitched. "No. It comes in a box. A mixture of popcorn and crunchy stuff. I eat it when I go to ball games, another one of my many addictions."

He'd wondered how long it would take her to get around to the pennant taped to her closet door. Obviously not long. He took another puff on his cigarette, a necessary affectation of his con that he could do without.

"You have just mentioned an aspect of American culture I find fascinating."

"When we both know this nation has too many overweight people, you're being very diplomatic."

"I was not talking about the enjoyment of nonnutritious food. American women seem to enjoy watching sports as much as the men do. I like that. Natasha never had an interest. Tell me, are you a fan of football or basketball?"

"Depending on the team, I like just about every sport."

"Except for bowling, I, too, am enamored of most sports on American television. The lady who owns my apartment house lets us watch them in the lounge room."

"You don't have your own TV set?'

"No. She does not allow us to keep one in our rooms because of the noise. It is a good rule for me. Otherwise I would stay in bed and flip the channels all day."

"You're catching on to the American way fast. You didn't think I kept the TV at my office solely for my clients, did you?"

"I decided you must use videos to explain information to them in their native tongues."

"That's very perceptive of you, and of course, you're quite right. But I ascribe to the theory that all work and no play makes Jill a dull girl."

"I have heard that idiom before, but I think another name was used."

"Jack."

"Jack! That is it." He inhaled on his cigarette one more time for effect, then stubbed it out on the plate she'd given him.

"I believe I have all the information I need on your fiancée. In a few days I'll let you know if I can get her temporary student visa approved." She moved out of the chair and put the notepad on the table. "Thank you again for the delicious dinner."

She was getting rid of him, and there'd been no mention of stickball. That would come later. Ms. Peris knew exactly what she was doing. Two steps forward, one step back.

He got up from the couch with the plate to take it into the kitchen.

"That's all right, Anatoly. I can do that." She reached out to take it from him, but he slipped past her.

As he dropped the cigarette stub in the wastebasket, then washed the plate, he said, "I did not come here to make extra housework for you. You are doing me a great favor. Tomorrow morning I will be here at five to seven. On the way we will stop at the place where they have taken your car. I will make arrangements to have it towed to the garage where the Audi is being repaired."

She shook her head, causing her ponytail to swish. "None of that will be necessary. I plan to take the bus."

He finished drying the plate and put it away in the cupboard. Then he turned toward her with his hands on his hips. "I have offended you in some way?"

"No, of course not."

"Is it because I am Russian?"

"Your nationality has nothing to do with anything."

"I will be a naturalized citizen very soon."

"Anatoly," she said in exasperation, "you are putting words in my mouth."

"That is because you insist on hiding the truth from yourself."

She frowned. "I don't know what you mean."

"You are in the business of helping immigrants, but you still consider us untouchables."

"That's not true!"

If he'd slapped her hard, her dark eyes couldn't have looked more hurt or surprised. What a superb actress she was, letting him believe she was horrified by the accusation! In reality she was no doubt afraid she'd overplayed her hand and needed to rectify the situation so he wouldn't get away from her.

He shrugged. "What is it you Americans say? If the shoe fits..."

"Well, the shoe doesn't fit *this* American. The reason I didn't want to accept any more help from you is that I was afraid you'd think I was trying to take advantage of your good nature."

"But you are doing legal work for me."

She heaved a deep sigh. "It will probably take me an hour, no more. It hardly compares with a couple of weeks' worth of chauffeuring me around."

"But you went to university to learn exactly what to say in that hour. That is why you are entitled to the fees you charge. Since I have already taken up your time talking about Natasha, that makes two hours I owe you."

"Have you forgotten I caused the accident that deprived you of your company car?" she exclaimed. "Look. I don't want to talk about it anymore. If you want to drive me, fine. I'll be very grateful. Tomorrow I don't need to leave for work until eight."

"Then if I come at seven, we will eat breakfast together at the Jukebox Café first. It is on the way to your office."

"I know where it is." She shot him an amused glance. "You have a fascination for fifties music and waitresses who wear bobby socks and chew gum?"

He smiled back. "I have a fascination for everything American. You are the most American woman I have ever met.''

''What do you mean by that?''

''You do everything. You have opinions on everything. You are afraid of nothing. You are never boring. You are more like a man.''

''That's high praise, Anatoly.'' She opened the door for him. ''Good night.''

He put a hand to her flushed cheek one more time and felt her tremble. That was one response she couldn't possibly fake. Either she wasn't well or she was afraid. Whether of the situation or of him, he couldn't tell yet. Considering she was mafia, her reaction was a revelation.

There was one infallible way to find out if her attraction to him was fake. But he needed answers to a whole host of other questions first and so was forced to slow down the pace of their relationship.

It had only been about thirty-five hours since they'd met, and already he had trouble controlling the trembling of his own body when he got within touching distance of her.

''You feel warm. Do you wish me to buy you something to relieve it?''

''I have medicine in the cabinet, but thank you.''

''You are welcome. Sleep well, Gabriella.''

He left her apartment, resisting the urge to brush his mouth against her lips. The door closed behind him. When he heard the click of the lock, he hurried out of the building and around the corner to the van.

As soon as he got in the driver's seat, he put on the earphones. If there was nothing coming from her end, he'd phone the guy doing surveillance from the carpeting van parked around the corner. Max wanted to know the gist of her phone conversation earlier in the evening.

GABY SAT in the overstuffed chair, shaken by what could only be described as unassuaged desire. For one brief moment she'd thought Anatoly was going to kiss her. When he didn't, she couldn't believe how disappointed she was. The business about a widow being lonely and vulnerable wasn't funny.

Before things went any further, she needed answers to a couple of burning questions. If Anatoly wasn't who he said he was....

Grabbing her cell phone, she called her uncle in Atlantic City. For years he'd been a police detective who now worked for the criminal investigations department. He had excellent contacts.

She knew it was late, but he loved her like a daughter and would forgive her when he understood why she was calling.

"Yes?" He always sounded gruff when he'd been wakened from sleep.

"Uncle Frank? Forgive me for phoning you and Aunt Marion this late but—"

"Gabriella! You can call me anytime," he said. "What's wrong?"

"This isn't an emergency. I'm not dying or anything, but I do have to talk to you."

"The family has been waiting for the latest update. You know the one I mean."

"Yes." She swallowed hard. "That's why I'm calling."

"Does this mean you followed my instructions?"

"Yes." *I took off the rings.*

"And boom—you and this man you were told to watch for have collided on cue?"

Her eyes closed. Trust her uncle to refer to her meeting a man as a "collision." In Anatoly's case, it had been literal.

"Yes." It wasn't love of course. But her attraction to him was strong enough that she needed to do something about the situation.

"You've made progress. That's terrific. Tell me. Have you informed the family? This is the news they've been waiting for."

Her uncle understood how upset her parents had been over Paul's death. For Gaby to find another wonderful man and marry again was everyone's greatest wish.

"They'll have to wait a little longer. Until I tell you otherwise, this must stay between you and me."

"You know I won't say anything until you give the word."

"Thank you. Uncle Frank, you've always been the one who said that if something looked too good to be true, it probably was."

"I've survived by following that motto." After a little silence, "If your instincts are telling you something's wrong, then trust them and get rid of him. *Now.*"

I wish it was that easy. "Before I do as you say, I need information only you can provide." She gave him Anatoly's name and asked him to find out if Anatoly was a wanted man back in Russia. Her uncle would phone his contacts at the CIA and Interpol. "Do you think you could get it for me by quarter to seven in the morning my time? He's taking me to breakfast."

But maybe Russia wasn't even his real birthplace. Though she didn't want to even entertain the thought, with his superior intelligence and grasp of English, Anatoly could be a ringleader in the Russian mafia, operating under several aliases.

Natasha might even be a relative of his with her own criminal record. It was possible that since Anatoly had found out Gaby was an immigration attorney, he'd decided to use her to get this other woman into the country under the noses of the port authorities.

Before she saw him again, she needed to find out whatever she could, be it good or bad. It was a case of self-preservation.

"Expect a call from me by 6:30 a.m. at the latest," her uncle replied.

"Bless you, Uncle Frank."

MAX PULLED behind Gideon's unmarked car at the AmerOil truck stop in Balboa Park. No matter the time of night, the big round-the-clock gas station did a brisk business. It was a perfect rendezvous spot.

In a tank top and shorts, Gideon looked as if he'd just come from the beach. He'd already started to fill his car with gas. Max got out of the van and reached for a hose. They stood ten feet apart, never acknowledging each other.

"The phone call to her apartment came from Girls' Village. It was one of the teens in the accident wanting to know more about a picnic they were going to have on Saturday."

Armed with a squeegee, Max walked to the front of the van to clean the windshield. "I heard she made a phone call."

"Yes. She was reporting to her uncle Frank in Atlantic City about your accident."

Atlantic City.

He took a deep breath. So far his hunches where Gabriella was concerned had turned out to be correct.

"That's not all. She smells a rat. Are you listening, Max? Her uncle apparently gives the orders. He told her to get rid of you, but she said she needed more information on you before she acts. Karl wants you off the case *now.* So do I."

Max lifted the windshield wipers to clean under them. "They won't find anything on me I don't want them to find. I need more time to get closer to her."

"Is that your brain or your libido talking?"

His friend knew him too well.

"Probably both," Max said. "But since she's led us to her uncle, I'm wondering if her family set up Girls' Village for a front. Maybe that's her contact.

"At the accident she told the investigating officer she was a volunteer, but I find it odd she would receive a nighttime phone call at her apartment from one of the girls, even if the staff allows them phone privileges."

Gideon tightened the cap on his gas tank and put the hose back. "So you think the teens are being used to make the call as some kind of signal for her to report in?''

''Possibly. If I could cultivate a friendship with a couple of the girls, they might say something that could help us blow this ring wide open.''

''Not if they do the same thing to you first.''

''According to that phone conversation, it won't happen yet. She's out to learn all she can first. I'm going to let her have her way and see where it leads. In the meantime I want you to find out what you can about her activities in Miami.''

Max proceeded to tell him about her law office, the degree from Rutger's. ''She said her husband died in a freak boating accident last year. It could be a lie, but check it out, anyway. She called him Paul. I don't have a last name. Let's find out how much of what she told me is legit.''

''I'll get on it, but I still say you should pull out while you can. She's not worth it, Max. Nothing's worth ending up getting crushed inside a pile of twisted metal next time around.''

With that warning, Gideon walked off to pay for the gas. In case anyone was watching them, Max checked the air pressure in his tires, then put the hose back and headed for the cashier inside. They passed each other outside the door without changing their stride.

When Max got back in the van, Gideon had already disappeared in the opposite direction. His friend's warning came from the gut, but Max couldn't imagine calling it quits, not when this could be another way to get names of the ringleaders. Certainly not when the thought of seeing her first thing in the morning was consuming him.

Once back at his apartment, he spent a restless night. By 5:30 a.m., he'd showered, dressed and was on his way to her place. He parked around the corner as before, then made contact with the guy on surveillance in the truck parked across from her place.

"Calder here. What have you got for me?"

"Her uncle phoned her at 5:00 a.m. We're doing a background check on him now. He told her his sources hadn't found out anything that raised a red flag. But he trusted her instincts and warned her to lie low while he did some more digging. Then he'd get back to her."

That meant she probably wouldn't be at the apartment when he called for her. There would be a note stuck to the outside of her door with some excuse that she'd had to leave early.

"Just a minute ago she made a phone call to a Linda Early in Mira Mesa. Ms. Peris is going to buy a bicycle from her on her lunch hour today. That's it.'

Max's tactics were working. Already Gabriella was squirming because he was moving in too fast for her.

"Check the name of the person who pays the bills at that phone number. Get me anything and everything you can about the people at that address in case someone there is one of her contacts."

"Yes, sir."

"If Ms. Peris leaves her apartment before you see me go inside, let me know if she went on foot, rode the bus, took a taxi or was picked up."

"Right."

He thanked his informant, then became filled with fierce determination. *If Mohammed wouldn't come to the mountain...*

CHAPTER FIVE

GABY QUICKLY PULLED on the jacket of her suit, hoping she would make it outside in time to catch the bus. Otherwise she'd have to spend a lot more money on a cab.

Hard as it would be to deprive herself of Anatoly's company, she knew her uncle was right in warning her to stay away from him until there was definitive proof that he wasn't involved in anything criminal.

On her lunch break she planned to buy the bicycle she'd seen advertised in the newspaper. She realized she'd wakened the girl with her morning call, but Linda Early, a college student, had been nice about it because she was desperate for the cash. Gaby had been to college and knew the feeling of being broke before the end of the month. Buying the girl's bike would help out both of them.

With that done, Anatoly couldn't use the excuse that she needed his services any longer.

After stuffing her briefcase with her sneakers rolled up in a pair of jeans, she hurried into the living room to grab the note she'd written to Anatoly explaining that she'd had to leave early.

"Oh!" she cried softly when she opened the door

to find him blocking her path. In her confusion, the note dropped to the floor.

"Good morning, Gabriella." In a deft movement, he picked up the piece of paper and handed it back to her without looking at it. The green of his eyes seemed darker in the dimly lit hallway. She could tell he'd just come from the shower. He smelled good.

"We are both early. I assume that means you are as excited about our date this morning as I am. I did not sleep well last night thinking about you."

That makes two of us. She locked the door, all the while attempting to pull herself together.

"When I discovered that the Jukebox does not open as early as I had supposed, I bought breakfast for us and rushed over here. It is out in the van. I thought we could take advantage of the beautiful morning and drive down by the water to enjoy it."

Her thoughts reeled. After the conversation with her uncle, she knew what she should say to Anatoly. But since he'd surprised her like this, it would be churlish to refuse him, especially when she'd already agreed to have breakfast with him. If he just hadn't gone to the trouble to buy them anything....

But as she was coming to find out, it was typical of him to be thoughtful to a fault. In her heart of hearts she had to admit she liked that trait in him. Maybe too much.

If everything he'd told her was the truth and he'd spoiled his fiancée the same way, then Gaby could understand why the woman was so anxious to come to America and marry him.

He cocked his dark head. "You are quiet this

morning. We do not have to go any particular place. If you would rather, I can bring the food from the van and we can eat here.''

Not a good idea. The living room was too small. The smell of the roses was still too strong. Everything felt too intimate when he came inside and shut out the world.

''Actually, I have a lot of work to do at my office this morning. Can we eat while you drive me?''

He stared at her through narrowed lids. ''If that is what you wish. On the way, shall we stop and make arrangements to have your car towed to the shop I told you about?''

She shook her head. ''That's very kind of you, Anatoly, but no. I'm going to be using a bike to get to and from work from now on, so I'm not in such a big hurry for it.''

He followed her down the hall. ''You mean a motorbike?''

''No. I plan to get around the old-fashioned way. I'm going to pedal.''

Though he moved behind her on the stairs, he managed to reach the front door of the building ahead of her and opened it. ''Where do you keep it? I did not see it in your apartment or your office.''

''That's because I'm buying it today.''

As before, he cupped her elbow to guide her around the corner. She wished he wouldn't touch her. Every part of her came alive at the slightest contact.

''How much are you planning to spend?''

''There's one advertised in the paper for two hundred twenty-five dollars.''

"You must not buy a used bike," he said in an authoritative voice. "It will fall apart the first time you ride it. Let me take you to get a new one on your lunch hour. I can purchase it at fifty percent off."

"You're talking about the store where you have to have the club membership to get in."

"Exactly. My friend sells everything there, all the major brands."

That was what worried her. A legitimate company couldn't sell top-of-the-line merchandise at such a discount. No doubt it was full of a lot of hot property she didn't want to know anything about. Like stolen cars, for instance.

Once they were ensconced in his van, he handed her a warm croissant and a cup of coffee still hot in its container. He'd brought fresh fruit and yogurt. All foods she loved.

Anatoly was like her own gorgeous-if-not-corrupt genie who appeared as if by magic. He had this uncanny ability to anticipate her needs. Nothing was beyond his ability to produce. It was just as she thought. He really was too good to be true, yet the more she was around him, the less she seemed to mind.

She was in trouble.

They pulled away from the curb to merge with the traffic.

"As much as I appreciate the offer, Anatoly, I would rather ride a used one. That way it won't get stolen as fast." She reached for some fat green seedless grapes that were so sweet they tasted like candy. Where did he find produce this fabulous?

Anatoly's mouth lifted at the corners, making him

too attractive for so early in the morning. "You are sounding very cynical for a beautiful woman who does not look anything like an attorney, Gabriella."

"I'm afraid I became jaded after my apartment was cleaned out twice when I was living in Miami."

He flicked her a penetrating glance. "While your husband was still alive?"

Why had she said anything? "Before, a-and after."

"Now I understand why you keep your valuable things at your office."

That wasn't the reason, but she had no intention of telling him the truth. As it stood, he already knew more about her than she wanted him to know.

"This food is delicious. Thank you."

"You are very welcome. We will have to go to the Jukebox on Saturday for lunch. That way you can sleep in as long as you want first."

She stirred in her seat. "I'm afraid I can't, Anatoly."

"Since I met you, I can't sleep in, either. No woman has ever disturbed me so much before, not even my fiancée."

His line amused her—it was ten miles long—but it didn't seem to matter, because she could feel a growing attraction to him in spite of it. Perhaps even because of it. Before meeting him, she would never have thought "amusing" could come packaged with such a sensual charge.

"I didn't mean that. What I was trying to say is, I have other plans."

"Yes?" He had that Russian ability to sound sad down to an art form.

"Yes."

"Your lover?" he persisted.

She bit into a ripe plum so hard she cut the soft inner lining of her lip against the pit. "I'm spending the afternoon at the park with the two girls who were in the accident."

"Fine. We will all go to lunch first, and then enjoy ourselves for the rest of the day." He grinned cheerfully. "Did I tell you the owner of my apartment house has a croquet set she will let me borrow?"

Croquet? Good grief. Gaby thought that had died out by the end of the forties. "Your landlady didn't vote for Roosevelt by any chance, did she?"

His eyes lit up. "Yes. How did you know?"

"Just a wild guess."

"Do you not agree croquet will be a good activity for girls who are going to have babies? Better than Frisbee?"

She sighed. "Yes."

"Then it is settled. We will play in teams. You and I against the young mothers. We will let them win."

Oh, Anatoly.

She cleaned up the mess she'd made. "I thought you had to deliver flowers."

"Not *this* Saturday. Karin's husband is doing them that day."

"How come?"

"Ever since you phoned my work, Karin has insisted that I take time off to be with my sweetheart."

"Do you have any idea what that word means?"

"Of course."

There were several empty parking spaces in front

of her office. He pulled into the one closest to the door and shut off the engine. Afraid he planned to follow her inside, Gaby reached for the door handle, wishing she'd never made those calls to the florist shop.

"Then you need to tell her *yours* is still in Russia."

"Karin says I should concentrate on my new one in case the old one does not work out."

"I don't suppose Karin knows I'm the person trying to help you get your fiancée here."

"She doesn't want Natasha to come."

Gaby frowned. "Why not?"

He shrugged. "She says I do not act like a man in love."

"Did you tell her that's the whole point? That you need to see her again?"

"Yes. But Karin says that if I loved her, I would never have left Russia in the first place."

The same thought had crossed Gaby's mind.

"I have to go in. Thank you for the ride and the breakfast."

His hand reached for hers. "You don't have to keep thanking me. Tell me what time you plan to leave to get your bike, and I will be here."

"I'm taking a taxi."

"You are a very stubborn American woman," he murmured, rubbing his thumb against her palm. Her legs turned to jelly right there. "That is why I like you so much. My job is to deliver flowers all over San Diego. Tell me what area you have to go to."

"Mira Mesa," she said of her own free will. Her

uncle Frank would have a coronary if he knew. She was practically having a coronary herself!

"I always have deliveries in the northeast part of the city. I will come for you at noon. We will pick up your bike and make those deliveries at the same time. It will be fun."

She moaned.

"Since I met you, I have dreamed of us working together," he said. "You are a very intriguing woman, Gabriella. I find that I want to be with you all the time." His husky voice underlined what his hand was still doing to hers.

She snatched it away. "If you don't get going, you'll be on a permanent vacation from your second job."

"When I tell Karin why I was late, she will give me even more time off with pay."

Gaby could believe it. That's what was scary.

WHILE MAX WAS delivering the last order of flowers for the morning, a message had come in on his cell phone. As soon as he got back in the van, he called his contact.

"What did you find out about the address in Mira Mesa?"

"It's a single-family dwelling, four school-age kids, both parents work. The father's an employee at Larson Heating and Air-Conditioning. The mother works at the Diamond T Mini Mart in Mira Mesa. She has a speeding ticket in a school zone on her driving record. The eighteen-year-old has a debt from a CD company. It's been sent to a collection agency."

The report sounded innocuous enough, but that in itself could be misleading.

"Call me if you notice anything suspicious happening at Ms. Peris's apartment."

"Will do. The house in Mira Mesa will be surrounded by the time you get there."

"Thanks for the information."

It was ten to twelve. Max turned the van around and drove back to East Village, aware of an excitement he couldn't suppress even though he knew he was playing with fire.

In the distance he spotted Ms. Peris on the sidewalk in her pale blue suit. With that gorgeous figure and legs to match, you couldn't possibly miss her. The way a couple of delivery guys were eyeing her on their way into Jack's Guitar and Drum Shop, he realized he wasn't the only male enjoying the view.

When she saw the van, she hurried toward it. Max reached across to open her door. It pleased him to watch the guys' faces fall as she climbed inside, unaware her every move was being scrutinized with blatant masculine interest.

He felt a juvenile urge to flip them off until he remembered that what he'd been doing to her since she'd driven her car into the Audi was much worse. There was a name for a man who took pleasure going through a woman's closets and drawers, handling her most intimate apparel, listening in on her conversations, riffling through her mail.

But there was also a name for a woman who set a man up to be killed. He intended to get to know her a lot better before he knocked the car ring out of commission and sent all the players to prison.

She fastened her seat belt, then turned to him. "Why don't we stop for hamburgers at a drive-thru on our way? My treat."

With that inviting smile, he couldn't picture her as a woman who was fast headed for incarceration without parole.

"Some of my compatriots do not like the American hamburger, but I am not one of them. There is a Jack-in-the-Box down the street."

"That sounds good. I love their cheesecake."

"I do, too." He covered her hand, which was resting on the seat. "We have so much in common, I feel we must have known each other in a former life."

"I doubt we had cheesecake then." She slid her hand out from beneath his.

He smiled. "What a boring existence it must have been." He paused and shifted topic. "You are not a Mormon by any chance, are you?" One of Max's close friends in the FBI belonged to the Mormon Church. He'd taken Max to one of their Sunday meetings when his third baby was christened.

A gentle laugh came out of her. "No. Much to my parents' chagrin, I don't espouse any particular religion."

Having seen the crucifix and missal in her bedroom, he'd been waiting for *that* lie.

"It sounds like the missionaries have been to your door, as well, Anatoly."

He'd pulled off the street to follow the cars funneling into the drive-thru. "Since I arrived in San

Diego, I have been visited by Mormons and Jehovah's Witnesses. Like you, I listen to their messages, but I have not yet decided what I think. We had no Church in Russia.''

It was their turn to order. ''What would you like on your hamburger?''

Within a half hour they'd eaten their lunch and had found the address in Mira Mesa. He pulled up to the curb and killed the engine. There were several unmarked cars parked along the street, but not in front of the house or in the driveway.

''Will you come to the door with me?''

Though he didn't believe she planned to have him finished off here, it wasn't beyond the realm of possibility. That was what his backup was there for.

''I am glad you asked, because I would not let you go up to a strange house alone.''

''I knew you'd say that. The thing is, a college girl is selling her bike. If she has a man with her, like a family member or a boyfriend, he might try to change the price on me. Unlike most women of today, I'm not above asking a man for help. It's still pretty much a man's world out there.''

He pretended to be flattered while his mind was busy working out what she was really up to. ''You want to do the talking while I stand by?''

''If you wouldn't mind. Your presence will guarantee a fair deal.''

''Of course I do not mind. I will also check out the bike before you hand over the money.''

''Thank you, Anatoly.''

She got out of the van before he could go around

to help her. Together they walked up to the porch. The second she rang the bell, a young blond woman of about eighteen opened the door.

Max couldn't see anyone else in the background. He was depending on the guys to know those details.

"Hi." The girl seemed shy.

"Hello. I'm Gaby Peris, the woman who called about your bike. This is my friend, Mr. Kuzmina. Are you Linda?"

"Yeah. Just a minute and I'll get it." She left the door ajar, then walked the bike out a second later.

At first glance, the bike looked in good condition. After inspecting it closely, Max could tell it had been well oiled and lubed. There was no rust. He took it for a ride so he could shift the gears. So far he couldn't see a problem and felt the bicycle was worth the asking price.

When he rode up, he nodded to the woman who'd just called herself Gaby. She was too feminine for that name. He preferred to think of her as Gabriella.

Max shouldn't have been surprised she would take his opinion about the bike without question. After all, she had a plan to ingratiate herself to him. But it brought him no pleasure for reasons he didn't want to think about.

He'd never enjoyed a woman's company to this extent before. Not even his ex-wife's. *Lord.*

She pulled the cash from her purse and gave it to the girl. Then she produced a bill of sale, which they both signed. Once that was accomplished, the girl wished her well with the bike and closed the door.

He pushed the bike toward Gabriella. "You want to go for a spin?"

"I'll wait until after work."

"Fine. Then I will load it in the back of the van."

"Thank you for all your help," she said when they were on the road again. "You've made the aftermath of the accident a very pleasant experience. When we go to the park on Saturday, I should have the information you've been waiting for about your fiancée. Hopefully you'll be able to make plans for her visit in the very near future."

Draw me in. Push me away. She'd chosen the wrong man to mess with.

"If you can make that happen, you are truly an amazing woman, Gabriella."

"I haven't promised a miracle, but I'll try my best."

Of course you will.

He turned down her street and double-parked in front of her office building. "One moment. I will get your bike and take it down to your office."

"I can do that."

"That is not the point. I like to do things for you."

She whispered her thanks and opened the door for him. An Asian was waiting for her at the bottom of the stairs. She opened her office door so Max could take the bike on through.

"I will put it in the back," he murmured near her ear where the scent of her shampoo lingered.

She nodded to him before greeting the man, who looked to be in his late twenties. He could be a mafia contact or a client.

Max set the bike against the wall, then returned to her office. She approached him. "I think I left my purse in the van."

There was no way she would have done that without a reason. Maybe the whole business about the bike was an elaborate scheme so she could be alone with the other man for a moment.

He didn't know if she'd found the bugs in her office and apartment. Perhaps she'd done this to see if he would take this opportunity to plant one in her cell phone.

On the other hand, someone in the mafia might have wanted to deliver a message in person, and this was her way of getting rid of Max for a few minutes while still looking totally innocent.

"I'll get it."

Taking the stairs three at a time, he hurried outside and found her purse on the floor of the van. Without opening it, he dashed back down to her office. She looked surprised that he'd returned so fast.

Tit for tat, Ms. Peris.

"Thank you, Anatoly. Have a good week. I'll see you on Saturday. Shall we say one o'clock in front of my apartment?"

Sorry, sweetheart, but you're going to see me a hell of a lot sooner than that. "I will be there with the croquet set. We will have a wonderful time."

A stillness emanated from her. "Why do I get the feeling they play croquet in Russia and you were world champion?"

"Not croquet," he teased.

"What then?"

"That is for me to know and you to find out."

"You're terrible," she grumbled, but her eyes were alive with curiosity, almost as if she couldn't help herself. Those warm, chocolate-brown depths were seducing him in ways for which he had no defense.

Watch your back.

He could hear Gideon's warning. But it was coming from a long way off and didn't carry its usual punch.

"Other women have told me that before, but they were not as exciting as you, Gabriella."

The trouble with that statement was that it was true.

Max went out to the van and headed for the florist shop. He needed to load the afternoon orders and get them delivered in time to carry out his next plan of attack.

En route he checked in with the guy manning surveillance in a construction trailer near the corner of her office complex.

"Tell me about the people who've been to see her today."

"So far they've all been legitimate clients talking to her about petitions for various types of visas. The guy who was there when you took in the bike was inquiring about a fiancée visa."

"What about phone calls?"

"Except for one incoming call, everything else has been work-related."

Max's hand tightened on the phone. "Who was it?"

"Someone from a Dr. Karsh's office in Miami, Florida, returning her call. They made an appointment for a phone consultation on Friday at two o'clock her time.''

''Find out what you can on Dr. Karsh. I'll get back to you later.''

If she knew she was being bugged, she wasn't about to give anything away she didn't want Max to know about.

Clicking off, he got busy on the afternoon orders, then stopped by his apartment house to change into shorts and load his bike in the van. It was four-thirty by the time he'd parked it on the side street next to her apartment. After he'd removed his bike from the back of the van and had locked the doors, he took off for the office of one Gabriella Peris.

WHEN ANATOLY CARRIED her bike downstairs, he'd made it look so effortless. Getting it back up the steps was somewhat difficult, and Gaby wasn't exactly the picture of grace.

Already short of breath before she even sat on it, she almost stopped breathing altogether when she saw an incredible-looking stranger seated on his bike outside Jack's Guitar and Drum. He was lounging against a street pole obviously waiting for someone.

Her gaze darted to his hard, powerful legs. She tried not to stare. Good grief. She'd already made an appointment with Dr. Karsh to talk about her obsession with a certain Russian. Now she was thinking she'd better phone her regular doctor to find out why she was being bombarded with excess hormones.

She couldn't prevent her gaze from wandering up his well-defined chest covered by a blue T-shirt. From there it was only a little jump to his face, which had a familiar look. Then her attention was snagged by the well-worn baseball cap on his head. The rim had been turned to the back, and she could read the printing.

The words Bronx Knights sprang out at her before she realized who the guy was she'd been devouring with her eyes. He looked so American dressed like that, her mind hadn't been able to make the leap to Anatoly.

A wave of heat swept through her body. "Where did you get that hat?"

"I traded one of my Russian tapes for it with a guy at the beach."

"But why *that* one?"

"You do not like it?"

Not those sad eyes again. "Please don't take everything I say so personally, Anatoly. All I meant was, I'm surprised."

"Because I want to look like an American?"

"No—"

"I already told you I am going to be naturalized very soon," he cut in on her. Apparently she'd really offended him. "I had hoped to please you, but I can see that you will always think of me as Russian. What can I fix so you will like me better?"

She rubbed her forehead. She could feel a headache coming on. There wasn't anything to fix. He was quite perfect the way he was. The Russian traits only made him more attractive.

"Tell me the truth, Gabriella," he said in a hurt voice. "How can I change myself so you will be happy to be seen in my presence? If it is the way I speak, you could help me get rid of my accent. I would pay you.''

She bowed her head. ''Your accent is very charming.''

''Then it is the way I look. Shall I cut my hair in a buzz like all the college guys around here?''

''No!'' she cried without thinking, and felt her face grow hotter.

''Then I do not know what else to do. I thought I would ride home with you to make certain you arrived there in one piece. But I can tell you do not want me to come along because you will always see me as a Russian immigrant. A beautiful American like yourself is not interested.

''I understand if you do not want to spend Saturday with me. Promise me you will not get into another accident on your way home. On that bike you have no protection against a fast-moving car. Please, Gabriella. Be careful. If not for me, for yourself.''

Quick as lightning, he joined the traffic on the street with the agility of a Tour de France racer.

''Wait, Anatoly!''

She slid onto the seat and started pedaling as fast as she could to catch up with him.

''Slow down!'' she cried when he changed lanes. She crossed after the light had changed red and kept on going. Several cars honked. People yelled at her. She didn't care. It was imperative she reach him before that tragic streak in his nature convinced him she really didn't like him.

Her uncle would tell her this was the perfect time

to let him go. But watching him ride off like that had left her with a sense of loss more disturbing than the possibility that he could be involved in illegal activities.

If they weren't of too serious a nature, she was convinced that with the right incentive, Anatoly could be rehabilitated. She knew her thinking was faulty. That was why she'd phoned her psychiatrist. But right now none of that seemed to matter as she raced along the street, slowly gaining on him.

"Anatoly!" she called out one more time.

He looked over his left shoulder, then moved on to the sidewalk and came to a stop while he waited for her to join him.

She rode up to him, gasping for breath. As she brought her bike to a halt, his hand shot out to steady the handlebar. He studied her flushed features with brooding intensity. "You should not have tried to catch up to me."

"When you knew I was following you, why didn't you stop?"

"Because I am a selfish man, Gabriella. I wanted to find out how much you cared."

Oh, brother. "Of course I care! I'm trying to help you get together with your fiancée. If you persist in believing that because you're an immigrant you're not valid, people really aren't going to like you. No one enjoys being around a person who is always feeling sorry for himself. It's a major turnoff!"

He nodded and answered seriously, "As it happens, I believe what you say. I promise I will never consider myself your unequal again."

She wasn't sure that was correct English, but he got his point across. "Good. I'm glad we have that matter settled."

When he smiled like that, her heart seemed to expand. "Shall I go for the van and drive you home from here?"

"No, thank you. If I rest for another minute, I'll get my second wind."

His gaze held hers. "This is very nice, Gabriella. All these people rushing around us, frantic to get where they are going. Yet you and I are standing in the middle of them on our own special little island, content."

CHAPTER SIX

ANATOLY HAD A UNIQUE WAY of expressing himself that had nothing to do with his being Russian. From the beginning, his ability to tap into her innermost thoughts had created an almost tangible connection.

It was strong, like the bond she'd had with Paul, maybe even stronger in a way because it had happened so much sooner with Anatoly. He was the complete opposite of her husband, who'd been safe, cautious.

Gaby had to admit she'd enjoyed every second of the time spent with him. She really didn't want to believe that he was a criminal. Part of her was afraid to hear from her uncle Frank again. If he told her awful things, that meant the teasing would have to stop. The excitement would have to end. She wasn't ready for that. Not yet.

"I think I can make it to the apartment now."

"Then follow me. I know many shortcuts."

"That explains how you zip around San Diego delivering flowers so fast. I'm afraid I won't be able to keep up."

"We will proceed like the turtle."

"I'm not *that* bad!"

He laughed deep in his throat. It was infectious,

and she laughed too. She couldn't remember the last time she'd let go like that. She was finding that being with Anatoly was an experience she didn't want to miss. Not for a single second.

Once he'd sobered he said, "Are you ready?"

For the oddest reason she got the impression his question was asking something more of her than the obvious. How cruel fate was to place this particular man in her path!

When Paul had been killed, part of her heart had died with him. It might be early days, but if she were to learn that Anatoly was operating on the wrong side of the law, she had an idea the other part just might shrivel up, leaving her without the ability to feel.

"Ready for what?"

Still staring at her, he removed his hand from her bike. "We will go through one alley after another, but do not worry. I will be there to protect you."

"I'm not worried. Back home my neighborhood had its alleys. A lot more action went on in them than the ones around here."

"You mean in New Jersey?"

"You must have seen my degree on the wall."

"I notice everything about you, Gabriella."

So he did.

"You are afraid of nothing."

I'm afraid of you, Anatoly. Afraid of the way you make me feel.

"It explains why you live and work where you do."

"The rent is cheaper."

His half-veiled eyes studied hers once more. "I

have decided you are the most noble woman I have ever met.''

"Careful. You're making me out to be a paragon.''

"That is the word for you. Everyone in America wants to get rich. You could be driving a Porsche, living in an expensive beach house like all the other attorneys who charge six hundred dollars an hour. Instead, you work to help immigrants who have very little money when they first arrive in America.''

After what he'd just said, particularly the way he'd looked at her as he'd said it, she was in danger of embracing life again. *Damn!* she cried inwardly. Embracing life was good, but why did it have to be because of a man who might be a criminal?

"Don't be deceived,'' she said. "I make an adequate living. One day I intend to live at the beach and drive around in a Mercedes. But for now, this bike suits me fine. Shall we go?''

He caught up with her. They waited at the corner until the light changed. Then he moved ahead and made a detour. She followed him to the middle of the block, where he turned into an alley.

Soon she realized she was having fun, following him as he swung wide to the right, then the left to avoid kids, delivery trucks and other obstacles. On bare stretches they rode abreast, in perfect synch. It was more than fun, it was exhilarating, and she was disappointed when their ride was finally over. They'd come out on the street where she lived.

When they drew up in front of her apartment building, he was off his bike and holding the door open for her before she'd even dismounted.

"That was great!" Flushed and slightly out of breath, she pushed the bike on through. "I felt like a kid again."

"You look happy," he murmured before resting his bike against the wall opposite the mailboxes. "I will take your bike upstairs for you."

There was no point telling him he didn't have to. As he disappeared, she reached into the box for her mail. To her surprise she found a postcard along with a free sample of a new cereal. She turned the card over.

Dear Gaby,
Depending on the traffic, I should arrive at the apartment by dinnertime Saturday night. I'll wait for you no matter how late you come in. I'm on the verge of making a decision that will affect both our lives.
Love,

Hal.

Gaby tapped the card against her cheek. Hallie had been hovering on the brink of becoming a professed nun. Now it appeared she'd made up her mind. If this was what she really wanted, then Gaby was thrilled for her.

But it meant looking for another roommate. Hallie was such a wonderful person, Gaby knew she would never find her equal no matter how long and hard she searched.

Maybe it would be better to live alone until she

had enough money for a really good down payment on a condo.

"Gabriella?"

She looked up to discover Anatoly walking toward her carrying a large box of pizza, green salads and canned cola.

"Today you bought us hamburgers, so this afternoon I phoned ahead for pizza to be delivered here at six-thirty. If we do not eat it now, it will get cold."

Gaby had been waiting to hear back from her uncle. But already it was too late. The damage was done. Anatoly had become an addiction. Tonight she didn't want to think about what life would be like to lose him and Hallie at the same time.

BEFORE MAX HAD CARRIED her bike up the stairs, Gabriella had been glowing. If all else was playacting, her pleasure in their ride was a hundred percent genuine. You couldn't fake that kind of emotion.

But he'd come back downstairs to find her countenance changed. "The exercise has drained you. The sooner you eat some food, the better you will feel."

"I have to admit, pizza sounds good."

She moved past him and started up the stairs. His glance darted to her hand which still clutched a small sample package of cereal and what looked like a postcard.

When they reached her apartment, she pulled keys from her jeans pocket and opened the door. While he put everything on the table, she followed with the bike. Once it rested against the wall beside the window that looked out on the street, she turned to him. "If you'll excuse me for a moment, I'll be right back in."

"Of course. I will set the table."

To his surprise she tossed her mail on the kitchen counter before disappearing into the back part of the apartment. Like the handbag she'd purposely left in the van, she never did anything without an agenda. He knew she wanted him to read the card.

But he wasn't thinking professionally at the moment. He'd just watched her go up the stairs. Those womanly hips and legs molded by snug jeans were still fresh in his mind. The swish of her ponytail had distracted him to the point he was ready to set her hair free with or without her permission.

While he got the plates and glasses out of the cupboard with one hand, he turned the card with the other so he could read the writing. It had been mailed from Los Angeles. After absorbing the contents, he put it back the way it had landed and finished setting the table.

According to the postcard, she had a lover who was about to propose marriage. It was all bogus of course. He didn't doubt she had a lover somewhere, but it wasn't Hal.

Was her uncle the brains behind this calling card? His way of telling his niece he'd found something on Max, so she should go ahead and get the job done? If he had orchestrated this little trap, he showed a lot of cunning.

How shrewd of the uncle to make him think Gabriella had a lover. What better way to ignite his jealousy so he would insist on coming back to her apartment on Saturday night hoping to get a good look at his rival, maybe even confront him.

Hal was probably the hit man who would finish the job she'd started by running into the Audi. They would call it a crime of passion.

As Max had theorized to Gideon, someone in the ring had become suspicious, and the mafia family back East had sent Gabriella to investigate. Now it seemed her uncle had given her the sign for Max to be rubbed out.

As if thinking about her had conjured her up, she walked into the front room. "The bathroom's free if you want to freshen up."

"I used the kitchen sink. Come and eat before the pizza gets cold."

She'd barely started on her second piece of pizza when the phone rang.

"Excuse me." In a jerky motion she jumped up from the table and hurried over to the chair in the living room to answer it.

Max kept eating, unable to make sense of hushed snatches of conversation, since her back was turned toward him. After a few minutes she clicked off, but didn't immediately rejoin him.

He got to his feet and crossed to her. "Something is wrong. What is it?"

"One of my clients is in trouble. I'm afraid I'm going to have to go downtown."

"Now?"

"Yes."

"To your office?"

"No."

"Where?"

She lifted her eyes to him. He couldn't decipher their expression. "It's not your concern, Anatoly. Thank you for the dinner. I'll put my salad in the fridge and eat it when I get back."

"How will you get where you have to go?"

"On my bike."

"No. I will not allow it. Though it is not dark yet, it will be soon. You will not be safe. Let me drive you."

"How can you do that when you came on your bike?"

"My van is around the corner, parked in its usual place."

She shook her head. "You mean you rode your bike from here to my office just to accompany me home?"

"Yes."

"But you must be exhausted!"

"Not at all. I love to be active."

"You're amazing." Her eyes were alive once more.

He groaned. After all these years, why did it have to be this particular woman who attracted him so?

"I had hoped we could play cards after dinner, Gabriella. I have a deck in my pocket. Since that will not be possible now, allow me to be with you, if only to take you to your destination and back."

She caved in on cue. "I will on one condition."

"What is that?"

"Let me pay you for the gas."

"If you like, you may pay me right now."

"I *would* like. I'll get my purse."

She ran into the bedroom once more. While she was gone, he put everything in the refrigerator. Seconds later she returned and thrust ten dollars in his hand. "That's for all the other times, too." He stashed the money in his pocket.

When they left the apartment, she held the bottom door open for him so he could guide his bike outside. After they reached the van, she got in the passenger side while he put his bike in the back. Then he joined her.

"Now will you tell me where I should drive you, or shall I guess?"

That brought a smile to her lips. "Go ahead. Make my day."

Make mine, instead, by telling me you have nothing at all to do with the mafia. "The city jail," he said.

Her head swung around. "Nothing gets past you, does it, Anatoly."

"The kind of clients you see on a regular basis do not need you at night unless they've been arrested."

"You're right."

"You are sad about this?"

"Yes. This is a troubled young man with a sick mother. He made some mistakes after he arrived here and was hit with an HB 3488."

"What is that?"

"A new law for repeat car thieves."

"I do not understand. A few days ago you became very upset when I said that I hoped your car would be stolen. It provoked a magnificent speech."

Color filled her cheeks. "This is a unique case. Given the right help, I know my client could be rehabilitated. To sentence him to thirteen months in jail wouldn't accomplish anything. I was able to prevail on the judge to give him a shorter jail term and probation, so he could get counseling and take care of his mother."

Impressive, he thought. The mafia had many uses for Gabriella, including setting her up in her own law firm to get their guys off the hook.

"I take it he hopes you will bail him out again."

"Yes. He swears he's innocent, and I tend to believe him. But the police raided the auto body shop where he works and everyone was arrested. Unfortunately he's in this country on an H visa status, which has little clout."

"That is true."

"The thing is, I know this judge. She'll invalidate his visa and show no mercy. He's going to get deported and there isn't a thing I can do except tell him the bad news."

You're right about that, sweetheart. That little body shop probably strips eight to nine thousand stolen cars a year, sending insurance rates through the ceiling.

"I understand your concern for him, Gabriella. I would not like to be in his place if he has to return to Russia." Since détente, none of the governmental heads of countries that made up the former Soviet Union wanted to accept criminals back inside their borders.

"Actually, he's from Belorussia," she said in a quiet voice. If Max didn't know better, he could believe she was actually suffering over this young man's problems.

But part of her con was meant to give off mixed signals. Just when Max thought he had a fix on her, she said something that completely threw him. No doubt she'd been indoctrinated at a very early age to be this good at what she did.

He drove down the ramp to the parking beneath the jail to let her off. "I will wait for you."

"Thanks, Anatoly. This won't take long."

"I am in no hurry."

As soon as she'd disappeared inside, he drove out again and found an empty parking spot in the next block. As soon as he switched off the ignition, he phoned Gideon.

"I'm glad it's you, Max!"

Gideon's tone caused an adrenaline rush. "What's happening?"

"We've learned quite a bit, but nothing necessarily points to a family tie-in to the mafia. Her full name is Gabriella Peris. She's the youngest of three children born to David and Ellen Peris. He's the current CEO of Eastern Hospital Care."

Max blinked. "Isn't that the big hospital group in New Jersey?"

"Right. The uncle she talked to is Frank Cracroft, a longtime detective with the Atlantic City Police Department."

His heart knocked against his ribs. "You're kidding!"

"Most of what you've learned has been the truth. She did graduate from Rutger's with a law degree.

After passing the New York bar, she went to work for a legal firm that deals in immigration and naturalization law with an office in New York. The home office is in Miami. I'm presuming they sent her here to open up a branch in San Diego.

"She married Paul Andrew, a native of Miami Beach, who was an ESL teacher in the Coral Creek School District in Miami. Two and a half years later he was killed along with another teacher while they were out deep-sea fishing. I saw the newspaper article. There was a squall and they were lost at sea."

Max grew restless. "So what do you think? I know what I saw on her legal pad."

"I hear you. Maybe she got involved with the mafia in Miami."

"That's what I was thinking. Maybe her husband found out and somebody eliminated him."

"That's a real possibility. It means the same thing could happen to you."

"There's no way I'm pulling out, Gideon."

"Forget her!"

"I couldn't if I wanted to," he replied. "But more to the point, I'm being set up for Saturday night. Before Karl takes me off this case and sends me to another part of the country, he needs to understand this could be the opportunity we've been waiting for to get those names pinned down."

"He won't go for it!"

"He will when he hears my plan. Just listen to me. I'm going to need your help."

AT FIVE AFTER TWO on Friday afternoon, Gaby saw her client to the door, then walked back to her mini fridge for a drink while she called Dr. Karsh on her cell phone.

The receptionist put her through to him.

"Gaby? How are you, my dear?"

"I'm fine, Dr. Karsh. Thanks for letting me talk to you over the phone."

"Any time. You know that. How does San Diego feel to you by now?"

"At first it was hard living here, but I've learned to enjoy it."

"I'm proud of you, Gaby. You could have gone home to your parents. Instead, you've stuck it out on your own. I'm sure you're stronger and better for it. When you lose a spouse through death or divorce, you need a few years to find out who you are again. That doesn't happen as easily when loved ones surround you and try to remove all the hurdles."

"You're right. As you know, my family is the type to suffocate you with love."

"Lucky you."

"Yes. I'm very blessed."

"All right. So who's the lucky man in your life?"

She almost dropped her cola. "What do you mean?"

"I presume you've met one. Isn't that the reason for this call?"

"Well, yes, but it's not what you think," she declared, pacing the floor.

He chuckled. "You're attracted and feel guilty about it. That's very common for a woman who had a solid marriage like yours and wanted children.

Would you have expected your husband to stay celibate if you'd been the one who died so young?"

"Of course not, but it isn't that simple. This man has a fiancée."

"If he's seeing both of you at the same time, then you don't need me to tell you what's wrong with that picture."

"No. She's in Russia." *At least I think she is. Uncle Frank hasn't phoned me yet to tell me otherwise.*

"Except for one visit in six years, they've been separated the entire time. I'm working to help her get a visa through so she can come for another visit. Before he left Russia they were planning to be married, but now he's not sure. He'll be an American citizen soon and says he needs to see her again before he can make a commitment."

"That sounds reasonable. I'm assuming the attraction between the two of you is mutual."

"It's very strong on my part," she said honestly. "He acts like he's interested in me, too. But how can I know for sure? With us everything's so complicated."

"How long have you known him?"

She felt her face go hot. "Less than a week."

"Your feelings are this intense already?"

"Now do you understand why I'm calling? Is there something wrong with me?"

"No, of course not." He chuckled. "Once in a while chemistry can be very powerful, almost overwhelming, between people on a first meeting."

"That's my problem, you see. This is the first man

since Paul. I seem to have come back to life with a vengeance!''

Last night when he'd driven her back home from the jail, he'd dropped her off in front of the building, then waited until he'd seen her light go on in the apartment. She'd thought he would want to come in. When he didn't, she couldn't believe how disappointed she was.

''That's good. Healthy. Are you feeling extra guilty because you slept with him?''

''No! I mean, I haven't slept with him yet, but I *want* to. And yes, I feel guilty for having such thoughts.''

''Because you feel you're betraying Paul's memory?''

''Maybe.''

''There's no maybe about it. But I sense something else going on. Tell me. Did you sleep with your husband before you were married?''

''No.''

''Why not?''

She could hear her mother's voice. *Nice Catholic Girls don't do things like that until after the marriage, Gabriella. You listen to me. I know what I'm talking about.*

''Partly my upbringing. Partly because Paul was a good Catholic boy. He wasn't aggressive, and I didn't know anything,'' she mumbled.

''But with this man, everything's different.''

''Yes.''

''Tell me how.''

"I don't know exactly. He's very sensual. Demonstrative."

"The opposite of Paul?"

"Yes. Paul was shy."

"And now that you've been married, you know what goes on."

She blushed again. "Yes."

"Why do I get the feeling this man isn't a good Catholic boy?"

"Are you psychic, Dr. Karsh?"

He scoffed. "Since I know you stopped going to Mass years ago, it sounds to me like you're feeling guilty for not picking someone who would please your parents."

"Not if he ends up being imprisoned or deported."

After a long silence, "You think he's some kind of criminal? Russian mafia maybe?"

"I don't know!" she blurted in agony.

"What kind of proof do you have?"

Quickly she related the story about the accident and Anatoly's subsequent pursuit of her.

"In other words, you have no evidence, only fear."

"Yes."

"Then this is my advice. Until he provides you with something concrete, give yourself permission to get to know him, but don't complicate things by sleeping with him. It's too soon under any circumstances. Your judgment will be much sounder if you won't allow the physical side to take over."

"Have you got any ideas how to prevent that from happening?" Every time Anatoly's hand clasped hers, which seemed to be all the time, her body turned to liquid.

"I'm afraid all I can do is counsel you the way I've done my daughters. Enjoy activities where you're not alone, say good-night before you want to. That sort of thing."

"Wise counsel, Doctor. I'm going to try to follow it. Thank you for listening to me blab."

"It was my pleasure. Call me anytime, Gaby."

"Don't worry. You're not rid of me yet."

"Be careful, won't you?"

"I will."

She clicked off and finished the rest of her drink.

What she'd really wanted from Dr. Karsh was for him to tell her Anatoly wasn't doing illegal things. But that wasn't in his power. She would have to wait to hear from her uncle on that score. Still, she was glad she'd talked to her doctor.

He'd helped her survive Paul's death to the point that she'd made a new life in California, and she really was starting to enjoy it. As long as she kept taking his advice, she couldn't get into too much trouble. Just talking to him had helped clear away some of the cobwebs.

CHAPTER SEVEN

"YOU'RE LATE from school, Irina," Nikolai said. "What kept you?"

It was Friday afternoon. Irina knew her mother's boyfriend would be at the apartment, and so had put off coming home as long as possible. The brawny, dark-blond man terrified her.

"Where's my mother?"

"Like her daughter, she, too, is late getting home." He kicked the door shut behind her.

Irina's mouth went dry. "Dance club went on longer than I expected," she lied. "I'll just put my things away." She dashed to her bedroom.

Another dreaded weekend was here again. Nikolai's associates came to her mother's apartment on Fridays. They talked until the middle of the night while they ate and drank and filled the rooms with their disgusting cigarette smoke. They did other things, too.

Last week one of the men had opened her bedroom door after she'd gone to bed. Irina had screamed and it had brought her mother.

"It's all right, Irina," she'd tried to reassure her daughter. "Alexey was only looking for the bathroom. He didn't mean to frighten you. Go back to sleep."

Irina had known exactly what was going on. Those things had happened in Russia to girls much younger than her. It was a curse to be attractive. Now that she'd turned sixteen, guys at school were starting to look at her differently. So were the men. It wouldn't be long before one of them made it to her bedroom and her mother wouldn't be able to stop him.

Since the death of her father almost a year before, there had been several men who'd slept over, but in time they'd moved on. She'd hated all of them, but it wasn't until her mother had brought home Nikolai that Irina had entertained the idea of getting a gun and killing him.

After the first week of knowing her mother, he'd taken over their lives and told Irina what she could and could not do in her own home. He had a key and acted as if he lived here.

She'd pleaded with her mother not to let him come around with his friends anymore, but her mother had said it was okay because they'd started living better than they had before. There was more money for food and nice things.

Irina didn't care about that. She wished their family had never come to America in the first place. After they'd arrived, her father had changed into someone she didn't know. He'd grown secretive and argued with her mother, who'd cried a lot at night. Before his fatal car crash, he'd at least been there to protect them. Now there was no one....

Nikolai followed her into the kitchen. Having arrived ahead of her and her mother, he'd left the usual supply of vodka and cognac on the counter. He'd also made tea.

"Our guests will show up any minute now and they'll be hungry. We have a lot of business to discuss and are starting early. I expect you to do as you're told and give the men what they ask for."

She had a feeling he didn't mean just food.

With the blood pounding in her ears from fright, she hurried over to the refrigerator. Inside was a large pot of stew her mother had prepared the night before. Irina put it on the stove to heat up.

"I'll make *bliny* to go with the *rassolnik*," she muttered, praying for her mother to get home.

"We'll want plenty of sour cream and jam with those."

He lounged against the counter smoking a cigarette, watching her through hooded eyes. She could sense something horrible was going to happen.

With jerky movements she assembled the ingredients for the pancakes. It was when she reached into the bin for the flour that he moved close and pinned her against the counter with his powerful body. Then he began a slow exploration of her thighs with his hands.

She broke out in a cold sweat. "Please don't do that," she begged.

"Why not?" he inquired in a silky voice, his cigarette dangling from his lips. "Don't you like it?"

She averted her head. "No."

"In time you will."

"Irina?"

By some miracle her mother was home. *Thank God.*

"I'm in the kitchen," she called out, faint with relief. Nikolai smiled, making her skin crawl, before he removed his hands.

He knew she wouldn't dare tell her mother anything. The repercussions wouldn't be worth it. Nikolai had a violent temper, one that flared for no good reason. He would beat her mother savagely if she tried to protect Irina.

"What took you so long, Galena?" he demanded as her mother entered the kitchen. But instead of allowing her to respond, he tossed his cigarette in the sink and began kissing her.

"Nikolai, not in front of—"

"Your daughter's a big girl now. Almost as beautiful as her mama. She understands these things."

Irina turned away. Bile rose in her throat. But if she vomited in the sink, her mother would want to know why. Then Nikolai would inflict his punishment. She had no choice but to continue making the pancakes.

"Oleg and Alexey came in the door with me," she heard her mother whisper.

"Then you'd better take tea to them."

When he ordered her mother around like that, Irina wanted to plunge a knife between his shoulder blades.

After her mother left the kitchen with the tea tray, Nikolai turned to her again. "You're a very smart girl, Irina. In some ways prettier than your mama. An important man will be here in a few minutes. His name is Yevgeny Babichenko.

"If you please him, he'll give you things you never dreamed of. Clothes, a car. Maybe even your own apartment. If you don't please him, that will not please me. You understand what I'm saying?"

Irina nodded, but inside she was shuddering.

"Finish the pancakes, then go put on a nice dress."

After what had happened in the kitchen just now, Irina would rather die than let any man touch her again. As she was finding out, rape was something that happened everywhere, not just in Russia. No place was safe for a girl. She vowed it would never happen to her.

"I only have one good dress. It's downstairs in the laundry room. You know, where I iron for other people on Saturdays."

His eyes glittered. "What color is it?"

She swallowed hard. Nikolai had seen through her ploy.

"It's a blue-flowered print."

"I'll get it for you."

Now that she'd made that vow to herself, a calm came over her. "You'll need a key to the laundry room."

She pulled it from a hook next to the window overlooking the back alley. As she handed it to him, she said, "You'll have to hunt for the dress. It's hanging on the line with some other things."

"While I'm gone, put a little makeup on." He pinched her cheek so hard the pain brought tears to her eyes. "You're too pale. We can't have that. Yevgeny is expecting the surprise I told him about to be special."

He finally left the kitchen. Through the crack in the door she watched him greet his friends before he headed for the apartment entrance.

"Where are you going?"

"Relax, Galena. I'm doing an errand for Irina. Why don't you finish pouring the tea for our guests, hmm? I'll be right back."

The second he disappeared, Irina moved the case of vodka to the floor beneath the window. With heart pounding, she undid the lock and tugged on the handle with all her might.

When it opened enough to let her through, she stepped on top of the case and climbed out onto the fire escape. After closing the window, she raced down the three flights of stairs.

Under any other circumstances she would have been afraid to make the huge final drop to the ground. But fear of Nikolai had her running on pure adrenaline.

She held on to the bottom rung, then dangled in the air for a moment before letting go. Thankfully she was wearing sneakers. The impact wasn't as jarring as she'd thought it would be.

Free at last, it didn't matter where she went now. The only important thing was to get as far away from Nikolai as possible. As soon as he discovered she was missing, he would send his network of people, including the men at the apartment, on a relentless search for her.

She dashed to the end of the alley, then cut across the main street. It was close to six o'clock now. Everything was crowded with people going home from work. Unable to dodge the traffic on the sidewalk fast enough, she managed to get on a bus headed for the Marina District.

Twenty minutes later she got off at a corner where there was a park, then started running across the grass. If she remembered correctly, there was a big shopping center beyond it. She would lose herself inside until she found a phone.

There was only enough money in her pocket to make one call. The woman at the school assembly had said the number was easy to remember. Just dial VILLAGE.

AFTER MAX MADE his last delivery for Friday afternoon, he headed for Gabriella's apartment. On the way, he called the guy running surveillance at her office.

"Calder here. Tell me what went on today."

"She had clients coming and going until two. Around three, there was a call from someone in the State Department named Joe who sounded on friendly terms with her.

"He told her that the temporary student visa for Natasha Azarnova, which had been denied, has now gone through. He had it sent to her address in Moscow."

So…Ms. Peris *could* move mountains. But she still didn't have a clue that all that information had been planted.

"After his call she had two more clients, then she left."

Max pursed his lips. "You can't account for the time between two and three?"

"No. But she didn't leave her office."

That meant she'd been talking to the doctor. "What did your research turn up on Karsh?"

"He's a renowned psychiatrist who has run a top psychiatric hospital in Miami Beach for over twenty years. He's a native Floridian, president-elect of the Florida Psychiatric Association."

He rubbed his eyes. Was Dr. Karsh a link in the Miami mafia chain?

Gabriella had either removed the bug from beneath her monitor or she'd purposely walked to another part of her office with her cell phone to have her conference.

Then again she might have decided to leave the bug alone. There was no way of knowing.

A groan escaped his throat. She would have made a damn fine FBI agent. *She'd make an even better lover.* He shoved the thought aside.

"Keep up the good work." He clicked off and phoned the undercover officers tailing her.

"This is Calder. Give me a progress report."

"Yes, sir. She rode her bike home, then left a few minutes later for a Laundromat two blocks away. It's the Maple Street Laundromat in the middle of the 1300 block, west side. Officer Barr followed her inside. They're both still there."

She could have arranged to meet Hal there. No telling how many calls she'd made on her cell phone between two and three.

"Did she go on foot?"

"No. Her bike. She dangled a laundry bag on the end of her handlebar."

"Call me the second she leaves the Laundromat, and don't let her out of your sight."

"Right." There was a click.

When Max reached Little Italy, he pulled into a parking space for delivery trucks a block away from her apartment. He waited for what seemed like hours—in reality it was only twenty minutes—before his cell phone rang. He clicked it on.

"What's happening?"

"She just walked out the door with her laundry and is taking off on her bike headed north."

Max started the van and backed out of his parking place. "Put Barr on as soon as you can."

"He's on his way to the car now."

Thirty seconds later Max got the call. "This is Officer Barr. While Ms. Peris was getting ready to put in a wash, I checked all the units on the pretense of looking for something I'd lost. There were no notes left anywhere for her to read. After she loaded the washer, she sat down to work on a crossword puzzle she'd pulled from her laundry bag."

It was probably the same one Max had seen on the table by her bed.

"There were half a dozen people in there, but she didn't talk to any of them or make eye contact. She got up once to put her things in the dryer. When they were done, she put everything back in the laundry bag and left. I checked the washer and dryer she used to see if she might have dropped a note inside for someone. Nothing."

"Good work. Keep it up. I'll check in with you later."

Max took off for her apartment. It was time to make his next move.

GABY WAS HALFWAY between the Laundromat and home when she heard her cell phone ring. She pulled it out of her jeans pocket to glance at the caller ID. To her surprise it was the Girls' Village dispatcher. She hadn't had an emergency phone call from them in more than a month.

She came to a stop in front of a magazine shop and clicked on.

"Gaby, this is Janene. We've got a critical situation. Go to the back parking area of Greenbrier's Department Store at the Marina District shopping center. There's a sixteen-year-old girl hiding in the middle Dumpster near the loading dock. She's wearing a pink T-shirt and jeans. Her name's Svetlana."

Another Russian. Probably an immigrant. "I'll take care of it."

Gaby clicked off, then phoned for a cab. What a time to be without her car!

After turning off her phone, she put it in her pocket, then rushed inside the shop with her laundry bag.

"Excuse me, sir."

The man at the cashier's desk looked up. "Can I help you?"

"Yes. I've been called to an emergency situation and am waiting for a cab. Could I leave this laundry bag and my bike here? I'll come for them both as soon as I can."

After a slight hesitation, "Of course. Bring your bike inside. I'll put it behind the counter."

"That's very kind of you. I'll think of a way to repay you later."

She handed over her laundry bag, then went outside for her bike. Within a minute she was ready to go. "Here's my business card." She pulled one from the wallet of her back pocket and laid it on the counter before hurrying out the door again.

In a couple of minutes a taxi cruised up to the curb. She scrambled into the back and gave the driver instructions. The traffic was horrendous, but when she told him the nature of her errand and showed him her official identification for Girls' Village, he said he would hurry.

When they finally reached the shopping center, the back parking lot was full of cars and people. She told him to head for the middle Dumpster. As soon as he pulled up beside it, Gaby got out, leaving the door open.

Walking over to large trash bin, she lifted the lid. "Svetlana? My name is Gaby. I'm from Girls' Village. Don't be afraid."

In a second she heard noise, then a strawberry-blond head emerged above her. Finally she saw a lovely, but frightened, young face appear.

"Come on. Let's go."

Gaby helped the girl down. She was taller than Gaby by several inches, but very slender.

"Get in the taxi and crouch on the floor."

The girl did as she was told. Gaby followed her

inside and shut the door. The driver knew where to go. They were off.

"Thank you very much," the girl whispered in heavily accented English. She sounded like Anatoly, only her accent was far more pronounced.

"You are very welcome. How did you hear about Girls' Village?"

"At school. This lady told us we could call."

"Mrs. Apgard?"

"I do not know."

The girl's legs were pressed up against Gaby's. Her body trembled like a leaf in the wind. Gaby wondered what awful situation she was running from.

"Well, I'm glad you called us. We can help you."

"I glad, too."

"Is anyone else in trouble besides you?"

"Yes. My mother. Her boyfriend might kill her because I run away."

Tears stung Gaby's eyes. "Do you want the police to go there and help her?"

"No!" the girl cried. "Maybe he not kill her if no police come."

Sandra, the teen who was expecting a baby soon, had told Gaby the same thing when she'd plucked her from a life-and-death situation at an amusement park last spring. The girl had asked that no police be called in because she was terrified harm would come to her family.

Gaby pulled out her cell phone and called security at Girls' Village. "This is Gaby Peris. I'll be arriving with a new girl named Svetlana in approximately five minutes by TransCab."

"We'll be ready for you."

She put the phone away, then patted the girl's back. "We're almost there, Svetlana. You'll be treated with love and concern."

"Since my father die, I not safe anyplace."

"You will be now."

It wasn't long before she directed the driver to take the road around the side of Girls' Village to the gate, where they were allowed on through. Again she asked him to wait while she took Svetlana inside to the admittance wing.

Liz, one of the volunteers on night duty, was there to greet them. Gaby turned to the girl. "We're all on a first-name basis around here, Svetlana. Liz will help you get settled and then you can have dinner."

Her gaze flicked to Liz. "After her orientation, why don't you ask Sandra to be her buddy for tonight? I think the two of them will be able to relate without problem."

"Sounds like a good idea. Come with me, Svetlana."

The Russian girl hesitated. She stared at Gaby. "Thank you. You save my life."

Again she could hear Anatoly in the girl's words and voice. Everything about this girl tugged at her heart.

Gaby gave her a hug. "Knowing you're safe is all the thanks I need."

"You work here?"

"I come whenever my job lets me. As a matter of fact, I'll see you tomorrow afternoon."

Tomorrow Gaby would be with Anatoly. Just the

thought of him created an excitement she couldn't quell.

Gaby's comment produced the ghost of a smile on Svetlana's face before the girl followed Liz down the hall.

Trying hard not to think about Svetlana's home situation, Gaby hurried out to the taxi. One glance at her watch and she realized it was too late to go back to the magazine shop. It didn't matter. She could walk over there in the morning to get her things.

Right now she had a lot more on her mind than cleaning the apartment for Hallie. On the chance that Svetlana was the girl's real name, Gaby could run it through the State Department's computer and come up with some matches. Since the school district couldn't legally give her the information she sought, she would go about it her own way.

The father was dead. He could have brought his family over on several types of visas, hoping to get naturalized at a later date. Gaby would find out soon enough.

She gave the driver directions to her office. Fortunately she had some cash in an envelope at work she'd forgotten to deposit in the bank. She asked the driver to wait while she got the money out of the drawer. When she paid him, she gave him a big tip, thanking him for all his help. Then she dashed down the stairs, locked her office from the inside and got busy on the computer.

UNTIL MS. PERIS HAD TAKEN an unexpected detour on her way home from the Laundromat, her activities for the day hadn't set off any alarm bells.

Now their ring was deafening.

Max followed the taxi at a discreet distance. When it finally pulled away from the curb in front of Jack's Drum and Guitar Shop, he drove to the same spot and parked the van.

While Gideon ran a background check on the owner of the magazine shop where she'd stashed her things, Max had kept in touch with the guys tailing her. Their account of a teen being taken from a Dumpster to Girls' Village in such a clandestine manner fit with recent information that the mafia brought girls from Russia, then forced them to work as strippers and prostitutes.

Girls' Village was an established institution, reputed for the good it did in the community. But the mafia could have infiltrated it, and Ms. Peris was being used for a variety of activities. It would make the perfect laundering house for homeless immigrant girls.

Gabriella made the perfect Mata Hari.

Max gave her two minutes to reach her office, then moved stealthily down the stairs. She was already seated at the computer. Something was so vital she'd come here, instead of going straight home.

Determined to find out what that something was, he knocked on the door. Through the glass he saw her head swivel in his direction.

"Gabriella?" he called.

As he'd hoped, she jumped up from the chair without touching the keyboard. When she unlocked the door and opened it, he expected anything but what he got.

For one thing, there was nothing furtive about her demeanor. For another, she gave the appearance of someone who held the weight of the world on her shoulders. But that impression was a fleeting one as her gaze lifted to meet his and the sadness changed to pleasure.

"What are you doing here?" Her eyes roved over his features, warming places in his body he hadn't known were there.

"I went to your apartment to have a serious talk with you. When you were not there, I decided you must be working late, so I came here. What I have to say is very important. I do not mind waiting while you finish what you are doing."

"It couldn't keep until tomorrow?" But she'd asked the question with a smile hovering at the corner of her lovely mouth.

He inhaled sharply. "No. It could not. I must speak to you about my fiancée. I have decided I do not want her to come, after all."

She looked stunned. He didn't think it was an emotion she could fake.

"I'm afraid it's too late."

"What do you mean?"

Her beautiful arched eyebrows knit into a frown. "Come in, Anatoly."

He followed her inside and locked the door behind him.

She walked over to her desk but didn't immediately sit down. They stood a few feet apart. He could see the monitor over her shoulder. A list of names stood out on the screen, but he needed to get closer to make sense of them.

That was going to be difficult. In the shadowy light without the door between them, the curves her T-shirt and modest shorts revealed had robbed him of his concentration.

"Please explain about it being too late."

"Just today I learned that Natasha's student visa went through. I was going to wait until tomorrow to surprise you with the news. I'm afraid it has already been mailed to her."

He let out a stream of Russian invective. "Is there any way to stop it from reaching Moscow?"

"Not that I'm aware of." After a brief silence, "You know what I think?" She flashed him a teasing smile. "You're having an attack of prewedding jitters. It happens to American men all the time."

"It happens to Russian men, too, Gabriella. But that is not what is wrong with me. This morning when I woke up and found myself wanting to spend the whole day with you, I realized something earth-trembling was happening to me."

"Earthshaking," she corrected him.

"Yes. That is the word I meant. Please...do not laugh at me. You think this is some kind of a joke, but I assure you it is not."

She looked startled. "I would never laugh at you, Anatoly."

Such earnestness deserved some kind of award.

"It is no secret that I have enjoyed women as much as the next man. But never in my life did I want to spend every minute with one, not even my fiancée. When I met you I thought, this is an attractive American woman, but the novelty will wear off.

"But three days and nights have gone by. I am more excited to be with you now than the morning you crashed into me."

"Maybe that's the reason your interest has lasted so long."

"Now you are being sarcastic. You wound me, Gabriella."

A sound of exasperation escaped her lips. "Not at all. Anatoly, if you had been the one to crash into me, not only would I have been furious, I'd have been prepared not to like you at all. But that would have been impossible, because you are very likable.

"I think maybe you're still fascinated with me because the way we met was beyond your control, and you're a man who likes to orchestrate your relationship with a woman."

How did you know that about me?

"That is true. I have been caught off guard and should have recovered from my infatuation by now. But that has not happened yet. With feelings this strong, I realize I cannot marry Natasha. I have no desire to see her."

"Anatoly, you're jumping to conclusions."

"No. Karin was right. If I had truly loved my fiancée, I would not have left Russia. I should not have asked you for help with her visa. It was a foolish move, and I did it to fight my attraction to you. I must call Natasha and tell her not to come. She must be made to understand that a future with me is not possible."

He glanced at his watch. "There is an eleven-hour time difference between here and Moscow. She will be awake and getting ready for work. May I use your phone?"

Max moved over to the desk where he could see the words on the screen. She'd been researching the Russian name Svetlana from an immigration data bank. He memorized what he could while he pulled twenty dollars from his wallet.

"You're going to call her from here?" She sounded incredulous.

"If it is all right." He put the money on her desk. "When the bill comes, it might be bigger. Naturally I will pay. Please, go ahead and work while I stand here and make the call."

"But, Anatoly…you need privacy."

"In case you are trying to tell me that you understand Russian, let me assure you that I have nothing to tell her you cannot hear."

"I only know a few words," she said in a quiet voice. "But I should think you would still want to be alone."

He held the receiver of her desk phone in his hand. "If I wanted to be by myself, I would not have spent my time looking for you. When we are both through here, I will put your bike in my van and drive you home."

"No. I mean…I don't feel like doing any more work tonight."

For once she'd lost her cool.

"I have made you uncomfortable. Forgive me, Gabriella." He put the receiver back on the hook. "I was so anxious to let you know I was ending my relationship with Natasha, I did not stop to think that this is your place of business and I am the intruder. It will not happen again."

"Anatoly—" she said as he turned to leave. He paused midstride to look back at her. "You didn't intrude. I don't have my bike tonight and could use a ride home. Give me a minute and I'll be ready to go."

"Do not tell me this if you are only feeling sorry for me. That I could not take."

"I might feel many things for you, but sorry isn't one of them."

"Yes? Many?" He smiled. "What are these things?"

She ignored his question and sat down in front of the computer to shut it down.

Obeying a compulsion he could no longer fight, he slid his hands onto her shoulders, enjoying the warmth of her flesh through the thin cotton material. He felt her body tense.

"You must relax, Gabriella," he whispered. "Let my hands help you."

He'd been wanting to touch her like this since the accident. Too late—he forgot to read the last few names at the bottom of the screen before she closed the file.

It didn't matter. He knew where to find it again.

Right now he had found something else. Something tactile. Something throbbing with life.

He lowered his mouth where his thumb had been and brushed his lips against the flawless, satiny skin of her neck.

"I want to unlock your hair. May I?"

CHAPTER EIGHT

ENJOY ACTIVITIES where you're not alone. Say goodnight before you want to.

Gaby slid out of the seat, removing herself from danger by mere inches. "You like to unlock things?" she teased with a smile. "How about the door?"

He stood there with that hurt expression in his eyes. "I think you like to torture me."

I think you are torturing me a lot more than I do you, Anatoly.

"Don't look now, but the manager of the hair salon is waving to us from the stairwell." Gloria had probably seen him come in through the front door and couldn't wait to be introduced.

In a lightning move he reached the door and unlocked it. Gaby preceded him through it.

The striking blond divorcée was so busy looking him over, she forgot to greet Gaby. For the first time in her life, Gaby understood what it meant to feel territorial about a man.

"Hi, Gloria. How are you?"

"I'm great. You don't usually work this late, so I thought I'd come down and say hi."

Sure you did. "Gloria, this is Anatoly Kuzmina."

She turned to Anatoly. "This is Gloria Stewart. She runs the very successful hair salon upstairs."

"How do you do, Gloria," he said in his serious voice before shaking her hand.

"Are you one of Gaby's clients?" The hope in those baby blues could have lit up a small city.

"No. Gabriella is my sweetheart."

"Oh."

Gaby stood there in a euphoric daze.

"I am happy to know that you and Gabriella watch out for each other. She is very important to me. That is why I am here. To drive her home."

"Oh," she said again.

"Do you have transportation?"

"Oh…yes…my car's right out front."

"That is good you do not have to walk far. It was very nice meeting you, Gloria. I am sure we will see each other again."

"Yes. Right." Her stunned gaze flicked to Gaby's. "Well, good night."

"Good night, Gloria. Have a good weekend. See you Monday."

While she charged up the stairs, Gaby ran back to her desk for the twenty-dollar bill. "Here." She handed it to him. "I didn't want you to forg—"

The rest of the words never came out because Anatoly's mouth had found hers. She'd been wanting this to happen for days. But it was over almost before it began, because he didn't try to deepen their kiss. A protest of frustration escaped her lips. For a first try, it left a lot to be desired.

Embarrassed and red-faced because he knew how

disappointed she was, Gaby rushed down the stairs ahead of him.

"Do not be upset, Gabriella. I told you I am a selfish man. It is in my nature to test the waters first before I plunge in."

"Your idea of a test and mine must be two different things! Something *your* country invented?"

She pulled hard on the handle of the van's passenger door to get away from him. It didn't budge. All she managed to do was break the tips of two nails. Oh, well. She needed a manicure, anyway.

"Soon you and I will belong to the same country." He used a key to let her inside, then went around to the driver's seat.

"Don't count on the waters being the same temperature again," she grumbled.

"I do not need to count on anything." He started the van and backed out. "The temperature between us has always burned hot. It is as I told you from the beginning. We are compatible in every way. You and I make fire."

Oh, brother. She looked out her window as they drove down the street.

"I now have proof you have put the memory of your husband away in a safe place."

He was right about that. Paul hadn't once entered her thoughts. She waited for an accompanying stab of guilt, but it didn't come.

"Since meeting you, Natasha no longer takes up space in my heart, either. That is why I must talk to her tonight. So that tomorrow when I come to you, I come as a free man."

It would be crazy to believe anything he was saying. But damn, damn, *damn,* she wanted to believe him. She wanted him. She wanted Anatoly Kuzmina, a dangerous man. A man probably leading a double life. She was out of her mind to get involved with him.

She would be out of her mind to fall in love with him.

She couldn't tell her family. Any hour now she expected her uncle Frank to phone with news that would kill all these burgeoning feelings.

Was such a thing possible now?

"I have made you nervous." They'd come to a stop in front of her apartment building. "I, too, feel shaken by this intensity between us. Go inside, Gabriella, before I do something more than unlock your hair."

"Undo," she corrected him in order to break the tension.

"Yes. That is what I meant. I will be here for you at one o'clock tomorrow."

Before she got out, his eyes captured hers. "We will be a man and a woman on our first official date together. We will smile and laugh with the girls in the sunshine. Do you know how good it is to feel joy inside here?" He put a hand to his heart.

Yes. I know. I never expected to feel this way again. In fact, I don't know that I've ever felt like this before. Not in my whole life.

"I'm looking forward to tomorrow, too. Thank you for the ride home, Anatoly." She hurriedly shut the door and dashed inside the building before she did something dumb like turn around and beg him to come in.

Once inside her apartment, she turned on a light so he would know she was safe.

Gaby wished she didn't have to wait until tomorrow night for Hallie to come home. Hallie had lived through tragedy few people would ever experience. It had set her on a different course and given her rare insight into life. But unfortunately she wasn't here. Their talk would have to wait.

With so much excess energy needing release, the only thing to do was get busy housecleaning the apartment. She wouldn't be able to make the beds with clean sheets until she went back to the magazine shop for her laundry bag. That was okay. The secondhand refrigerator needed defrosting. She would do that.

For the next hour her mind vacillated about what to wear to the park tomorrow. Not that she had a huge wardrobe. But if they were going to play croquet, she'd better wear something comfortable. That meant slacks or walking shorts.

When she finally turned out the light and slid under the quilt, she still hadn't decided on an outfit. If she bought something new, it would be an admission that she'd taken Anatoly seriously about this being their first official date.

On the other hand, everything in her closet had been worn to death. Maybe when she went for her laundry bag, she would ride her bike to the mall and see what she could find on sale.

He'd only ever seen her in a ponytail. Should she

wear her hair long to surprise him, or would that be sending out too blatant a signal? But if she pulled it back the way she always did, he might think she was challenging him to "unlock" it.

Gaby chuckled in the darkness. Once in a while he said a word or phrase that was so funny—so-o-o Anatoly.

She wondered if he would wear something new. He always dressed well. She hadn't seen him in the same outfit twice. Anatoly looked good in anything. In a hand-tailored suit and Italian leather shoes, he'd do lethal damage.

Wouldn't she love to walk into a family gathering with Anatoly on her arm! Her female relatives would be sick with envy. Wait until he opened his mouth and they heard him talk...

Gabriella is my sweetheart. She is very important to me.

Anatoly had been kind to Gloria, but he'd let her know how things stood between them. In a way, she felt kind of sorry for Gloria.

But not *too* sorry.

WHEN MAX WAS within two blocks of his apartment house, he got a call from the guys providing backup.

"Calder here. What's going on?"

"You picked up a car at the last light. A gold Passat."

That would be Oleg. Max glanced at the rearview mirror. There were several cars behind him with their headlights on.

"Is he alone?"

"Yes."

"Thanks for the warning."

If Oleg was on official business, someone else would be with him. Wondering why Oleg hadn't called him, Max took the initiative and punched in the digits of his cell phone. Oleg didn't pick up.

Unwilling to wait until they reached the apartment, Max pulled over to the curb and sat there with the engine running until he saw the Passat slow down and pull even with him. He put his window down. Oleg did the same with the passenger window of his car.

"I saw you behind me," Max lied. The other man looked surprised that he'd been spotted. "How come you didn't answer your phone?"

"My cell's shot until I get batteries. There's trouble."

If it was official mafia business, why hadn't Nikolai phoned Max himself?

"Nikolai didn't call you yet?"

"No." More puzzled than ever, Max said, "Meet me in the produce section of Shopwise three blocks from here on Sycamore."

The other man nodded and took off. Max waited to let a couple of cars pass, then he phoned his backup and told them his destination before heading there himself.

The Shopwise parking lot was full. Max had to wait a few minutes until someone vacated a spot. Then he grabbed an abandoned shopping cart and headed inside.

While he was here, he'd pick up some items for his outing with Gabriella and the girls tomorrow. By the time he reached the produce section, he found Oleg pushing a cart in front of a mound of apples. Max stopped to fill up a bag with some Jonathans.

"Be glad you weren't at the meeting at Galena's apartment tonight," Oleg started without preamble. "Nikolai was in a rage."

Ever since Max had infiltrated the mafia, Oleg had been the closest thing he had to a friend. When Oleg was in a confiding mood, Max was able to pick up a lot of valuable information.

"I've never known Nikolai when he *wasn't* angry about something. He hates my guts."

"You're right about that. He'd just as soon slit your throat as see you made capper of the beach cities." Those comprised the coastal cities of San Clemente, Laguna Beach and Newport Beach, where a larger percentage of the population drove some of the highest priced cars.

"Is that what he was raving about tonight?"

The other man shook his head. "No. This wasn't like our normal drivers' meeting, Anatoly. Nikolai was planning something big tonight, but it never came off because Galena's daughter ran away."

The news didn't surprise Max. Alexey had been after the attractive young teen ever since they'd been meeting at Galena's. One of the reasons Max was angry he'd been temporarily barred from mafia business was because he knew Irina needed protecting.

Her mother could do nothing about the situation. She was Nikolai's helpless victim. At least when Max was there, he could run interference.

"That's not good. She knows our names."

"It's worse than that, Anatoly. While we were at the apartment, Nikolai said she knew something that could bring down the whole San Diego operation if the feds were to hear about it."

Max's hand stilled on one of the apples. That meant Irina knew the names of the mafia bosses. Or at least one of them. She could only have learned it from Nikolai. Max's thoughts reeled as he contemplated what Oleg had told him about tonight's meeting being different.

Was it possible Nikolai had planned to procure Irina for the head man's pleasure in order to curry favor? Was that what this was all about, and the girl had been frightened enough to run?

"He sent all the drivers at the meeting to look for her, Anatoly. We're not supposed to come back to Galena's without her. If you haven't heard from Nikolai yet, you will."

For Nikolai to break down and call Max, his mortal enemy, it would mean he was in the deepest kind of trouble.

"I figured that if we found the girl, he might not be so vocal about his hatred of you."

Oleg's motives weren't totally altruistic. The man was hoping that once Max had been made a capper, he would prevail on the powers that be so that Oleg could be a driver for Max in the beach cities.

"I appreciate your concern. Believe me, there's nothing I'd like better than to find the girl." *But not for the reasons you're thinking, Oleg.* "How did she get away?"

"Through the kitchen window and down the fire escape to the alley."

Irina must have been desperate. Thank God she'd gotten out of there. "How could Nikolai have let her slip through his fingers?"

"That's the strange part. He told Galena to pour us tea, then he said he had to do an errand for Irina. He was gone about five minutes. When he came back, he went straight to the kitchen, but she wasn't there. A case of vodka had been dragged to the base of the window, so he knew what had happened."

Smart girl.

"While he sent Galena to talk to the neighbors, we were all assigned a section near the building to cover. But I didn't see a sign of her. It was the dinner hour. People were coming home from work. I thought I'd go over to your apartment house and see if you had any ideas where to look."

"She probably ran to a place where she could get lost among a throng of people."

"Like a mall?"

"That's where I'd go until I figured out what to do next."

"There are four of them within easy walking distance of Galena's place."

"Most of them will be closing their doors soon. Get some batteries for your phone so you can call me, then drive around the Three Points Mall and Colonial Square. I'll take a look at Nine Palms Court and Fashion Place."

"What if we don't come up with anything?"

"Then we'll check bus terminals and hotel lobbies."

"She could be anywhere." Oleg didn't sound the least bit happy. Max couldn't blame him. None of the drivers wanted to face Nikolai empty-handed. He put the fear in all of them. As if their paranoia wasn't bad enough.

"Nikolai hasn't phoned me yet. Maybe she's already been found," Max theorized.

"She *has* to be found or we're history."

Unfortunately for you, Oleg, that's true.

"Tell you what. As soon as you get some batteries, call Nikolai and find out what's going on. Then phone me."

The other man nodded before taking off.

Max reached for a bunch of bananas, then walked to the express-line counter. Once he'd paid for the fruit, he headed for his car. By the time he'd driven a block from the store, Oleg phoned.

"Nikolai's still searching and ordered me to do the same." The news that Irina hadn't been found filled Max with relief. "He sounds demented. I have to admit I'm scared, Anatoly."

"Keep your head. She can't be far. Let's proceed as planned."

The minute they clicked off, he phoned Gideon to brief him.

"This is a fantastic development, Max!"

"It is, provided we can find Irina before something unforeseen happens. Her English is only so-so. I doubt she trusts anybody. Since she was running away from a horrendous situation, I don't imagine she'll use her real name with anyone. Luckily I can give you a detailed description.''

After Gideon had the facts, he said, ''I'll get out an all-points bulletin.''

''The counselor at her high school might be able to tell us who her friends are. They could shed light on her whereabouts. We've got to find her before Nikolai does, or no one will ever see her again.''

''I hear you. Where are you headed now?''

''To the Nine Palms Court and Fashion Place. Oleg might decide to come looking for me.''

''Okay. Stay in close touch. Before we hang up, I was thinking about the teen Ms. Peris picked up in the Marina District and drove to Girls' Village.''

Max hadn't been able to stop thinking about that whole situation. Was the girl she rescued named Svetlana? Or had Gabriella been looking up that name for an entirely different reason?

No matter what she called herself, if by the remotest possibility the girl in the Dumpster was Irina, then Max couldn't take the chance on her seeing him at Girls' Village. He would have to learn what he could from the girls on their outing at the park tomorrow.

''That would be too easy, Gideon. I'll check it out. Is everything set for tomorrow night?''

''Yes. We'll have our guys in place as roofers. You'll be covered.''

''Sounds good. Talk to you later.''

He clicked off and headed for the mall. It was going to be a long night.

AT FIVE TO ONE Saturday afternoon, Gaby looked out the apartment window. Anatoly waved to her. He'd come for her in a car. She had no idea whose it was, but she felt her heart do a little skip just to know he was outside the building waiting for her.

Another talk with her uncle hadn't produced any new information. At this point she decided to stop worrying about Anatoly and simply enjoy the day with him.

The apartment was as clean as she could get it. Everything was ready for Hallie. She'd stocked the fridge with food. The roses still looked beautiful. Hopefully Anatoly would like her new outfit. She loved the tan walking shorts and white knit top with the tan horizontal bands.

In the end she chose to wear her hair in a ponytail, but she'd secured it with a white chiffon scarf to dress things up a little. Before walking out the door, she stashed a small instamatic camera in her purse. Though the pictures would be for the girls to keep, she'd sneak one of Anatoly and put it in her wallet.

After locking the door, she hurried down the hall to the stairs. Anatoly met her halfway. In baseball cap, navy shorts and matching pullover, his masculinity pretty well overwhelmed her.

She read the appreciation in his green eyes. "I like a woman who is always ready on time, especially when I did not sleep all night waiting to be with her again. You look like vanilla ice cream floating in champagne, one of my favorite Russian desserts, Gabriella. I think I must have a little taste right now."

He brushed her lips with his. "The scarf is a lovely temptation. Tonight I intend to take it off and see your hair fall around your face. Now—are you ready to go?''

''Yes,'' was all she could manage.

''That is good.'' He kissed her again, more thoroughly this time, before he turned around and started back down to the lobby. She prayed her legs would support her as far as the car.

Once they were inside, she gave him directions to Girls' Village and they were off. ''Tell me something, Anatoly. I want the truth now.''

He darted her a serious glance. ''This is Karin's car, in case you wanted to know. If you are asking about Natasha, I can tell you that as of seven o'clock this morning, I am no longer engaged. She will not be coming to America.''

The news on both counts shouldn't have filled her with so much joy. She averted her eyes. ''If that's a relief to you, then I'm happy for you.''

His hand slid to hers and grasped it. ''I think you know how happy I am, Gabriella.''

Maybe it's better you don't know how I'm feeling right now, Anatoly.

''Actually, what I wanted to know was why you traded your Russian tapes for that particular hat. Why did you?''

His head jerked toward her. ''*That's* the serious question you wanted to ask me?''

''Yes.''

''Why are you so curious?''

''Because if you're trying to be American, then you need to know that the Bronx Knights aren't a baseball team.''

He frowned. "What do you mean? I saw in the newspaper that they are coming to San Diego to play."

"They are. But it won't be baseball."

"I do not understand."

"They play stickball."

"Stickball?"

"Yes. It's a game that started back East. I used to play it with all the kids on the block. When I got older, I went to the league games and rooted for my favorite team, the Barrio Gents."

"I like the names. Do you have a cap?"

"I did. But it got lost in my last move. When you take me home, I'll show you my pennant."

"That I would like to see. You really know how to play this stickball?"

"Yes."

His face broke out in a smile. It took her breath away. "You will show me when we get to the park?"

"I thought you were into croquet."

"We will do both!"

"I'm afraid we don't have the proper equipment, but I guess we can improvise."

"That is what I love about you, Gabriella. You are game for anything."

"Well, we can't have you running around San Diego in a Bronx Knights cap when you don't know the fundamentals."

"It will be exciting with you as the teacher."

She flashed him a mischievous smile. "Are you a sore loser?"

"What does that mean?"

"Will you get angry if I can do something better than you? Some guys don't like that."

"I want you to be better than me."

"You say that now."

"I mean everything I say, Gabriella. You are an expert at some things. I am an expert at others. We balance each other. That is the way it should be between a man and a woman who are as perfectly matched as we are."

The more he kept talking like that, the more she wanted to believe him.

To her chagrin he had to let go of her hand to make a turn at the light. The Girls' Village facility loomed on the right. He pulled up at the curb.

"Do you want to come in with me?"

He shut off the ignition and put his arm behind her seat. "I want to do everything with you." In the next breath he kissed the side of her neck. The tang of the soap he'd used in the shower assailed her. "But in case the girls are shy, they might like it better if you introduce us after you bring them out to the car. By the end of the day I will hope they will like me enough to ask me to come in next time."

Somehow Anatoly always knew the right thing to say and do. "I'll be back in a minute."

She fumbled for the door handle, and he came around to her side to help her out of the car. His gaze captured hers. "I will be here waiting impatiently for you." His hand tugged the end of her ponytail. She felt a finger of delight travel through her body to her toes.

To ward it off, she dashed up the walk to the front

doors. The girls were waiting in the lobby on one of the benches.

"Hi!" they both said at once.

"Hi, yourselves! How are the lovely young mothers-to-be today?"

"Okay." Juanita stared at her. "You look beautiful."

"Well, thank you."

"That's a new outfit, huh?"

She nodded to Sandra.

"Is it for that man you ran into?" Juanita wanted to know.

Gaby chuckled. "Yes."

The girls exchanged glances and smiled at her.

"All right. Let's go, but don't tell him I bought this just for him. He's going to take us to lunch at the Jukebox Café, and then we'll go to the park. How does that sound?"

"Cool."

"Just one more thing. Have you girls ever played croquet?" They both frowned in puzzlement. "I didn't think so. Listen, when Anatoly sets up the game, will you go along with him? He brought it especially for you because he knows you're pregnant, and he doesn't want you to strain yourselves. The thing is, he's very excited about it."

They both nodded.

"Come on. I'm starving and I bet you are too."

TWO HOURS LATER the girls had gotten the hang of croquet. Out of the six games, Max and Gabriella let them win four times. Sandra and Juanita were both good sports and fun to be with. If Gabriella was using them for a front, Max thought, they didn't seem to know it. In fact, they seemed crazy about her.

So was he. And falling harder every second.

"I think you ladies must be tired, so we are going to rest while Gabriella shows us a game she learned to play when she was a young girl."

"I'll have to set it up first. See that monument over there about fifty feet? We'll use that."

"For what?" Juanita asked.

"You'll see," Gabriella answered mysteriously. "I'll be back in a minute." She'd grabbed four croquet mallets and a ball before she started walking away from them.

That was when Max knew Ms. Peris hadn't been lying to him about her knowledge of stickball. At least the way it was played on the streets of New York and New Jersey.

With knees raised, he sat on the grass between the two girls. "Do you think some of your friends at Girls' Village would like to come to the park with us another time?"

"All of them would!" Juanita declared.

"Are there any girls from other countries?"

Juanita nodded. "We've got one from India, and another from Mexico."

"Just last night we got a new girl from Russia. She roomed with me," Sandra confided. "I asked her if she wanted to come with us today, but she said no. Her English isn't good like yours."

Max peeled a banana and began eating. "If she only came recently from Russia, it will probably take time for her to feel comfortable. She is lucky to have you for friends.''

''I don't think Svetlana can trust anyone,'' Juanita commented. ''She's afraid to go outside for fear she'll get killed.''

''That is very sad.''

Sandra said, ''I used to be scared the same way because my stepfather took drugs and used to beat me and my mother all the time. But he finally got caught by the police for armed robbery. Now he's in jail, so I'm not afraid anymore.''

''That is good, Sandra. Did this Svetlana tell you what happened to her?''

''Yes.'' Sandra nodded. ''She ran away from her mother's boyfriend. He and his friends were going to rape her, so she climbed out the kitchen window and ran as hard as she could down her alley. She took a bus to a park and then ran to a store where she called Girls' Village. Gabriella picked her up.''

''How did Svetlana know to call?''

''She learned about it at school. So did I. Gabriella was the volunteer who came to get me when I called Girls' Village.''

''Gabriella is very courageous, just like you girls. How long ago did that happen to you, Sandra?''

''About six or seven months.''

''Hey!'' In the distance Gabriella was waving her hands over her head. ''Come on! I'm doing all the work!''

''Let us go, ladies.''

They followed Max over to the monument. ''Okay,'' Gabriella said. ''You girls sit behind that

line where I put the mallet. We'll pretend there's a
strike box drawn here on the monument. About fifty
feet away you'll see another mallet—it serves as the
pitcher's mound. I'll have to be the whole team today.
Anatoly, you'll pitch the ball and play the field.''

She handed him the ball, then took the other mallet
and stood over by the monument.

He walked to the pitcher's mound, trying hard not
to smile. ''Are you ready?''

''As I'll ever be.''

She crouched in her batter's stance, holding the
mallet by the head. He'd been the star pitcher on his
block. Deciding to be kind, he threw a soft underhand.
The next thing he knew he heard a whack and the
ball sailed at least a hundred feet. The girls cheered
and clapped.

''Anatoly? While you field that ball, pretend an
imaginary runner has snagged first base. When you're
ready, pitch me another one.''

He found the ball in the grass at the bottom of a
tree. Damn, if she wasn't good.

Next time he'd throw the ball with a little more
force.

Even from the distance, he could feel her fighting
spirit. He warmed up, then pitched. But he put a little
spin on it to throw her.

Whack!

This time the ball sailed at least a hundred and
twenty feet, if not more. The girls let out more
whoops. By the time he'd emerged from a thorny
bush with the ball, he was no longer smiling.

"We have two runners on base now!" she announced. He could hear the smile in her voice.

Will you get angry if I can do something better than you? Some guys don't like that.

I want you to be better than me.

Like hell—

Making no concessions this time, he threw the ball overhand.

"Steeeriiiiikkkke one!" she called out. "That was a pretty good pitch, Kuzmina. You keep improving like that and you'll be ready to coach a whole team of girls from the Village. Try it again. Faster!"

Faster? Don't say you didn't ask for it.

The ball and bat connected, but he heard a sharp crack.

"Aieee!"

CHAPTER NINE

"OH, NO!" Gaby cried. The stick of the mallet had come apart in several splinters.

Anatoly ran up to her. "Are you hurt, Gabriella?"

She shook her head. "No. But we should be playing with a rubber ball, and I should've known better than to use your landlady's croquet stick for a stickball bat. I feel terrible about this."

He took the pieces from her hands. "It is my fault. I threw the pitch too hard. Tomorrow we will go to a store together and find a replacement." His gaze held hers. "You are a magnificent stickball player."

"You think?"

"How did you get so good? Tell me!"

"I played every night till dark out by Wilson's garage door. When I didn't show up because I had to do homework or something, the guys would come to my house and get me."

His eyes gleamed. "That I can believe."

"You're a good stickball player, too. Somebody taught you how to spin your pitch. Fess up, Anatoly. You've played the game before."

One corner of his compelling mouth lifted. "Maybe I told a little white lie."

"There's no maybe about it. I bet you play on the beach every chance you get."

"Not for the past four days."

No. The past four days they'd spent every possible moment together.

"We will go to the big-league stickball games together, yes?"

She sucked in her breath. "Yes." *I can't wait.*

"Can we go, too?" Juanita asked.

"Speak for yourself. I'll probably be in the hospital having my baby."

Gaby put an arm around Sandra's shoulders. "I'll come and visit you."

"We will both come," Anatoly said. "I have never seen a baby right after it was born."

"You're joking! My mom had seven kids. I took care of most of them."

Gaby felt for the poor girl. "Anatoly never jokes," she couldn't resist saying.

He flashed her a wry glance. "I can see I am in a little trouble with you."

"Quite a bit, actually."

"Good. I cannot wait to receive my punishment."

"I'm glad to hear you say that because all the croquet equipment needs to be gathered up before we go."

"I'll help," Juanita said.

As the girl walked with him, Gaby pulled the camera out of her purse and snapped another picture. She'd taken several throughout the day when Anatoly wasn't looking. She couldn't wait to get the film developed.

"Come on, Sandra. You're looking flushed. It's time to get you back to the car and home." They started walking.

"Anatoly's good-looking. Funny too."

"You're right on both counts."

"I think he loves you."

"In four days?"

"I guess not. But you should see his eyes when he looks at you. Some day I hope I'll meet a man who looks at me like that. Months ago I decided it would be better to give up my baby for adoption. Seeing you so happy with Anatoly makes me realize I'd like a life like that one day. My baby deserves to be with people who really want it and can take care of it."

Gaby hugged her hard. "What will you do after it's born?"

"The counselor is going to help me finish high school, then I'm going to go to college."

"I admire you more than you know. You're very courageous, Sandra."

"I was thinking the same thing about Svetlana."

"So she talked to you?"

"Yes. After her father died, her mother's Russian boyfriend took over their apartment. The night she ran away, he touched her where he shouldn't and told her an important man was going to give her things if she cooperated. She was afraid of being raped, so she climbed out the window and jumped off the fire escape."

Gaby shuddered. "Thank heaven she was able to get away."

"She says Russian men are horrible. Maybe her

mother is dead by now, but she's scared to call the police.''

"She said as much to me in the taxi. I'm glad she could talk to you about it, Sandra.''

"I told her what happened to me. She knows she's safe at Girls' Village. But I'm afraid she'll never go outside again.''

"It's too early to know what the future holds for her. She's going to get counseling. In the meantime, if you can be her friend, that would be wonderful.''

"I'll try.''

"I know you will.''

By the time she'd helped Sandra get her swollen body strapped into the back seat, the other two had joined them.

Juanita had been having the time of her life. Gaby had never seen her smile and laugh so much. Anatoly had a way with everyone.

He has a way with you, Gaby Peris.

It was a good thing Hallie would be at the apartment when he took her home. The way she was feeling right now, she could easily toss Dr. Karsh's two hundred dollars' worth of sage advice into the surf and watch it get carried out to sea.

TWENTY MINUTES LATER, Gaby had said good-night to the girls. She rejoined Anatoly.

"Thank you for being so wonderful today. Juanita has a huge crush on you, and Sandra thinks you're funny. Those are both great compliments coming from girls who've had no reason to trust anyone or anything.''

"I liked them, too. It has been a fantastic day. I never want it to end."

"Neither do I."

She felt his eyes on her. "You are keeping something from me," he said. "What is it?"

"Much as I would like to spend the whole evening with you, I can't."

"You have work at your office?"

"No, it's nothing like that. My roommate is back in town."

Before she could blink, Anatoly had pulled over to the curb. He shut off the engine and turned to her.

"This is the first I have heard about a roommate."

She swallowed hard. "I'm sorry. Before today I didn't feel it was necessary to tell you. But since you've broken your engagement and we've had our first date, you're entitled to know more about my life."

"Were you lovers before he went away?" Anatoly sounded quite desolate. Was it the Russian in him coming out again, or was he really upset?

"Anatoly, I said roommate, not lover. Hallie is a woman! She was the first person to befriend me when I moved to San Diego. We hit it off immediately, and decided to room together."

"Hallie?"

"Yes. I know it's a rather unusual name. She's been gone for several weeks. The other day I received a postcard telling me she was coming home tonight. She said it was important that I be there because she needs to tell me something that could affect both our lives."

He stared at her through shuttered lids without saying a word.

"You don't believe me?"

"Yes, of course I do. I am waiting to hear if there is anything else you want to tell me."

She bit her lip. "I wouldn't believe me, either. You probably think I'm making this up."

"I will believe what you want me to believe. You say she is there now?"

"Probably."

"Then I must get you home."

"You're not angry?"

"I am more disappointed than you can imagine. But I am not angry."

He started the car. Once again they merged with the traffic and headed to her apartment.

"Would you like to meet her?"

"Not if I am going to be interrupting something important. Does she know about me?"

"No. We haven't been in contact. But when she sees your roses, she's going to suspect something. I'm too big a tightwad to ever spend money like that on myself."

"They will stay beautiful for another week at least." He didn't sound quite as unhappy as before.

"Anatoly?"

"Yes, Gabriella?"

"I'd like you to meet her."

"Then it is settled. But I will not overstay my welcome."

She chuckled. "I'm not worried."

Within minutes he'd pulled the car to a stop at the side of the building.

"I am excited," he said as he helped her out of the seat and shut the door.

"Why?"

"I want to know everything about you. You have lived with this woman for many months. I am curious to see what kind of friend you have chosen."

He put his arm around her shoulder. It felt so right, so natural, as they walked around the corner to the outside door of her apartment. Each time their hips brushed, a jolt of electricity went through her body.

It was on the tip of Gaby's tongue to tell him she'd like to meet his friends. But she held back because she didn't want to know anything that would force her to have to stop seeing him.

He followed her up the stairs.

"I'll just slip inside and see if Hallie's arrived. If she has, I'll tell her to make herself presentable."

MAX WATCHED her disappear into her apartment.

Hal was a woman named Hallie? His would-be assassin?

How could Gabriella have been living with a roommate all these months and the guys hadn't turned up any evidence?

Good grief, what in hell was going on? Were they all flying blind?

Max hadn't seen the guys on the apartment roof, but he knew they were in position to protect him physically.

What he needed was emotional protection, but it

was already too late for that, because today he'd crossed a line with Gabriella.

The line they warned you about in training.

The line that said proceed beyond this point at your own risk. The line that meant you were in so deep you couldn't think clearly anymore.

Karl had wanted him off the case two days ago. So had Gideon. But Max was beyond listening to them. It was as if Gabriella had given him some kind of drug that dulled all voices except hers.

It was possible that Svetlana was Irina. The details Sandra had offered fit Nikolai's profile. But they also fit any number of mafia types. He needed to get on top of that right now. Yet here he was at the mercy of a woman who'd been setting him up all week.

The door opened. "Anatoly? You can come in."

Lord. How could she smile at him like that and do what she was about to do.

Her eyes beckoned him. Could traitor's eyes be so velvety brown and beautiful?

It was time to get this over with. He moved inside, prepared to hit the floor to escape the line of fire from his colleagues.

To his shock he caught sight of an attractive blond woman, taller than Gabriella. Wearing a long white robe, she stood in the room next to the lamp where he'd planted one of the bugs.

"Hello," she said in a friendly voice. "I understand you're Anatoly. My name's Hallie."

Trying to get a grip on the situation, Max advanced into the room. "How do you do." They shook hands.

Gabriella was in the kitchen pulling sodas out of

the fridge. "I've made submarines, and we've got plenty of chips and dip. Let me put everything on the table, then you two can help yourselves."

A few minutes later Gabriella joined Max on the couch with her plate. Hallie had seated herself in the easy chair.

The rush of adrenaline he'd felt in the hallway had made him ravenous. His hostess must have noticed because she brought him another sandwich without him having to ask for it.

"We played stickball this afternoon," Gaby said to her roommate.

Hallie smiled. "That explains the appetite."

Both of them were looking at Max, whose mouth was too full to respond.

"He plays croquet well, too. Anatoly's a man of many talents."

"Tell me how you two met."

"I don't want to tell you, Hallie." Gabriella's eyes slid away from his. "It's too embarrassing."

"What happened? Were you body surfing and crashed into him on purpose?"

Max almost choked on the last of his sandwich.

"You got the crash part right. You're beginning to sound just like Uncle Frank. He wanted to know if I had collided with a man yet."

Both women chuckled.

Max smiled at them. "It was my lucky day."

Hallie didn't seem capable of being an assassin. For the first time in four days Max was beginning to wonder if Gideon hadn't been right about Gabriella being a total innocent.

Watch your back. Gideon's warning rumbled from a great distance off.

"Would you believe that after almost killing him, Anatoly brought me those roses?"

Hallie's curious gaze flicked to Max. "Every woman should be so blessed. Neither of you were hurt?"

"No. But both our cars are in the shop."

"How are you managing?"

"Anatoly's been my taxi service. He uses his company van to whisk me around."

"A knight in Russian armor."

Max liked Hallie already. Hell.

"He helped me buy a bike."

"I noticed it when I came in earlier. If I had known all this was going to happen, I would have gone away sooner. I bet you never even missed me."

There was a heartbeat of silence before Gabriella answered. "Of course I did, Hallie."

The blood flowed to Gabriella's face. That wasn't a reaction she could summon on cue. Max was starting to feel another adrenaline attack coming on. But this was different from the one he'd experienced out in the hall when he thought he might be taking a bullet in the chest.

Caught in the grip of intense excitement, he couldn't sit still. Needing to channel his energy into something physical, he got up and took everyone's plates to the sink.

Get out of here, Calder. You're enjoying this too much. Your head's not on straight. It hasn't been on straight since the accident.

"Thank you for the dinner, Gabriella. Now I must go. What time shall I come for you tomorrow so we can shop for a new mallet?"

"Don't leave on my account."

His gaze flicked to Hallie. "Gabriella told me you have important things to talk about. I do not wish to intrude."

"Please stay," Hallie said. "What I have to tell her won't take long, then I'm going to bed."

"It is up to Gabriella. Do you wish me to go?"

Hallie lifted her foot to nudge Gabriella's leg. "You know you don't want him to leave." To Max, "She wants you to stay."

While Gabriella's blush was still in evidence, he walked back to the couch and sat down next to her. Without conscious thought he reached for her hand. Hers responded to the pressure.

"I know what you're going to say, Hallie. Your postcard prepared me."

The other woman's expression sobered. "If I have a regret, it's leaving you to find another roommate. Actually I have one more, but you don't want to hear it."

"What? That I won't renounce the world and join you?"

Max couldn't contain his curiosity any longer. "You sound as if you are leaving to go on some sort of pilgrimage."

Gabriella let out a deep sigh. "She is. Can I tell him?"

"Of course."

She turned her head to look at him. "Hallie's a lay

nun. I met her through the San Diego Welcome Mission. She helps arrange temporary housing for new residents.''

"I could have used you when I first came to America," Anatoly murmured.

"Poor Anatoly had to sleep in the same apartment with how many immigrants?"

"Thirteen."

Hallie shook her head. "How awful."

"We survived."

Gabriella squeezed his hand. 'But it shouldn't be like that, Anatoly. Anyway, Hallie and I got along so well we decided to room together, and we found this furnished apartment.''

His mind leaped to the crucifix and missal in the other room. At the time he remembered thinking a nun slept here.

"When I realized Hallie had given up all her worldly goods, I decided it wouldn't be nice to tempt her with my stuff, so most of it is still in storage."

"*That* is why you have such a beautiful office."

Hallie nodded. "I've had several close friends in my life, Anatoly, but none of them would sacrifice for me the way Gabriella has. Nuns everywhere could take lessons from her."

"Anatoly's not buying any of it, Hallie. He already knows I don't go to church."

At this point Max didn't know what he knew anymore. But he'd come to one conclusion. Either *everything* was a con, or else he was sitting with two innocent, extraordinary women.

"My grandfather used to tell me church is what a person carries inside of them," he said.

"It is!" Hallie agreed with him. "I'm not as inherently good as Gaby. That's why I've decided to live the cloistered life for a time."

"Oh, stop!" Gabriella jumped up from the couch. Hallie's adulation appeared to embarrass her.

"All right. I won't say another word, but it's still true. Before I enter the convent, I want to help you find a new roommate."

"I don't want another one."

Max looked at her. "How much do they charge for this apartment, Gabriella?"

"Twelve hundred dollars a month."

"I know of a place where they only charge eight hundred dollars a month and pay the utilities."

Her dark eyes flashed with impatience. "I've heard of that place too, Anatoly. Isn't it in Death Valley?"

"That wasn't nice, Gaby," Hallie said, chuckling.

"Gabriella is a constant source of amusement to me. That is why I do not want her to be out of my sight."

"I feel the same way about her, Anatoly. Giving up Gaby for the religious life is going to be like cutting off an arm or a leg."

"Will you be allowed visitors?"

"Once in a while."

"Then we will come."

"I can't imagine anything nicer."

Gaby had gone to the fridge for another soda. "How soon do you have to enter the convent?"

"I can go at any time."

"You probably want to leave tomorrow."

"What I want is irrelevant. I'm not going anywhere until I know you'll be all right."

Max rose to his feet. "Gabriella's going to live with me."

Both women stared at him in astonishment.

"The Frenchwoman in my apartment house has gone to live with her children in San Francisco. The landlady needs a new renter, but she won't take just anyone. They have to come on the recommendation of someone she knows well. If I vouch for Gabriella, Mrs. Bills will be happy to have her move in."

Gaby drew closer. "What's the place like?"

"You will love it. It is an old Victorian house that belonged to her family. She had it remodeled into apartments."

"Gaby loves old things," Hallie interjected before standing up. "It sounds like a perfect solution. Now that you know about my decision, I'm going to say good-night. It's been wonderful to meet you, Anatoly. I hope to see a lot more of you before I go."

"I feel the same way. Good night, Hallie."

When she'd disappeared he turned to Gabriella. "Let me drive you to the apartment house."

Her head lifted in surprise. "You mean right now?"

"Yes. It is a very nice apartment. Tomorrow is Sunday. Mrs. Bills will show it to potential renters. By the end of the day, it will be gone. Tonight I will give you the sneak preview."

The corners of her mouth lifted. "I'm not sure it would be a good idea to move into the same apartment house with you."

"I think it would be the next best thing to paradise."

"Don't talk like that!"

"How can I help it? When I learned that your friend was going to leave, I found myself wishing that we had known each other for several months so you would not be shocked if I asked to move in with you.

"But as it has not even been a week since you crashed into me, I realize I must give you more time. From the beginning I have wanted to be with you day and night. If you live with me, then after we say goodnight, I will know exactly where you are. You will be lying in your bed on the other side of the wall from mine. We can tap on it to send each other messages. It will be very exciting."

"I don't know, Anatoly."

"It will solve several problems for us. I will have less driving to do, and Mrs. Bills will watch to make certain we do not break the rules."

"What rules?"

"There are six people in the apartment house. All are single. We can mingle as much as we want in the lounge. But after ten o'clock, we cannot have anyone else in our own apartment. She is very strict about that."

"As good as that sounds, we might start fighting, and then we'll be sorry we live under the same roof."

"That is one of the things we have not experienced yet. I am looking forward to it."

Gaby looked at him incredulously, then asked, "Does she make you sign a lease?"

"No. She only asks for the rent for the first and the last month."

"It all sounds too good to be true, including the price."

"She charges more for the larger apartments upstairs. Ours are on the main floor. She cut one side of the downstairs into two parts. That is why they are smaller, so she charges less money for them. But they do not seem small to me because the ceilings are so high. It feels like a home, not an apartment. I like that."

"We can watch ball games in the lounge?"

Despite the fact that he had no proof she wasn't mafia, a warm feeling crept through his body. This woman made him feel beyond happy. "Yes."

"Well, I guess I could take a look, but I'm not promising anything, Anatoly, even though I appreciate the suggestion. You have to understand that."

He loved it when she went all serious on him. "Of course. To stay on Mrs. Bills's good side, we will not tell her about her broken croquet mallet until after you have made your decision."

"I forgot about that."

"Do not worry. I will assure her we had such a wonderful time we want to keep it a while longer. Shall we go? I want to beat everyone to the jab."

"The punch, Anatoly."

"Yes. I meant to say that."

She reached the door ahead of him. "Have I told you how impressed I am with your fluency in English? I haven't had to correct you hardly at all."

"Three times."

"That many?"

"Yes. I am keeping a list. I want to sound like an American when I become a naturalized citizen."

Her eyes searched his. "How much longer?" she asked with an earnestness that confounded him.

"One month."

"Have you been studying for the test?"

"Yes. However, I need a tutor to make certain I get every answer perfect."

"You're about as unsubtle as a sledgehammer, but if you want my help, I—"

He lowered his mouth to hers. This was the last of the brief kisses. Next time was going to be different. "Thank you, Gabriella," he whispered against her lips. "You will come to watch me take the oath?"

"I'd be honored."

"We will celebrate afterward."

"What do you think you'll want to do on your first night as a new citizen?"

"The way I am feeling right now, it would be better if I did not answer that question. If you do not understand, please do not ask me to explain. I am trying very hard to do the right thing with you. This is one of those times when I need your help to keep me strong."

He heard her breath catch before she opened the door and preceded him into the hallway.

YOU'RE A VERY SMART GIRL, Irina. In some ways prettier than your mama. An important man will be here in a few minutes. His name is Yevgeny.

If you please him, he'll give you things you never dreamed of. Clothes, a car. Maybe even your own apartment. If you don't please him, that will not please me. You understand what I'm saying?

"Svetlana?"

Irina felt a nudge on her shoulder.

"Svetlana? It's okay. You're having a bad dream."

She could hear a voice, but it wasn't calling her name.

"Come on. Wake up."

The overhead light went on. Irina blinked and raised her head. Sandra was standing over her. "What?"

"You were crying out in your sleep. A couple of times you moved around so hard I was afraid you'd fall on the floor."

Irina sat up all the way, pushing the hair out of her eyes. "I have bad dream."

"That's what we call a nightmare. I used to get them all the time, too. After you've been here a while, it won't happen as often. Do you want me to keep the light on or off?"

She rested her head on her upraised knees. "I not care."

"You can call the nurse if you want. Maybe she'll give you something to help you sleep without dreaming."

Tears rolled down Irina's cheeks. "My mother..." She could hardly talk as she rocked back and forth.

"I know you're worried about her. Listen. You know the woman who picked you up? Gaby?"

She nodded.

"She's really cool, you know? If you told her your address, she could find out about your mom."

Irina wiped the moisture from her face. "How?"

"That's her job as a volunteer. She does a lot of things to help. You can trust her."

"Too dangerous."

"Not for her. She's an attorney and can get information without anyone knowing what she's doing. Sometimes she wears disguises."

"I do not understand."

"She changes her hair, puts on costumes."

"Yes?"

"Yeah. Nobody can tell who she is. She did that for me a couple of times to find out what was going on with my family."

"No police."

"No. She has to come here for a volunteers' meeting in the morning. You can talk to her after she's through. It will make you feel a lot better if she can find out about your mother."

"Maybe. Okay."

"Do you still want to talk?"

"Yes."

"Let me turn off the light first." After she'd done that, Sandra got under the covers of her own bed. "What do you want to talk about?"

"Your baby?"

"Do you like babies?"

"Yes. Do you?"

"Yes, but I'm going to give mine away to a couple who want a baby and will offer it a good life."

The tears gushed once more. "I wish my mother give me away."

CHAPTER TEN

"MRS. BILLS? Do you accept personal checks, or would you prefer a cashier's check from my bank?"

"A personal check will be fine. Anatoly tells me you are his attorney. That is a good enough reference."

It was clear the landlady liked Anatoly a lot. So did Gaby, but if she had any brains, she wouldn't be jumping from the proverbial frying pan into the fire.

Maybe something was wrong with her that she would obey a compulsion stronger than her good sense to take this drastic step. But if he was leading a double life, then this was about as close as she'd be able to get in order to keep an eye on him without actually living with him.

During their comings and goings, surely he would make a slip at some point to prove his guilt. With tangible evidence, she would have to walk away from him.

It would kill her to do that. She didn't even want to think about it.

Right now she was trying to remain positive. When he smiled at her as he was doing this very second, she pretty much felt immortal.

The three of them were congregated in the lounge

of the Victorian apartment house located in an older section of City Heights. The apartment she'd rented was a little bigger than the size of the apartment she'd been living in with Hallie.

Dark moldings and cornices graced the ten-foot ceiling. There was a window seat with a tall window, the top portion of which was made of stained glass. The hardwood floors shone with a rich patina. The kitchen and bathroom were small, but obviously newer than the original house.

The bedroom came furnished with a queen-size bed and an armoire with a floor-length mirror. Most people would kill to find a place this nice anywhere.

So far she'd met three of the five occupants. Four if she included Anatoly. One guy with a beard worked for a graphic design studio. Another man, who'd gone prematurely bald, was finishing up his internship at Bay Shore Hospital. The Amazon upstairs ran her own weight-lifting club and had already told Gaby she could come in for a free visit.

The whole time she talked to Gaby, Anatoly kept a poker face, but she knew he was laughing. Gaby was tempted to take the woman up on her offer, if only to rid herself of the excess energy built up by being around him for hours on end.

She finished writing out the check. "Here you are, Mrs. Bills." The older woman gave her a smile, obviously pleased to have the apartment rented again.

"You can move in any time."

"Thank you. It probably won't be until next week. Possibly Tuesday or Wednesday."

"That's fine. Anatoly will show you the place around the side to park your car."

"Thank you. For the next few weeks I'll be riding a bike. Where can I put it?"

"There is a bike stall on the same side, which you can lock."

"That's great."

"Good. Then all is settled."

"Thank you very much, Mrs. Bills." She glanced at Anatoly. "I guess I'd better get back to Hallie."

Before she reached the front door in the large foyer, a strong pair of hands slid to her shoulders from behind. "You are in a great hurry to leave me?" he murmured against her hot cheek.

"No. But I feel guilty leaving Hallie on her first night home. She needs to talk about the decision she's made. Knowing I'm going to be moving here will be a relief to her."

"Have you considered *my* relief? At least now I can be magnanimous and let you have your time with her. But be warned. I will only stay patient a little longer before I get you all to myself without fear of interruption.

"Come. I will whiz you home." He kissed her hair. "Just so you know, I *meant* to say whiz."

AFTER DROPPING Gabriella off, Max returned Karin's car to the back of the florist shop, then headed for the apartment house on foot. No one on the block seemed to be out at this time of night. Before he reached the main street, a motor home pulled around the corner.

Max walked faster. The motor home drew alongside him, a door opened and he climbed inside, shutting the door behind him.

Gideon greeted him with a clap on the shoulders. "Good to see you, bud."

"You, too." He punched Gideon's arm.

"How about a beer?"

"Oh, yeah."

His friend moved to the mini fridge. He retrieved two cans of lager and gave Max one of them. They sat down on opposite benches facing each other.

Max emptied half his can without taking a breath. Expelling a heavy sigh, he lounged back and extended his legs in front of him. By now the motor home was weaving through night traffic.

Gideon grinned, transforming his craggy features. "Tell me what it felt like to walk into that apartment and discover Hallie was a nun."

"Let's just say it was an experience I'll never forget."

"You know what all the buzz around the department's about..."

His eyes closed. "I can imagine."

"No. I don't think you can. With everything bugged, you've had about as much privacy as two elephants in the middle of Times Square. I have to tell you. Your con is the greatest thing going since the invention of pizza. Karl's thinking of getting the tapes printed into a manual to help teach rookies what real undercover work is all about."

"Oh, hell."

"Seriously. He can't figure out how you keep coming up with the stuff you do. The guys think they should do a remake of *The Great Valentino,* world's greatest lover. Only they're calling it *The Great Anatoly.* With you and the sexy Gabriella starring in the film, you'd pull in millions.

"You want to know how famous you are? Get this. The guys are starting to use some of your best lines for codes. Their favorite is, 'Come on over here so I can unlock your hair.' That's supposed to mean, I'll spell you off now."

Max finished the rest of his beer in one gulp.

"That's not all," Gideon said. "Bets are flying fast and heavy that you'll end up marrying the woman, *if* it turns out she's on the level. At this point Karl's about ninety-nine percent sure she's a person who just happened to be in the wrong place at the wrong time."

"Is that what you think? Even with those notes I found on her legal pad? The Russian dictionaries?" Max sat forward, dangling the empty can between his legs. "I'd go on your gut instinct over anyone else's facts."

The mirth left his friend's eyes. "I can't explain the notes. That's the only part that bothers me. As for the dictionaries, she deals with Russian immigrants, so I don't find that evidence suspect."

"Hell, Gideon. If it's all a con, she's a master at it."

His friend studied him in a way that pierced through to his soul. "After all these years, how come you had to go and fall in love with this one?"

Max jumped to his feet. "You think I'm happy

about it?'' He tossed the empty can in the wastebasket.

"A part of you is. I've listened to those tapes.'' He inhaled sharply. ''That's your heart I heard talking. It scares the hell out of me because it means you've lost your edge. I knew it the second you spirited her off to your apartment house across town.''

Max rubbed the back of his neck. ''I can keep a better eye on her there.''

"You don't need a better eye on her. We've got her under day-and-night surveillance.''

"Not completely,'' Max countered. ''Now that she's going to be living under my roof, so to speak, we've got all the bases covered. When I get back to the apartment house, I'll plant enough bugs that there aren't any parts of her place that won't pick up conversation. And tomorrow I'll put one on her cell phone when I take her shopping. If she's mafia, she'll eventually trip up. Then we've got her.''

Gideon nodded slowly. ''Let's talk about Svetlana. What did you find out?''

"After hearing Sandra's account, my gut instinct tells me the girl is Irina. Do me a favor and get into the Girls' Village files. They keep photo ID on every girl. All I need is to see a picture. If it's Galena's daughter, we'll come up with a plan to free Galena. Once they turn state's evidence, we'll put them both in the witness protection program.''

"I'll get on that first thing in the morning. Still no phone call from Nikolai?''

"No.''

"Not even through Oleg or Alexey?''

He shook his head. "The bastard doesn't want me anywhere around, not even to help find Irina. That's how much he hates my guts. But Oleg and I will pay him a visit, anyway, on the pretext that all our lives are on the line if Irina's not found."

As Gideon nodded, the driver honked the horn. "We're coming up on your corner."

"Yup. Got to go. Thanks for being there."

"That's what I was going to say. Max...I hope to hell she's clean. The chemistry between the two of you is burning up the wires."

Haunted by the sheer strength of his emotions, Max turned to his best friend. "Then maybe you can imagine what it's like being up close and personal with her." He patted Gideon's shoulder. "Thanks for everything."

GABY SPOTTED Juanita and Sandra the moment she left the volunteers' meeting in the west wing of Girls' Village.

"Good morning, you two! I'm glad you were waiting for me. It saves me the trouble of coming to find you. I've got a little present."

She opened her purse and handed each of them three pictures. "You guys look like real pros out there playing croquet."

"Next to Anatoly I resemble a big fat blob."

"Sandra!"

"Well, I do."

"I don't look much better and I'm not even showing yet," Juanita grumbled.

"I guess there isn't a woman alive who's satisfied

with her picture,'' Gaby sighed. "Maybe these photos weren't such a good idea.''

"Yes, they were. I'm sorry we complained. Thanks, Gaby,'' Sandra murmured.

"Yeah. Thanks.''

"Hey, Gaby?''

She darted Sandra a glance. "Yes?''

"Will you come to my room? Svetlana wants to talk to you.''

Gaby eyed the clock. "I can give her five minutes before I have to leave.''

"Is Anatoly coming for you?''

"No. I rode here on my bike. My roommate's expecting me. She's moving today and wants to take me to lunch before she goes.''

"Is she the nun?''

"Yes.''

"Where's she going?''

"To live at the convent in Los Angeles.''

"You mean, like, she'll have to wear those robes and never talk to anybody again?''

"Yes and no. Come on. I'll tell you about it on the way upstairs.''

It was closer to twenty minutes before Gaby said goodbye to the girls. When she left the building, her heartache was almost too great to bear.

On the ride back to the apartment, she tried to put herself in the Russian girl's place. Her name wasn't Svetlana. It was Irina Pedrova. Her mother's name was Galena, and she was being held hostage.

The only thing that would bring Irina any relief was

knowing if her mother was still alive, and please God, safe. At least for the moment, anyway.

There was no doubt in her mind Irina's mother had become a victim of the Russian mafia. Probably her father had gotten involved with it when they'd immigrated to the States. It was a life-and-death situation. Irina had every reason to be terrified of the man named Nikolai.

Armed with a description of him and Irina's mother, Gaby pedaled faster while she thought of a plan to check up on the mother.

Anatoly would be by to take her shopping after her lunch with Hallie. But much as she longed to confide in him, even ask him to help her, she didn't dare.

Because somewhere deep down you're afraid he might know those criminals, men who should be put behind bars for the next millennium.

Dear God. If she were ever to find out that Anatoly had anything to do with monsters like them...

Just the thought of it sent a pain through her heart so acute she had to struggle to stay in control of her bike.

When she walked in the apartment a half hour later, Hallie took one look at her and stopped drying her hair with the towel.

"What's wrong, Gaby? You look like death."

"I feel like it."

"Tell me."

Thankful to be able to unload on someone she could trust with her life, she related Irina's tragic story.

"The thing is, I wasted my time looking up the

fake name she gave me on the immigration database. But at least now I have the address of her mom's apartment. The girl's barely hanging on. I've got to go over to that place right now and find out what I can. Forgive me if we don't have lunch together?''

''Forget food. How can I help?''

''This isn't your problem, Hallie.''

''You hurt me when you say that. What do you need?''

''A plan, and a disguise.''

Hallie draped the towel across the top of her head. She held the ends down close to her cheeks.

''What do you see?''

''A ghost?''

''No. Look with a little more imagination.''

It took her a minute before comprehension dawned. ''Hallie!''

The other woman grinned. ''Who would question two nuns visiting the neighborhood, welcoming any and all to the local parish, passing out pamphlets with solutions to world hunger?''

''But is that legal? You know what I mean.''

''If we're on a mercy mission, can anyone say that it isn't? Besides, you're the lawyer.''

''That's right. I forgot. I think maybe there was a case back in Pennsylvania. As I recall, the man impersonating a nun at a convent went to prison. The thing is, it wouldn't bother me to go to jail, but I don't want you to get in trouble on the very day you're due to report.''

''An opportunity has presented itself to do an act of service. I see it as the greatest kind of omen for what lies ahead of me. I'm ready to go, except for my hair.''

Gaby followed her to the bathroom.

''After I finish brushing this mop dry, we'll drop by Our Lady of Mercy Parochial School in my rental car. Sister Paulina will help us.''

''Now we're going to get someone else in trouble.''

''She's a soft touch, just like you. Bring me the cell phone and I'll let her know we're on our way over.''

''I don't remember where I put it,'' Gaby said.

''Try the refrigerator.''

''Very funny.''

''I recall finding it in there once.''

''Yes, well, I had other things on my mind.''

The phone turned up on the dresser in the bedroom. Gaby hurried back to the bathroom and handed it to her. Hallie made short work of reaching the nun Gaby knew had been her friend's mentor for the past year.

''There. Everything's set.'' She handed the telephone back to Gaby, who went in search of her purse. After putting the phone inside her bag so she wouldn't forget it, she returned to the bathroom.

Casting her friend a fond regard, she said, ''How come you couldn't have been an attorney I met at one of my meetings? We could have gone into practice together.''

Hallie smiled. ''I was just thinking how great it would be if you entered the convent with me. But that would be cruel. Did I ever tell you about the recluse who lived next door to my parents in Bel Air?''

''I don't think so.''

"Well, she kept this huge, gorgeous white cockatoo in her house. But every afternoon around four, she brought it outside and put it on a branch of a tree overhanging her back patio. She would leave it there for about half an hour.

"It couldn't fly away because she'd clipped its wings. I used to stand at the bedroom window and cry while I watched that poor thing try to escape. All it did was kind of flop from one branch to another. It would cock its head while it watched the other birds flying around. You could feel it struggle to break free."

Gaby's eyes smarted. "If you told me that story to discourage me from entering the convent with you, then you've accomplished your objective."

"No. Besides, you know I won't be living there forever. One day I'll be sent to South America to teach. That's what I'm looking forward to. Gaby, I was only trying to paint a picture of you the way I see you. Dr. Karsh was right to encourage you to try your wings after Paul died."

When Hallie spoke, Gaby always listened.

"No one has to tell me how great the Peris family is. I've been a witness to and recipient of all their love. Your dad's a sweetheart, and your mom lives to make him and your siblings happy.

"But if you'd gone back to Atlantic City after Paul's funeral, you wouldn't have learned to really fly like you're doing now."

Gaby bowed her head. "Would you still say that if you thought I'd flown completely off course?"

"You're talking about Anatoly, aren't you. What's

that little adage? By their fruits you shall know them?''

"I've tended to go along with that philosophy all my life,'' Gaby said. ''But I told you what happened right after the accident.''

''You mean about his foreign friends taking off for parts unknown?''

''That, and the Audi.''

''He told you it belongs to the company where he does accounting.''

''What if he was lying? I can't account for the hours when I'm not with him. I know he delivers flowers part-time, but...''

''But what?''

''I don't know. His English is incredible for someone who wasn't born speaking it.''

''If his grandfather did business with Americans, then he probably encouraged Anatoly to learn English. The man has a university education. You saw it on the computer.''

''I know.''

''You told me the girls really liked him. Sometimes younger people can see things adults miss. They saw nothing wrong with him.''

''That's true. His employer and landlady are crazy about him. But I don't know any of his friends. He hasn't taken me around them. I haven't heard him even mention any.''

''It's early days, Gaby. If he's been working two jobs all these years in order to make money for him and his former fiancée, then he probably hasn't had a

lot of time to cultivate friendships. Give your relationship a little more time.''

''That's what Dr. Karsh said, but...''

''I keep hearing these buts. Let me ask you something. Think back to the moment you first entertained
doubts about him. Go through the sequence of events.
When was it, exactly?''

Gaby's thoughts flew back to the morning of the
accident. ''I remember walking over to him to tell
him once more how sorry I was. He was talking to
the passengers who'd been in his car.

''That's when this strange feeling went through me.
They were crowded around him while he spoke. I
couldn't hear what he was saying, but it was as if he
was orchestrating something. He looked dark and for-
midable standing there.

''His friends appeared nervous, but it didn't seem
like the accident was the cause of it. Nothing was
natural about the situation. I can't quite explain it.''

Hallie exhaled a heavy sigh. ''So your fear is based
on a dark feeling.''

''Yes. Just for a moment I felt chilled. Maybe it's
because I'd attended that seminar about the Russian
mafia accident ring. Everything the detective told us
to watch for seemed to fit Anatoly and his foreign
passengers, right down to the new black Audi.

''But later, when he showed up at my apartment
with the roses, all traces of that darkness had gone.
He's done nothing since to make me suspicious.''

''Yet you still think he could be in the mafia.''

Gaby took a shuddering breath. ''What if he is,
Hallie?''

Quiet reigned for a few moments. At last Hallie said, "Then naturally you couldn't trust anything." Her brow furrowed. "I can see you're convinced something's wrong, so maybe you'd better listen to yourself."

"You think there's something wrong, too, don't you!"

"This doesn't have anything to do with me, Gaby. I've lived with you long enough to know how stable you are. For you to have these kinds of reservations, despite the fact that your uncle couldn't find anything wrong, tells me you're probably being warned."

Gaby nodded. "I'm scared, Hallie. Really scared."

"Now you're making me nervous. Last night I watched him watching you. Even if the man's guilty as sin, he's got it bad for you. I hate to say this, but you'd have a difficult time getting rid of him if you tried to call it off now. Especially since you've made plans to move into his apartment house."

"You're saying I could become another victim, like Irina's mom?"

"In the sense that mafia boyfriends tend to be territorial and consider that they own you? Yes."

Another shudder racked Gaby's body. "I've played right into his hands, Hallie. It's the stuff movies are made of. A criminal finds the woman he wants, then charms her until she's crazy about him, willing to do anything for him.

"When she's proved her loyalty, the man's true colors start to emerge. By then, she's in too deep. I'm already in too deep!" Gaby cried softly.

Hallie's concern turned her expression sober. "If

he's a liar, then it wouldn't do any good to ask him point-blank if he's been lying. Conversely, you could hurt him a lot if you told him you were afraid he was involved with the Russian mafia and he wasn't. As I see it, there's only one thing to do.''

"I know what you're going to say."

Hallie nodded. "After we find out about Irina's mother, you're going to get on the next flight to New Jersey. Sit down and have a long talk with your uncle Frank. He can hire a couple of good private detectives to have Anatoly's activities monitored. Plan to stay under the protection of your family until there's word one way or the other.''

"But my clients!" she cried, aghast.

"That's easy. Make arrangements with a couple of colleagues—I know you've met other immigration lawyers here—to transfer your cases to them. They'll probably be thrilled for the extra money. As an incentive, you can even offer them free use of your office for a while.

"Ask Anita Garcia to start work now, instead of at the end of the month. She can help make all the arrangements. You can work with her long distance."

"That's true. Oh, Hallie. I can't believe it's come to this!"

"I don't want to believe it, either. But your instincts are telling you Anatoly isn't who you think he is. You need to act while he's still in the honeymoon phase of your relationship. He's not suspicious yet because so far you've given him everything he wants."

"Not quite. We haven't slept together. In fact, we

haven't even had a real kiss yet, if you know what I mean.''

"So he's just been teasing you with little ones."

"Something like that."

"No wonder you're both going crazy. Are you listening to me, Gaby?"

"Yes."

"I only spent a short time in his company last night. But it was long enough for me to be impressed by his superior intelligence. He's no grunt."

"No."

"A guy like Anatoly would be in a position of authority. If he's a mafia boss, one who's high up in the ranks, that makes him shrewd, powerful and very dangerous to you, because he would have connections everywhere."

"Thanks for making me feel better."

"You wanted gut honesty from me, so I'm giving it to you."

"Okay. Go on."

"Don't despair. There's a ray of sunshine in all this."

Pain screamed from every cell. "I don't see where."

"He won't be expecting you to disappear today."

I don't want to disappear. We have a date later on. I'm living for it.

"Gaby?"

"What?"

"Last night you paid good money for your new apartment. This is probably the only time you'll have the opportunity to catch him off guard. Hesitate and it might be too late to escape him.''

Much as she hated to admit it, Hallie was right.

''When we walk out of here in a little while, don't plan on coming back until your uncle can give you the okay.''

''What about the landlord here? Our lease isn't up for two more months.''

''Call him after you get to Atlantic City. Tell him we had to vacate unexpectedly, so he's free to rent the apartment to someone else. I'll pay what we owe him.''

''We'll both pay, Hallie. Poor Mrs. Bills. What's she going to think when I never show up?''

''She'll be two months ahead in rent and can find someone else in a day. Right now your life is more important. Let Anatoly put his own spin on your sudden disappearance.''

''Nobody spins better than he does.'' The tears spilled down her cheeks. ''Did I tell you how good he is at stickball?''

''Yes. After last night, I could write a book about him.''

''He's coming by for me at three.''

''But you won't be here.''

''Neither will you. Not anymore. The next time I see you, I'll have to bow or something.'' By now Gaby was sobbing.

''Oh, come here, you big crybaby.''

They hugged.

Hallie wiped her eyes. ''You'd better get busy

packing your clothes. Knowing your boyfriend, he might just decide to drop by early.''

''That's exactly what I was thinking. All I need is—''

They both jumped when they heard the rap on the front door.

Gaby's eyes flashed Hallie a signal of distress.

''You stay in the bathroom. I'll take care of this,'' her friend whispered.

''No,'' Gaby whispered back. ''If I don't make an appearance, he'll come up with a reason to hang around until I come out. He thinks you and I are going to lunch. We'll just let him go on thinking it. I'll get rid of him as fast as I can.''

CHAPTER ELEVEN

BY THE TIME Gaby opened the front door, she felt as if she was going to faint. She almost did when she saw Anatoly standing there with a gaily wrapped package in his hand.

A pair of white cargo pants covered his hard, powerful thighs. There was a classy elegance in the way the navy sweatshirt fit his broad shoulders and chest. The hood at the back of his neck brushed the tendrils of his dark, vibrant hair. Talk about a beautiful man...

Combined with the forbidden-fruit aspect of their association, she found him completely and utterly desirable. She could talk about her fears all she wanted when they were apart. Yet all he had to do was appear in the flesh. In an instant his male essence blotted out everything except her attraction for him.

It staggered her how much she wanted to throw herself in his arms and forget the world.

"Gabriella." His husky voice penetrated to her insides. "If I knew you were alone, there would not be one molecule of air separating us."

The way his eyes appeared to devour her, she could believe it. No doubt he'd registered her eyes feasting on him.

"Good morning, Anatoly."

"Good morning. Forgive me. I know you did not expect me until three. But I could not stay away. The thought of you moving to my apartment house is all that has kept me going since last night."

"I'm looking forward to it, too." It was true. Even though she was going to run away from him, *it was true*.

Their eyes clung. "I realize you are busy getting Hallie ready to leave for the convent. If she is presentable, I would like to give her this small gift as a going-away present."

"That's very thoughtful of you. Come in. I'll tell her you're here."

Afraid to linger before she willed him to touch her, she hurried through the living room to the bedroom.

Hallie took one look at her flushed face and shook her head in acknowledgment of an impossible situation.

"He has a gift for you," Gaby said.

"Your Russian does everything right, doesn't he."

Gaby nodded solemnly.

Together they moved out of the bedroom.

"Hi, Anatoly."

"Good morning, Hallie. This is for you."

"How thoughtful you are!" She took the present from him and undid the wrapping. When she opened the lid, Gaby heard her gasp.

Inside the box lay an exquisite corsage of gardenias and white roses.

"Th-this is beautiful," Hallie stammered. She

sounded shaken. "You shouldn't have gone to the trouble."

"I wanted to. You are about to embark on a life that will not allow you to accept flowers from a man. It would please me very much if you will wear these until you reach the convent."

Oh, no. Too late Gaby realized what was happening. "Hallie?" she said. "Why don't you take them in the bedroom and put them on while you finish packing."

"Yes. I-I'll do that. Thank you again, Anatoly."

She almost ran from the living room.

The second she was gone he grasped Gaby's upper arms firmly, forcing her to look up at him. Lines of strain marred his handsome face. "I have done something wrong. Tell me, Gabriella. How did I offend her? I thought every woman loved flowers. Why was she offended?"

Gaby shook her head. "She wasn't. I know she loved your gift, but I'm afraid it brought back certain memories she wants to forget."

"I am so sorry. If I could make amends I would do it. Help me to understand what I have done." He gave her arms a squeeze.

She couldn't think with his hands on her.

"Sit down and I'll explain."

He gave her arms another squeeze before releasing them to do her bidding.

"Hallie used to be an airline stewardess. She met a man from Chile and fell in love with him. He and his family flew to Los Angeles, where they were married. Then the wedding party flew to Santiago, Chile, to enjoy more festivities. Both families were on the plane with them. It crashed in the Andes.''

Anatoly groaned, making it even more difficult for Gaby to continue.

''Out of two hundred people, only five survived the ten-day ordeal at the crash site in mountain blizzards. Hallie was one of them.'' Tears trickled down her cheeks. She couldn't stop them. ''In that crash she lost everyone she loved.''

''That is not possible.'' He sounded as devastated as she felt.

''There was a nun on board, a native Chilean. She also survived and helped the other four hang on until rescue units arrived. It was her faith that got Hallie through.

''The survivors were flown to a hospital in Santiago. As soon as Hallie's broken leg was set in a cast, this nun found her a place to stay with a family where she could be taken care of. The two women formed a bond that I suppose only people who share such a traumatic experience would understand.''

Anatoly sprang to his feet and started pacing. ''That explains so much, Gabriella.''

She nodded. ''Hallie quit flying. She ended up staying down there and working for a Chilean-American concern. But her true interest was in the religious life and she became a lay nun. The other nun urged her to return to the States and get in touch with her roots before she took the step to be professed. With great reluctance Hallie came back to Bel Air, but she didn't feel her life was there anymore. She ended up coming here to San Diego where she found temporary work with some other lay nuns. That's when we met.''

She heard him expel a troubled sigh. ''Nothing I could have given her would have brought more pain than those flowers.''

''You didn't know, Anatoly. Hallie will cry for a while, but then she'll recover.''

''I already have.''

They both turned their heads at the same time. Hallie had come into the room. She wore the corsage on the shoulder of her cotton blouse.

Gaby watched her walk over to Anatoly and kiss his cheek. ''Thank you for the gift. You've given me another memory. A happy one.''

The sweetness of Anatoly's smile melted Gaby's heart. ''I will not take up any more of your time with Gabriella. I can imagine how precious every moment together must be now.''

His gaze flicked to Gaby. It said all the things he wasn't saying out loud. ''I will see you at three.''

You're killing me, Anatoly, her heart cried.

MAX DIDN'T REMEMBER the drive back to his apartment house in the van. What had transpired in Gabriella's apartment just now defied description. So many conflicting emotions were bombarding him, he felt as if he was losing his mind.

This was one time he needed a vacation badly. Instead, he had to pull himself together, because Oleg would be picking him up in a few minutes.

He'd just parked the van and had started walking

out to the street when his cell phone rang. It was Gideon. He clicked on.

"You called just in time. I got hold of Oleg. Any minute and he'll be at the corner of the street outside my apartment house. We'll be traveling to Galena's apartment. Did you get your hands on a picture of Svetlana?"

"I made a copy."

"Give me a description."

"Her hair is ash blond, straight, worn to the jaw-line. Blue eyes. She's sixteen. Five foot seven, a hundred ten pounds. Quite pretty. Full lips. Good posture and carriage."

"That's Irina! She moves like a dancer. Thank God she had the courage to get away from Nikolai! As long as she's in Girls' Village, she's safe for the moment. Unless, as we speculated, it's really a holding tank where some girls are sold into prostitution."

"I've had the guys checking on that. They've gone back in the records fifteen years. There's no evidence of that kind of activity going on here."

"We could stand a lot more good news like that. Unfortunately, that doesn't mean Gabriella's not using her job as a volunteer for other purposes. Furthermore, we can't celebrate yet when we don't know what's happened to Galena."

"I hear you. Don't be surprised if you get over there and find the apartment closed up. I hate to even think this, but she might have already paid the ultimate price."

"Maybe. Maybe not. Nikolai has to be enraged Irina got away. I'm more inclined to believe he's still hanging around there using Galena for bait. Something tells me he's counting on Irina to get desperate enough to try and contact her mother. In the meantime his thugs are turning the city inside out looking for her. He knows what'll happen if she gets to the police before he can muzzle her.''

"That's what worries me, Max. Nikolai's running scared. It's going to be hard to predict his next move. I've got a bad feeling in my gut about you going over there.''

"So do I, but when has that ever bothered either—'' He broke off as soon as he saw the Passat in the distance. "Gotta go. I'll check in with you later, on the way to Gabriella's apartment.'' His breathing grew shallow just anticipating being alone with her.

"Take care.''

"HI, SVETLANA. How's it going?''

Irina looked up from the bed she was making. She'd told the girls her real name in front of Gaby. But she'd begged them not to use it while she lived there.

"Hi, Juanita.''

"Where's Sandra?''

"With doctor.''

Juanita sat down on Sandra's bed. "Do you think she's going to have the baby?''

"No. No pains.''

"Oh. She probably went to an appointment, huh?''

The other girl nodded.

"Do you want to come to class with us? It starts pretty soon.''

"I— No, thank you."

"I know you're worried about your mom, but Gaby said she'd find out about her and get back to you. When Gaby tells you she'll do something, she will."

Irina nodded, but inside she wanted to die.

"This class is really fun. It's not like math."

"What is it?"

"On Saturdays we do different projects. This month we are learning how to fix our hair and makeup."

"Oh yes?"

"It's great! These ladies are beauticians. They bring all this good stuff we can try. You know. Blusher and lipstick and eye shadow. If it's your first time in class, they give you a makeover."

"What is that?"

"They study your coloring. Like you're a blonde and you have blue eyes. So they put the right colors and base on you to make you look good."

"They do to me?"

"If you want. I got mine last time. Today I have to remember what they did and try to apply it right by myself. Everyone has something different, depending on their hair and skin color."

"Hi, guys!"

Irina's eyes darted to the door. "Hi, Sandra."

"Are you okay?" Juanita asked.

"Yes. The doctor said I'll probably have the baby pretty soon. According to him, it is getting into position."

"You scared?"

"Kind of. But I'm so tired of feeling like a hippo, I can't wait for this to be over."

"Hippo?" said Irina.

"It's a huge animal, but if you don't know what it looks like, I can't explain."

Juanita said, "Haven't you got a picture of one in your scrapbook?"

"Oh, yeah. Gaby's taken us to the San Diego Zoo a couple of times."

"I'll get it," Juanita volunteered. "You'd better sit down and rest all that tonnage."

"You'll be sorry you said that to me five months from now."

"I was just kidding. Here you go." She emerged from the closet and handed the book to Sandra.

They sat down on either side of Irina. Sandra flipped through the pages of photographs.

"I see it!" Juanita cried.

"Yup. Here are some pictures. This is what we call a hippopotamus."

Irina took the scrapbook to get a better look. "Ah, yes. They dangerous."

"That's what the guide at the zoo told us."

"You not look like hippo."

Sandra gave her a squeeze. "Thank you. I'm your friend for life."

"Can I see all pictures?"

"Sure. While you do that, I have to go to the bathroom again. Guess what? They're showing *Titanic* after lunch."

Juanita turned to Irina. "Do you know the story about the ship that struck an iceberg and sank?"

"Oh, yes."

"Did you see it?"

"No."

Irina started at the front of the photo album, interested in all the pictures. Gaby was in many of them. It looked as if she'd taken the girls a lot of places.

"Do you want to?"

She lifted her head? "What?"

"Would you like to see the movie with us?"

"Yes." She kept turning the pages. "This is ship."

"Yeah. One time Gaby took us to the dock so we could watch people getting on the Cunard *Princess*. That one goes to Mexico."

"It is big."

"Yeah. It is."

Irina came to the last of the pictures. The second she turned to the final page, she saw a photograph that curdled her blood. She pointed to it with a trembling finger.

"Who is this?"

"He's a hunk, isn't he. That's Gaby's boyfriend."

"Boyfriend?" she repeated in a shaken voice.

"Yeah. He's Russian, like you. Last week Gaby was driving us to the beach, and the strap of her sandal got caught. Anyway, she couldn't stop the car. We crashed into this beautiful black Audi. He was driving. When he got out, he took one look at Gaby, and it was love at first sight."

Sandra joined in the conversation. "You can say that again. He's better-looking than a movie star. They're crazy about each other."

Irina could hardly swallow. "You not see him before accident?"

Juanita grinned. "Only in my dreams."

Sandra sat down next to her. "What's wrong? You look like you're going to be sick."

"Gaby not meet him before accident?"

"No, otherwise we would have met him a long time ago. She tells us everything. Her husband died over a year ago. She was so unhappy she moved all the way from Florida to start a new life. Anatoly is the first man we've ever seen her with."

Anatoly. A cold hand squeezed Irina's heart.

"What is it?" Sandra whispered.

"Gaby in danger."

"Why?" they both cried at once.

"Because he *bad, bad* man."

Sandra put a hand on her arm. "Is he one of the men who tried to rape you?"

"No." Irina shook her head. "He not there last time. But he come to apartment many times when Nikolai do business."

"You're positive this is the man you've seen with the others?"

"Yes. No man look like him."

"Maybe you're mistaken, Irina. Anatoly was so much fun and so good to us. He couldn't be evil."

"I agree," Sandra said. "Gaby wouldn't go out with a man she didn't trust. She isn't like that."

Tears stung Irina's eyes. "My mother think Nikolai good man. He give her money. Then he change. He criminal."

"Aieee!" Juanita cried. "This is a nightmare. What's his last name?"

"Kuzmina."

"That's what she called him! Kuzmina." Both girls moaned.

Sandra took the scrapbook and looked at the picture again. "This is going to break Gaby's heart."

"She not safe. Anatoly not let her go."

The three girls stared at each other in fear.

"We've got to get hold of Gaby," Sandra said.

"No!" Irina cried. "What if she with him?"

"That's right."

"Somebody's got to warn her!"

"No, Juanita. No police. She look for my mother now."

"I know."

Sandra stopped pacing. "Gaby will probably come over as soon as she has any news. Even if she's with Anatoly, she can't bring him to our rooms. Those are the rules. When we get her upstairs, we'll tell her then."

"I don't want to be the one to break the awful news."

"Neither do I, Juanita."

Irina got up from the bed. "I tell Gaby."

GABY HAD WRITTEN down the address of the Pedrovas' apartment in Core-Columbia. But when she saw the block of row houses on the east side of the street, it was easier to go by Irina's instructions.

Climb the third set of steps from the south end. Their apartment was on the fourth floor, number eight. Once inside, they could take the elevator or the stairs.

"Sister Paulina? This is the street. You can pull over to the curb the next chance you get. We'll start at the corner and work our way back to the car."

The older sister nodded. She just happened to be the head administrator for the nuns planning to serve in foreign missions. When Hallie had explained why she was asking such an unorthodox favor, Sister Paulina immediately agreed to help them.

Not only did she give them habits to wear, she offered to drive the convent car so their visit would appear official.

"Don't forget these pamphlets."

"No." Gaby took them from her. "Thank you, Sister."

The older woman smiled and made the sign of the cross.

"Let's go, Gaby."

It took some doing to be graceful as she climbed out of the back seat of the church limousine wearing the black habit and wimple.

Soon Hallie would don similar robes of the postulant. Garbed in the same clothing, but for entirely different reasons, Gaby felt closer to her dear friend than ever. She would always treasure this moment.

"Don't go getting all sentimental on me now," Hallie whispered as they straightened their skirts. "We're partners in crime. We could do time if we're caught."

Gaby blinked back the tears. Trust Hallie to make

a joke under such precarious circumstances. "I wish I felt like laughing."

"You don't have to worry about anything. Let me do the talking. This is my domain."

Thank heaven.

Before they reached the corner, a couple of children playing on the sidewalk ran up to them. Hallie greeted them with a cheery smile and told them to take a pamphlet home to their mothers.

As the boys disappeared into one of the apartments, Hallie turned to Gaby. "You see how easy it is? We're already spreading the good news."

Prophetic words. Within a few minutes more people seemed to come out of the woodwork to talk to them. All Gaby had to do was give out a pamphlet while Hallie chatted with them in her friendly way.

By the time they'd canvassed two buildings, Gaby figured six out of every eight apartments had someone inside. Those were good odds, even for a Saturday morning.

So far everything had gone well. But when they reached the fourth floor of the third building, Gaby's skin broke out in a film of perspiration. Unspoken messages flashed between them as they approached number eight. Her heart was slamming so hard against her ribs, she was surprised she couldn't hear it reverberating off the walls.

Hallie knocked on the door.

They waited. No response.

If Irina's mother was being held against her will, her boyfriend would make sure she didn't answer.

After another minute Hallie tried again, a little louder this time.

Still nothing.

Her gaze swerved to Gaby's. She moved her head to the side, indicating Gaby should slide a pamphlet under the door.

She knelt down and pushed it through, praying that if someone was inside, they would be curious enough to walk over and see what it was.

While still in a kneeling position, the door opened. Gaby stood up. Through the crack she found herself being scrutinized by a dark-blond male, the man Irina called Nikolai. He had the build of a boxer, just as Irina had described.

The dangerous glitter in those eyes would terrify anyone, especially a young and lovely teenage girl who would have no defense against him.

Gaby's fear turned to white-hot rage. Forgetting that Hallie was supposed to do the talking, she said, "Good morning. We're the new sisters from Our Lady of Mercy, in the area getting to know the community. If you have a few minutes, we'd like to come inside and go over the pamphlet with you to explain about a pro—"

"Not interested," came the words on a hiss. He tossed the pamphlet back at her. It fell to the floor. "Don't ever come here again."

He slammed the door in her face.

Gaby swallowed her disappointment before turning to Hallie in despair. That was when they heard a woman's voice cry out in Russian from the other side of the door. She sounded frantic.

He answered with harsh, staccatolike Russian phrases. Gaby thought she heard Irina's name mentioned. It didn't matter. Her mother was still alive! They had the proof they'd come for.

Hallie gave Gaby a thumbs-up.

She smiled back, then picked up the pamphlet.

They started for the stairs at the same time, not wanting to wait for the elevator. Nikolai might decide to take matters into his own hands and physically kick them out of the building. Or worse.

MAX HAD BEEN in Irina's apartment many times, but no missionaries had ever knocked on the door before. Certainly not any Catholic nuns who'd probably been frightened by Nikolai's reception.

As Max watched the smoke unfurl from the end of his cigarette, he wondered what the odds were that the nun who'd done the speaking had the exact same voice as Gabriella's. Probably in the millions...

That's your heart I heard talking, Max. It scares the hell out of me because it means you've lost your edge.

Gideon had been right. Max *had* lost his edge. The nun on the other side of the door couldn't possibly be Gabriella.

As he tossed off the rest of his vodka, Nikolai disappeared into the bedroom to quiet an hysterical Galena in a way that would produce bruises on her face and body by morning.

Oleg sent Max a glance that said to hell with this mess. Irina's disappearance had upset the fragile balance of Nikolai's underworld. When one of the bodies spun out of orbit, it started a domino effect. Tempers erupted with more frequency and violence. The men were frightened, and with good reason. Poor Galena was receiving the brunt of Nikolai's anger.

If the mafia bosses got wind of this glitch, the underlings would be eliminated with no questions asked. Their con would be over, anyway, if the law got to them first. Paranoia ruled the day.

Gideon had said it best. Nikolai was running scared. Every poor dumb lackey who owed him a favor was out scouring the city for Irina. For once, Nikolai hadn't started baiting Max the moment he'd appeared at the door with Oleg half an hour ago.

Max didn't know how much fear played into this drastic change in Nikolai's behavior toward him. Maybe it was that, coupled with the fact that Nikolai didn't have an audience to hear him attack Max.

Whatever the reasons, today Max wasn't the sole object of Nikolai's vituperation. Even Nikolai was coming to the conclusion that to save his kingdom from destruction, it might be wise to accept help from his bitterest enemy.

But Max would be more than willing to take the bastard on if it meant he stopped beating Galena. Max couldn't get Irina's mother out of here fast enough.

He extinguished his cigarette. "Nikolai?" he called to him. "We're wasting time. I have an idea to discuss with you before we go."

"Women!" Nikolai walked back into the front room, letting fly a stream of the grossest profanity. He lit another cigarette.

"So, Kuzmina, you think you can find her little whore when none of the men have been successful?"

"Do you want my help or not?"

"Let's hear your brilliant idea first."

"Ever since we started meeting here, Alexey has had the hots for Irina. She's only sixteen, still young enough to believe in romantic love. You know what I'm getting at. She didn't have the hots for him. Obviously Alexey scared her off, so she ran away.

"All this time you've lived in the hope that she would come back to her mother. But I can tell you right now, she won't step in this apartment again because she knows Alexey will be here."

"What makes you the expert on romantic love?"

"Did you never feel something in your heart for a woman, Nikolai?"

The man grunted. "Go on. What is your theory?"

"Irina had no papers on her. I have put myself inside her head. I believe she would stow away on a ship to get as far from California as possible."

Nikolai puffed on his cigarette, staring at Max through narrowed lids.

Oleg sat forward on the couch. "Anatoly's theory makes sense, Nikolai. She's a frightened girl, not a manipulative woman capable of striking back."

A long silence ensued. The bastard was listening.

Max leaned forward. "Tell me. How much longer am I going to have to wait until another accident is arranged?"

Nikolai's eyes slid away from Max. "I don't know yet."

Liar.

"You told me two weeks. One has gone by already. If that's the way things still stand, then I'll take a vacation from my other job and start a search for Irina. It won't be difficult to find out how many ships left port since her disappearance. Someone might remember her. I'll leave no stone unturned."

He stood up to emphasize his point. "My job as future capper for the beach cities is on the line, too, Nikolai. We are all in this together. What do you say? Am I to stay here and wait until you put me back to work? Or do I follow my instincts and hunt this girl down? It is your call."

Nikolai lounged back in the chair. "Go hunting, of course. But I expect you to report in every day. If one of my men should find her first, then I want you back here at once."

"Of course."

GABY LET HERSELF out of the service-station rest room carrying the habit and wimple over her arm. It felt good to be in normal clothes again. As long as she'd been wearing a nun's habit for a special purpose, she'd felt all right about it. But now that they'd accomplished their goal, she had no more excuse.

Though Sister Paulina had been great about everything, Gaby was relieved the older nun didn't have to cover for them any longer. When she drove Hallie back to the church for her rental car, she wouldn't have to explain anything—or answer any awkward questions—because Gaby wouldn't be with them.

Gaby ran around to the other side of the convent car and leaned inside the window.

"You look beautiful in those clothes, Hallie. I'm glad you're wearing them today. It's the way I'll think of you from now on." Tears smarted in her eyes, but she fought them. "We've had lots of adventures, but this one was the best, wasn't it?"

"The very best. Don't get me started, Gaby."

"I won't. That's why I wanted to say goodbye here."

"Okay." She sniffed. "Tell me what you're going to do. Let's go over it one more time."

"I'm going to take a taxi to Girls' Village. After I've talked to Irina, I'll take another taxi to the airport and fly to my parents." Gaby hugged her friend. "We'll always stay in touch."

After she released her, she walked around to the driver's door. "Sister Paulina?" Her voice trembled. "I'll never be able to thank you enough."

"The news that the child's mother is still alive was worth all the trouble."

"May I come and visit you one day?"

"You'll always be welcome." She made the sign of the cross, then drove off. Gaby waved until the black car disappeared into traffic.

Thankful she wasn't at her apartment where she had the luxury of crying her eyes out, Gaby pulled out her cell phone and rang for a taxi. While she waited for it, she went into the station's minimart and bought a couple of magazines to read on the plane.

On her way to the airport she would phone Anita, then make calls to a couple of her attorney friends and arrange to go over her clients' cases with them. There were other phone calls to be made, as well,

including ones to her landlord and her family. They
had no idea she was coming home.

But there was a yawning emptiness growing inside
her. In a little while she'd be leaving the world that
contained Anatoly. She couldn't comprehend never
seeing him again, never laughing with him, teasing
him, kissing him. Loving him.

Though he hadn't been her lover, she had felt
loved.

How on earth would she pick up the pieces of her
life a second time?

She honestly didn't know.

CHAPTER TWELVE

MAX BOUNDED UP the stairs to Gabriella's apartment three at a time. After she let him inside, he didn't plan on them coming out of there for a while.

His heart racing from long-suppressed hunger, he rapped on the door, desperate to have Gabriella in his arms. He would love her and take whatever she was willing to give him until proof of her duplicity made it impossible to go on.

"Gabriella? Open the door."

He knocked again.

After a couple of minutes he had to face the fact that she hadn't returned from her lunch with Hallie. He realized it would be hard for them to say goodbye. But Gaby had no idea how much he'd been anticipating this time alone with her.

His disappointment was so acute he couldn't stand to wait in the hall for her. It would be better to go out to the van. The guys tailing her could tell him her exact location. Maybe she was still at the restaurant. If that was the case, he would drive there and pick her up.

He punched in the number on his cell phone and waited for one of them to answer.

"Calder here. Where's Ms. Peris?"

"We followed her friend's rental car to Our Lady of Mercy Convent and Parochial School out on Fairfax. They both went inside. They've been in there all that time. A few minutes ago the other woman came back out alone and drove off in her rental car. Ms. Peris hasn't made an appearance yet."

Max frowned. They must have had lunch there. Maybe Gabriella had taken Hallie's departure harder than Max had imagined.

"Stay on it. Let me know the moment she leaves."

"Yes, sir."

For security reasons he'd never tried to reach Gaby on her cell phone. But right now he didn't give a damn about that.

One of the guys had gotten her number. Max had already programmed it into his cell phone. With a jabbing motion of his index finger he punched in the two digits. While he waited for her to pick up, a spurt of adrenaline charged his body.

"The party you wished to reach is not available. You may have reached this recording in error. If so, hang up and try again."

He tried it a second time and got the same recording.

Hell. She'd turned off her phone.

He was surprised, considering her many responsibilities, legitimate or otherwise. But if she was upset, it was reasonable she wouldn't want to be disturbed. Reasonable, but very unlike her.

In place of his former euphoria, he felt a strange foreboding that created a pit in his gut.

In a distinctly different frame of mind than he was

a few minutes ago, he started up the van and headed into traffic. If he exceeded the speed limit, it would take twenty minutes to reach his destination. But the traffic was impossible.

The faster he drove, the more convinced he became that something was wrong. He got on the phone to the guys tailing him.

"It's Calder. I'm headed for Our Lady of Mercy on Fairfax. Get me a couple of patrol cars to give me an escort. Siren and lights."

"We'll get right on it."

GABY ENTERED the front doors of Girls' Village and hurried upstairs to Sandra's room. No one was there. When she went back down to the main desk, she learned that most of the girls were still in the auditorium watching the end of *Titanic*.

Much as she hated to disturb them, she knew Irina was barely holding on while she waited for word about her mother.

Once Gaby stepped into the auditorium, it took a minute for her eyes to adjust to the darkness. Finally she was able to walk down the side aisle searching profiles. Sandra's advanced stage of pregnancy made it easier to find them.

Bending over, Gaby asked the girl on the aisle seat to pass the word that Svetlana was wanted out in the hall.

Barely through the back doors herself, the three girls caught up to her. "Come with me. We'll go to your bedroom." On the way upstairs, Gaby put an arm around Irina's shoulders.

"Your mother's all right," she whispered. The girl caved in right there and started sobbing. "I have a plan to get her out of there, but I'll need your permission to contact the authorities."

Irina stared hard at Gaby without responding, but at least she hadn't said no.

The second they reached the bedroom, Sandra pulled her aside. "Gaby? There's something important you need to know." Juanita shut the door as if to punctuate the seriousness of this meeting.

Alert to the urgent inflection in Sandra's voice, Gaby sensed she wasn't going to like whatever it was.

"All right. We're alone. Tell me what's wrong."

"Go on, Irina."

Her gaze darted back to the Russian girl. "I was hoping the news about your mother would make you happier."

"Yes!" she cried. "But now you in danger."

Gaby smiled. "Irina, you don't need to worry about me."

Irina acted as if she was in pain. "Yes. You know Anatoly Kuzmina one week. I know him twelve, maybe more."

What? "What do you mean, Irina?"

Juanita handed Gaby the scrapbook. It was opened to the last page where she'd put the photos of yesterday's outing. "Irina saw his picture and recognized him. He's one of the men who's been coming to her mother's apartment."

"No!" Gaby shook her head, dropping the scrapbook on the bed.

"All men at apartment are bad. Do bad business."

She felt so sick she had to sit down. "You *must* be mistaken."

"No. Anatoly very important man. Very smart. Much money. Big car. He bring flowers to my mother. Nikolai hate him."

Dear God. Gaby started to cry. She buried her face in her hands. The girls crowded around her, patting her back.

"We're so sorry, Gaby."

She finally lifted her head. "Was he one of the men who tried to come into your room?" Her voice shook.

"No. He nice to me and my mother. He there just for business."

If Irina had said anything else, Gaby would have died right there on the spot.

"Was he there when you escaped?"

"No. Nikolai say Anatoly take vacation."

I am on vacation from my second job, so I have time to take you where you have to go, Gabriella.

Shuddering uncontrollably, she got up from the bed. Irina's eyes followed her. "If Anatoly choose you for girlfriend, you never get away."

She sucked in her breath. "Thank you for telling me, Irina. Unfortunately your news leaves me with no choice but to talk to my uncle about this. He's a police detective. He'll advise me what to do so that you and your mother, and I, are safe. Will you trust me?"

The other girl nodded.

"I have to go now, but I promise I'll be in touch with all of you very soon."

Gaby left their bedroom so frightened and heartsick both at the same time, she could scarcely function.

But she had to! It was imperative she get to the airport as fast as possible.

She pulled out her cell phone and rang for a taxi to take her to the terminal. Thank God she'd listened to Hallie's advice. With her credit card, she'd already purchased her plane ticket.

Earlier in the day, Hallie had driven her to the bank. She'd withdrawn three thousand dollars from her savings account to make certain she had enough money on hand for any eventuality.

She'd been able to make all her phone calls to Anita and her colleagues. Hallie had talked to the landlord. He'd agreed to let a moving company come in and box up Gaby's things to be shipped to the East Coast. On the way to the airport she would call her parents and let them know she was coming. They'd probably have the whole family out to greet her.

After putting the phone back in her purse, Gaby hurried to the main staircase. Her legs wobbled so badly, she could hardly make it down the steps. Somehow she had to find the strength to pull herself together.

It was one thing to wonder if Anatoly might be involved in illegal activities. But hearing it from Irina's lips had changed everything. Gaby was no longer in denial.

"Gabriella?"

Dear God! He'd found her!

If Anatoly choose you for girlfriend, you never get away.

Earlier in the day she'd had to impersonate a nun when she and Hallie had gone to check on Irina's mother. Now it seemed her acting skills had to be called upon once again. Without question this was the most important role of her life.

Her first priority was to get Anatoly out of the building before Irina happened to come down the stairs. If he saw her, Gaby couldn't bear to think what would happen. She'd promised Irina she'd be safe here.

Propelled by fear for the frightened teen as much as for herself, she hurried toward him and grasped his hand. "Anatoly, I owe you an explanation, but I don't want to talk about it here. Is your van outside?"

He put his arm around her shoulders to guide her toward the front doors. "It is waiting for you."

One burden was lifted the moment they stepped into the late-afternoon sunlight, leaving Irina inside the building undetected.

"You look pale." He ushered her toward the van. "I am worried about you."

"You don't need to be. I had a call from Juanita while Hallie and I were eating lunch. She said Sandra was having labor pains and wanted me to come right away. Hallie dropped me off here before she left for Los Angeles in her rental car."

"Sandra is having the baby now?"

"No. It was a false alarm, but there was no way to contact you. I'm so sorry I wasn't at the apartment at three. How did you know I was here?"

He helped her inside the van. "When you did not come, I searched everywhere for you. I thought to look here, hoping one of the girls knew where you were."

Anatoly always had a logical answer for everything.

"At last we are going to be alone. My heart is racing too fast, Gabriella." He gave her a swift kiss on the lips before moving around to the driver's seat.

A shiver, part ice, part fire, ran down her spine.

Irina had said he was an important man. Powerful. He probably had spies everywhere. It was possible he knew she'd been lying through her teeth just now.

From the moment he'd surprised her in the hallway with the roses, he hadn't left her alone. Coming and going, she would barely blink and he'd be there, day or night.

Unless a man was a law unto himself, he didn't have the resources or the time to pursue his own pleasure to that degree. In Gaby's case, he'd been relentless in his pursuit of her since the accident.

Because she'd made the fatal mistake of trying to reach him at the florist shop the first time, she would never know if that phone call was the catalyst that had made him come after her.

If she was honest with herself, it was probably her instant attraction to him that had tempted her to contact him at all.

Obviously men who lived their lives in the underworld had women and families who loved them. There'd been hundreds of books written about such men, especially the Italian mafia dons.

How incredible that she, Gaby Peris, a New Jersey girl, now found herself deeply involved with a Russian mobster. A man whose physical and mental traits were perfect for her in every way.

It had happened so fast, so naturally, she'd become enamored without realizing the severe consequences of such a liaison.

Like Gaby, Irina's mother had been vulnerable after her husband's death and had fallen under Nikolai's spell. By the time she'd figured out why strange men kept invading her apartment on a regular basis, she'd tried to get away from him. No doubt that was when the beatings had started.

For the moment, Gaby recognized that she wasn't in mortal danger from Anatoly, not in the sense that she could expect to be eliminated any time soon. He wanted her too much for that. His desire for her was as great as her hunger for him.

Since she hadn't made it to the airport in time to escape, that meant she was going to have to be cunning and bide her time.

In order to survive, she would have to go on living exactly as she'd been doing. In case he'd put her under surveillance, even to the extent of tapping her phones, she'd tell no more lies so she wouldn't raise any alarm bells with him.

For the past week Gaby had been living in denial. There was no question about that. But she wasn't naive. Men like Anatoly did whatever it took to keep their women in line.

If she could lull him into a state of total trust, whether it took days or weeks, there would come a moment when she would be able to slip away and disappear from his world.

"You are more quiet than I have ever known you to be."

They had come back to her apartment, something she'd been looking forward to until Irina's damning testimony.

Her eyes traveled over him as they'd done earlier that morning. His impact on her senses was as profound as ever. But the blinders had come off.

Could he tell? Was he that shrewd? She knew she'd have to put on a convincing performance.

"Maybe it's because today marks the end of one era and the beginning of another."

She saw fire in his eyes. Her body started to tremble.

"I have been living for it." He reached for her hand. "Come over here."

Slowly, like a person being led through water, she followed him to the couch where he pulled her down on his lap. His hands went to her hair.

"Since the moment I walked up to your car and saw you at the wheel, I have been wanting to do this."

In an economy of movement he undid the elastic tie. The release felt electric as her hair sprang free to fall about her shoulders. He touched the strands experimentally. She heard his sharp intake of breath. "Your hair...it is heavy yet silky. Why do you never wear it this way?" His eyes flicked to hers. "You have done this to torment me. You know you have." Their lips were only centimeters apart.

"Long hair gets in the way, Anatoly. If you'd let yours grow out, you'd understand the necessity of tying it back. Come to think of it, you'd look pretty good like that."

He frowned. "Only pretty good?" But he was tracing the line of her lips with a finger as he asked the question. It was making her crazy.

"You want compliments now?" The tension between them had become unbearable.

A low sound of delight rumbled from his throat. "I want so many things, I hardly know where to begin."

"Don't take too long," she teased, trying to quell the frantic pounding of her heart. "There's an American adage that says, 'He who hesitates is lost.'"

She knew he was going to kiss her and realized she'd have to let him. But she had no intention of going to bed with him. If he suggested they move to the bedroom, she would use the excuse that she needed to start dinner.

His hands had moved to either side of her face. "There is an old Russian expression that says, 'He who devours caviar in one swallow does not deserve to feast.'"

"Is that what we're going to do? Feast?"

"You sound impatient. Breathless. First we will enjoy an appetizer."

She swallowed hard. "What kind?"

"Look into my eyes, Gabriella."

"No, Anatoly. Don't make me do this."

"You are shy. Tell me. Am I the first man to touch you since your husband?"

"Yes."

"It was good with him?"

"Yes."

"It will be different with me. But it will be good. Let me show you."

Then his mouth covered hers.

It wasn't like his kiss in the stairwell that had left her panting and unsatisfied. She found her mouth opening to the urgent pressure of his until there was a communion so total she couldn't think about anything except the way he made her feel.

This man holding her in his arms was kissing her as if he was starving for her. She couldn't tell where one kiss ended and another one began. Their hunger was mutual. Insatiable.

She couldn't stop moaning. Anatoly had turned her into a wanton. They should have satisfied themselves much earlier than today. Holding back until now had only fed the fire. She was on fire. So was he.

Somewhere in the cosmos she heard a phone ring. It had a different sound. One of his friends was trying to reach him.

"Anatoly? Your phone…"

Gabriella was beneath him. She pushed against his shoulders with her hands in an attempt to distract him.

"Let it ring. I have more important business right here."

Once again his mouth descended, sweeping aside everything in its path, igniting another feverish response from her as they clung, arms and legs entwined.

Gaby knew this insanity had to stop, but her body was slow to obey. A driving need to know his possession was pushing her closer and closer to the edge.

The phone rang again.

Keep ringing…

On a groan of protest, Anatoly finally tore his lips from hers and stood up to answer it.

Though dazed and weakened by the rapture he'd

created, Gaby found the strength to get off the couch. Somehow she managed to make it to the kitchen.

Never again, Anatoly.

If Gaby had felt frightened after leaving Girls' Village, that emotion was nothing compared to the fear she felt now.

And he'd only been kissing her!

Anatoly was like a fever in the blood. Since the accident, she'd known that it would be like this if he ever really kissed her. Given any more opportunities, she could easily imagine herself falling completely under his thrall and staying with him no matter what kind of man he was…

MAX TURNED his back on Gabriella and pulled out his phone. It was Gideon. He clicked on. "What's happening?"

"You're asking *me?* Good grief, Max, get rid of the bug or move to another part of the apartment. Otherwise you're going to cause the guys listening to every cry, breath, moan and syllable to forget why they're being paid."

Heat crept into his face. "I couldn't do anything about it without raising suspicion. Then things kind of got away from us."

"You don't need to tell me that. Listen. Karl's got a plan to rescue Galena without Nikolai catching on, but he needs your input. He's called a meeting."

"When?"

"Now. It'll probably be an all-nighter."

Max sucked in his breath.

"I'll be there."

He clicked off.

When he walked to the kitchen, he discovered Gabriella making tacos. The ground beef had started to sizzle in the pan with the onion salt. It smelled good, but nothing compared with the scent of her skin and hair.

He slid his hands around her hips to her stomach. She trembled when he pulled her body against him.

"Karin has called me with a big problem. The flowers shipped from South America did not come in on their normal flight. Now she has had word that they will be in on the next shipment. I have to go to the airport and wait for them to arrive."

"Do you want me to come with you?"

Gabriella—are you asking me because you can't bear to be separated? Or are you under orders to watch my every move? He turned her around so he could look at her.

"There is nothing I would love more. But if the plane is delayed, it could take much longer. Once the boxes come in, they have to pass customs inspection and it is a very lengthy process."

He rubbed her arms with growing insistence. "This is not how I imagined our first night alone would be. Already I am aching for you. But I will make it up to you tomorrow."

She smiled at him with those velvety eyes. "What is it you have planned for us?"

"How is it that you have forgotten? The Big League Stickball Tournament is tomorrow. It starts at ten in the morning and goes all day."

"That's right!" Her face lit with genuine pleasure.

"If it is too late for me to get back here tonight, I will pick you up at nine-thirty sharp. I will not forget to wear my baseball cap."

"I'll bring my pennant to wave."

"Gabriella, I do not want to leave you. Not even for one moment."

"I'll miss you, too, but I've got four new cases that need working on. I could use the time tonight to get going on them."

"Thank you for being so understanding."

Her mouth was irresistible. It was impossible to kiss her without wanting to devour her.

His friend Gideon knew that. It was why he'd interrupted Max during a moment of such intense pleasure it eclipsed all others—even memories of Lauren in those early days before their marriage.

If Gabriella had agreed to do this job for the mafia, she'd lost her way, just as he had.

This was something that happened on occasion in the department. An occupational hazard. Max had never imagined it happening to him. But the proof was in his arms, clinging to him.

Five minutes passed before he lifted his mouth from hers. Her lips were a little swollen. They quivered with longing. Could there be anything more enticing to a man than to know the woman he desired above all others wanted him every bit as badly?

"Tomorrow," he whispered before striding swiftly away.

GABY WATCHED him disappear out the front door. She gave him a minute, then hurried over to the front window in time to see the van drive off.

The urge to run had her jumping out of her skin. But one false move right now might turn him into someone like the monster who'd answered the door at Irina's apartment.

Searching back, the only time she'd ever seen a hint of a grimace on Anatoly's face was at the accident, right after the crash. But anyone would have been angry to have their car demolished. When he'd approached her, he didn't yell or act upset in any way.

Not under any circumstances could she imagine Anatoly being ugly like Nikolai. Irina had told Gaby he'd been nice to her and her mother.

But nothing excused his being involved with the mafia. He was either into stealing cars or crashing them. Both represented big business and million-dollar revenues.

How could Anatoly associate with men like that? Where was his humanity when he knew the other men were going to rape Irina? How could he sit back and allow Nikolai to beat Irina's mother? The more she thought about it, the less she could stand it.

Where to turn? She didn't dare venture outside or use her cell phone in case he'd bugged it.

Suddenly she got an idea and didn't know why she hadn't thought of it before. She could call her uncle Frank from the Arnolds' down the hall. She knew they wouldn't mind being bothered.

Making sure the stove was turned off, she covered the food, then ran over to the table for her keys.

Once the door was locked, she walked to the next unit and knocked. After trying it several times she remembered that they always went to church on Saturday evening.

Mrs. Boyd might be home.

Gaby darted across the hall and rapped on her door.

No luck there. She was probably visiting her children. Besides being the weekend, it was the wrong time of night.

Mr. Ortega in the other apartment was away on a business trip and wouldn't be back for another week.

Her neighbors in the next section would help her. She hurried down the stairs to the front door. But when she saw a strange man saunter by on the sidewalk and make eye contact with her, she feared he might be someone Anatoly had ordered to keep watch. It wasn't worth the risk.

Wheeling around, she retrieved her mail from the box, then dashed back upstairs to her apartment. She would have to wait until one of her neighbors came home tonight. Tomorrow would be too late.

Knowing Anatoly, he would show up with the sun. Then any opportunity to use someone else's phone would be lost.

Until she heard noises in the hall, she would work on her new cases and eat the tacos she'd made. No matter how late, she needed to unload on her uncle. Never in her life had she needed his love and professional advice more.

Three hours passed before the sound of Mrs. Arnold's voice reached Gaby's ears. She got up from the table and hurried out into the hall.

"Hello, Gaby. How are you? How's that handsome young man of yours?"

"He's fine." *He's in the mafia.* "Listen. I'm sorry to bother you, but my cell phone's not working properly and I need to make an important call. Would you mind if I used yours? It's a long-distance call, but I'll use my phone card."

"Come on in."

Breathing a sigh of relief, she followed the Arnolds into their cozy apartment. "Over there at the desk. Talk as long as you want. We're going to watch television for a while."

"Thank you so much."

Gaby moved to the love seat, then reached for the phone. After punching in all the numbers, she sat back and waited to hear her uncle's booming voice. When she got his voice mail, she let out a groan.

There was no way she could leave a message. Her aunt would tell Gaby's parents she'd phoned them. Then her mom and dad would be hurt that she hadn't tried to call them.

Gaby phoned home once a week without fail. But this week was different from any other. Crashing into Anatoly had turned her world inside out.

Maybe she could get through to her uncle at his office. She called information for the number of the detective bureau in Atlantic City. It took ten minutes to wade through all the extensions. She finally reached a dispatcher who gave her a number to call.

In the end, all she got was more voice mail. She would have to wait. Maybe tomorrow at the ball game she could excuse herself to go to the rest room, then find a pay phone.

She would find a way....

CHAPTER THIRTEEN

"WAY TO GO, Gents! Woo-hoo!"

Max slid his hand to the back of Gaby's neck. Watching stickball with her was almost as exciting as being in her arms. Several times the pennant she waved blocked his line of vision and he missed a play. None of it mattered as long as they were together.

He couldn't prevent his gaze from wandering over her glossy brown hair. She'd caught it back in a ponytail again. But it wouldn't stay that way for long. After being cheated out of last night, he was counting the hours until they returned to her apartment.

Unable to resist, he kissed the tip of her ear. "Are you hungry? Do you want me to buy you another hot dog while we wait for the next game?"

She turned to him with a fake look of compassion on her face. "I'm sorry the Bronx Knights are losing so badly, Anatoly. But more food isn't going to solve the problem."

"Maybe this will." He swooped down to capture her mouth. It tasted of orange drink and Cracker Jack. In fact, it tasted of so many wonderful things, he couldn't get enough and didn't care who might be watching.

When he released her, the teasing expression had

vanished. She looked as shaken as he felt. The chemistry between them was explosive.

Last night Karl had told him that as long as Nikolai expected Max to take a vacation from his part-time job to look for Irina, that was exactly what he should do. Let the department handle Galena Pedrova's escape. The guys would keep a close eye on Ms. Peris while Max cooled off.

On an intellectual level, he knew his boss was right. But Gabriella's mystique had him trapped so snug and tight, he couldn't bring himself to stay away.

"There are people walking up and down the aisles selling popcorn. I am going to buy us a box. We will feed it to each other. That is something I have never done with a woman, but I want to do it with you."

She flashed him a wary glance. "What's the catch?"

"Why do you always think I have ulterior motives?"

"Don't try that tragic Russian tone on me. It won't work anymore."

"What do you mean?"

"I'm on to you, Anatoly."

The oddest sensation swept through him just then. He had the distinct impression she was trying to tell him something.

Was it possible she'd fallen for him to the point where she was willing to warn him the mafia had a contract out on him? Did she care for him enough that she wanted to give him a fighting chance to defend himself?

If that was true, then it was also possible that somewhere down the road she could be reformed. Maybe she wanted to be free of the mafia, but needed help.

Too many thoughts converged in his mind at once, playing his emotions like a seesaw.

"Popcorn! Fresh buttered popcorn!"

Gabriella glanced at the vendor, then back at Max. Her eyes gleamed with mischief. "Go ahead and buy some for us. Make my day."

His eyes narrowed on her mouth. "I intend to do that."

They'd been sitting next to the aisle. He stood up and reached in his back pocket for his wallet. When he turned to the vendor, he saw Nikolai hovering nearby.

What the hell?

Nikolai's presence meant something big had come up. Otherwise he would never have emerged from the woodwork to find Max. Normally he'd send someone like Oleg or Alexey to inform him of an unexpected meeting.

For some reason he must have had Max tailed since he'd left the apartment house this morning. No doubt he was in a rage because Max had taken time off to be with Gabriella, instead of getting down to the business of finding Irina through the port authority.

Max nodded at the vendor. "How much?"

"Two-fifty a box."

"I will take one."

He gave him five dollars. "Keep the change."

"Thank you, sir."

As the man handed him the popcorn, Max read the

note Nikolai flashed from his hand at the same time. Then Nikolai moved on.

Max sat down, opened the box and extended it to Gabriella. "Go ahead and feed me a piece."

"What will happen if I do?"

"You will like it. I promise."

After a slight hesitation she picked one up and put it in his mouth. He caught her fingers and kissed the palm. To his surprise, her hand was shaking.

There was a difference between shaking and trembling. She was frightened. Suddenly the pieces of a puzzle he hadn't been able to put together started to form a design.

Nikolai had been sent by someone higher up to take Max out. Today was the day. Part of Gabriella's job had been to let Nikolai know where they'd be. But it hadn't been part of her job to warn Max.

If there weren't so much at stake, so many guys in the department depending on him, he'd convince her to disappear with him. They'd find their own private haven somewhere on the globe where they could relax and love each other into oblivion. But that wasn't the way it worked.

He let go of her hand. "You did not mind that too much?"

"No."

Unable to coax a smile out of her, he said, "Now it is my turn to feed you."

"Anatoly." She stopped him from reaching for more popcorn. "If you'll excuse me for a minute, I need to use the rest room."

"I will accompany you. Not inside, of course."

"That will be a relief to the other women."

They got up from the bleachers and headed toward the pavilion in the distance.

Another stickball game had started. Gabriella didn't comment on it. She was afraid for him. Max could feel it. He wanted to take her in his arms, tell her she didn't have to worry. His colleagues had him covered.

It didn't take long to reach the west-end rest rooms. She glanced up at him with an unfathomable expression in her eyes. "I'll be out in a few minutes."

"Take your time, Gabriella. I'll get a drink while I wait."

Once she'd disappeared behind the door, Max headed for Nikolai's car in the west parking lot where the note had said he'd be waiting. He sat behind the wheel of the white Mercedes. The engine was idling.

If Nikolai were going to shoot him, he'd wait until Max got in, then use a silencer on him. To his surprise, the other man climbed out of the car at Max's approach. That wasn't Nikolai's style.

He waved him over before pulling out a cigarette. The addiction would kill him if the feds didn't.

"What's going on? I thought you had better things to do than follow me to see if I'm doing my job."

He drew on his cigarette, then exhaled. "You told me a fairy tale about finding Irina on a ship."

"No, Nikolai. Like you, I have men loyal to me. One of them has located a boat headed for Australia with a stowaway aboard. A young blond female, underage. She'll be put ashore in Hawaii and flown back to San Diego. When my source can make a positive identification, I'll leave it up to you to figure out a plan to get her away from the authorities. Now, if you'll excuse me, I'm spending the afternoon with my girlfriend.''

Nikolai squinted at Max, as if not knowing whether to believe him or not. ''You think you're so damn clever. But I have news for you. It'll wipe that arrogant smile off your face. Don't you want to know the real reason I didn't put you back to work?''

''Not particularly. But I'm sure you're dying to tell me.''

''That woman who crashed into your car. Your girlfriend,'' he said mockingly. ''The bosses think she did it on purpose to get friendly with you.''

Max's heart did a thunderclap. ''Now you're the one telling fairy tales.''

''No.'' He took another puff of his cigarette. ''I sent your paperwork through normal channels. Boris did the usual checks and passed the documentation to those higher up.

''Someone recognized Ms. Peris's name. She's the attorney who was unsuccessful in representing one of our members working in the body shop where we pick up the cars. He's now been deported.''

The guy at the jail…Max remembered the night he'd driven her there to meet a client.

''It's possible he gave her names of the drivers in a plea bargain that went wrong, and now she's working on a lead, hoping to get more information out of you.''

''The idea of her running into me to get my attention sounds pretty far-fetched, Nikolai. Even if it were true, you think I would tell her anything I didn't want her to know?''

Max noticed how Nikolai's eyes slid away. ''It doesn't matter what I think. Boris told me to tell you to get rid of her by tonight. The bosses don't want her making trouble.'' He smirked. ''You aren't so cocky now, eh, Kuzmina? You think I have nothing better to do than track you down for the hell of it? You were a fool to get involved with an immigration attorney. It has cost you the beach cities job.''

''Boris said that?''

''The bosses aren't pleased with your choice of lover. They think you need more time to learn from your mistake before you are given heavier responsibilities. So you will continue to drive for me.

''You know, Kuzmina, we've all wondered why you haven't had a woman before now. Then you hand yourself to this one like a gift. The joke is on you. Such an easy target. Soft. That was your unlucky day. With such faulty judgment, you'll never make capper.''

He tossed his cigarette to the ground, then mashed it with his boot before getting back in his car. After he'd driven out of the parking lot, Max reached for his cell phone. Now he was the one trembling as he punched in Gideon's number.

Come on. Pick up.

''Max? I heard Nikolai paid you a visit at the game.''

''Thank God he did! I'm no longer living a nightmare.''

''What do you mean? What's happened?''

"I feel like I've been reborn. Gabriella's not working for the mafia. You were right all along. She's an innocent woman who was in the wrong place at the wrong time."

There was a pregnant pause. "How do you know for sure?"

"Someone sent Nikolai to find me. I've been given orders to eliminate her because she's under suspicion. I'll tell you about it later."

"Well, what do you know. Some dreams do come true. I'm happy for you, Max. It's too bad you have to turn right around and get rid of her."

"I can handle anything now that I know the truth."

"We'll ship her out to her parents today."

"First I have to talk to her."

"Then do it in the van. Just drive around while Karl and I decide how we're going to handle it. I'll get right back to you."

"Thanks, Gideon."

Feeling as though a miracle had occurred, he clicked off and raced toward the pavilion. Gabriella would be outside wondering where he'd gone. When he rounded the corner, he expected to see her standing outside the women's rest room.

There was no sign of her.

He got on his phone and called the guys tailing them. "Calder here. Did Ms. Peris go back to the van?"

"No, sir. After she left the rest room, she walked to the south parking lot. Pretty soon a man in a blue Accord picked her up. We're right behind them."

Max felt as if he'd been kicked in the gut. Something had frightened her before she'd gone into the rest room. If she was so scared, why hadn't she waited for him? It didn't make sense.

"Did she go with this guy willingly?"

"Yes, sir. She waved to him and ran over to his car."

Nothing was making sense. "Give me a description."

"He's Latino. Probably mid-thirties."

His hand tightened on the phone. "Where are they headed?"

"Down near the Old Town area."

"I'm on my way. Keep the line open."

"No problem."

What are you doing, Gabriella? What's going on inside that beautiful head of yours?

GABY LOOKED BACK over her shoulder. "I know we're being followed, Luis. I shouldn't have phoned you. Especially on your day off. But I didn't know where to turn for help."

"I'm glad you thought of me. I'm a cop, Gaby. You needed help."

Luis Aguirre, married and the father of two, was one of the police officers who worked with the court on cases involving illegal immigrants. Over the past months he and Gaby had become friends. But this was asking a favor that had put him in danger.

"This man is high up in the Russian mafia. Not exactly your average criminal."

"A criminal's a criminal. Some network better when they belong to a group whose members look out for each other. We've got men in the department who work with the feds on these kinds of cases. When we arrive at the precinct, we'll find someone who can put you in touch with an expert."

"I can't tell you how grateful I am. When I couldn't reach my uncle, I panicked."

"That's all right. We're almost there."

"If anything happened to you because of me…"

"Hey. I'm not exactly helpless, you know."

"No one can defend themselves in a drive-by shooting."

"That's true. If and when that happens, then I'll know it was my time to go."

"You're amazing."

"In this business if you're not a realist, then you'd better find another job." He turned a corner, then made another right. The driveway wound around and down to an underground parking area restricted to police officers only. "Here we are, safe and sound."

Luis helped her from the car. Together they walked inside and took the elevator to the third floor. He escorted her to the detectives' division and told her to sit down in the front office while he made some inquiries.

Ten minutes later he returned with a cup of coffee for her.

"Thank you, Luis."

"You're welcome. I've been told someone will be here before long to talk to you. Is there anything else I can do for you?"

"No. You've been wonderful. Go back to your family. Just be careful. Please?"

"You sound like my wife every time I leave for work."

"I'm sorry."

He smiled. "Don't apologize. It would worry me if she ever stopped saying it. See you in court." After giving her a hug, he left the room.

In an attempt to pull herself together, she took one of the magazines from her purse and glanced through it while she drank her coffee. Nothing captured her interest. It was impossible to concentrate.

She didn't think she'd ever recover from the shock of seeing Nikolai make contact with Anatoly at the ballpark.

"Ms. Peris?"

Her head shot up as an attractive guy in a crew-neck shirt and jeans swept into the room and shut the door. With dark brown hair and blue eyes, he reminded her some of her brother-in-law, Rick.

"Hi. I'm Detective Gideon Poletti."

She could see that on the official ID fastened to his shirt. After putting the cup and magazine on the end table, she shook his hand. He sat down at the desk opposite her. Nothing lay on it but a phone and a couple of paper clips.

"Lieutenant Aguirre said you've had a real fright."

She nodded.

"Why don't you start at the beginning. Try not to leave out any details. I'm going to tape you so that everything gets on the report when it's typed up." He pulled a recorder from the drawer and flicked a switch.

"For the record, state your name and address. Start

your story from the moment you lost control of your vehicle.''

Once Gaby began talking, it was like opening the spillway of a dam. She realized this was exactly like giving a deposition, only she had always been the one taping someone else's story.

The detective didn't interrupt until she brought Hallie into the conversation. He wanted her to explain what she meant by ''lay nun.'' Gaby obliged, then went on. When she'd told him everything she could think of, he asked another question.

''You say you saw Nikolai at the ballpark today.''

''Yes.''

''Do you think he recognized you?''

''I don't know. I don't think so. The habit I was wearing the first time I saw him covered everything except a part of my face. When I saw him in the bleachers, I was so terrified I turned my head away.''

He sat forward in his chair. ''That was a courageous thing you did for Irina.''

Gaby bit her lip. ''If you could have seen how frightened and worried she was for her mother, you'd have done anything to reassure her, too.''

''I'm talking about all of it. Picking her up at the Dumpster while Nikolai was out looking for her put you in grave danger.''

''At the time I didn't know what she was running away from, so I didn't worry about it. I've been doing volunteer work like that since I practiced law in New York.''

''Too bad there aren't more people like you around.''

"Don't give me any credit. To think that I let Sandra and Juanita come to the park with Anatoly...well, I ought to be shot. If he'd seen Irina while he was waiting for me in the foyer at Girls' Village, I shudder to imagine what might have happened."

"The good news is, everyone's all right. Tell me something—how much do you think Irina knows?"

"A lot."

"Do you think she would tell you?"

"I know she trusts me. But she's still learning English, and I don't know any Russian."

"Do you think she would talk if a translator were provided?"

"Maybe. Up to now she hasn't had a reason to believe in anyone."

"The authorities are aware of the Pedrovas' desperate situation. They have a plan to rescue the mother. But any light Irina could shed on the situation might mean the difference between success and failure."

"I'm sure you're right."

"What I'd like to do is set up a conference call from this room with a translator. You phone Irina. I'll leave it up to you how to get her to cooperate."

"I don't know if she will."

"You've had phenomenal success up to now."

She let out a shuddering breath. "All right. I'll try."

"Good. Use this desk phone." He moved it toward her. "Go ahead and call her. Tell her what we want to do. I'll be right back with the translator, then we'll get started."

Gaby called Girls' Village. She asked to speak to Liz and was relieved when her friend came to the phone. After explaining that she needed to talk to Irina in private, Liz said she'd arrange for them to use the office. No one would disturb her there.

While Gaby held on, she tried to think of the best way to approach Irina.

"Gaby?" the girl cried. "You with uncle now?"

Of course! Without realizing it, Gaby had already prepared Irina. This was one time when she knew she could be forgiven for telling a white lie.

"Yes. I'm back home with Uncle Frank and safe, just like you are at the Village," she said as Detective Poletti came into the room carrying a phone.

Another officer followed. He nodded to Gaby while the detective plugged the phone cord into a wall jack. When they sat down, he punched the speaker button. The tape was still rolling in the recorder.

"He help my mother?"

"Yes. In fact, he's right here with me and wants to talk to you. I'm going to put him on the phone. He doesn't know Russian, so one of his best officers is going to listen in. He will translate when it's necessary. Okay?"

"Okay." With the speaker on, her voice resounded in the room.

Detective Poletti flashed Gaby an approving smile.

"Hello, Irina. My Gaby has told me what a brave young woman you are," he said into the receiver.

"She brave, too," Irina answered back.

The ice had been broken.

"This is very important. Gaby says she'll never

speak to me again if I don't help your mother. So I want to do that. All right?''

"Yes."

"Good. Let's begin with the names of all the men who have come to your apartment. If you can give me first and last names, that is even better. If you know a nickname, I want that, too.'

"Nickname?'

"I'll let the translator take over now. He'll explain."

"Okay."

For the next hour Gaby sat there fascinated as Detective Poletti whispered one question after another to the translator, who then posed the questions to Irina in Russian.

Now that she could respond in her native tongue, she sounded like a different person. So much had been bottled up inside, the information gushed out of her. Sometimes there were long sentences punctuated with tears.

As Gaby listened, she realized Detective Poletti wasn't just any detective. By the kinds of questions he asked, she could tell he'd been working on this case for a long time. He was probably attached to a special task force cooperating with federal agents.

"Irina? You were wonderful! Thank you for being so patient. I assure you that with this information, we are going to free your mother and bring her to you. Okay?"

"Okay," she answered in a trembling voice.

"My niece wants to say goodbye."

"Okay."

Gaby took a deep breath. "Irina?"

"Gaby? I answer okay?"

"Better than okay. You've been so brave. Be brave a little longer. I promise to be in touch with you again real soon. Say hi to Juanita and Sandra for me."

"Okay. Goodbye."

"Goodbye." She hung up the receiver.

The detective stared hard at her. "You do good work, Ms. Peris. Have you ever thought of joining the force? You'd make a crack detective. It must run in your family."

She averted her eyes. "How can you say that when I've been cavorting with a known gangster? Worse, I put two defenseless young mothers at risk. I wouldn't say that qualified for any medals."

"There's no smoother operator in the business than Anatoly Kuzmina."

"You can say that again!" Her face went even hotter than before. "All the time I was falling for his con, I knew deep down something was fishy. All those foreigners in the sleek black Audi running away scared from the scene of the accident."

Detective Poletti nodded. "We've had him under surveillance for a long time. But there's a problem with the mafia. It's hard to pin a wrap on them that will stick."

"Anatoly's so slick he could give Houdini lessons."

He chuckled, then sobered. "I'm sorry. I realize this is no laughing matter, but I have to say I'm not surprised you caught his eye. The man's known for his discriminating taste. He just didn't realize who he was tangling with.''

An image of herself tangled on the couch with Anatoly sent a wave of heat through her body.

''I'm sure there've been thousands of other pathetic females like me who didn't see him coming until it was too late.''

''I think you've got that backward. You crashed into him, remember?''

''Don't remind me.'' Her voice shook. ''He should've stayed in Russia and married that fiancée of his. You know what I think? He must have left Moscow before she could find out what he was up to. Now that he's a millionaire, who probably owns half the Southern California coastline, he decided to send for her.

''He told me he'd ended his engagement, but now I know that's not true. Anatoly figured he'd have a little fun with me until she showed up again. To think I felt so sorry for him, I went to great lengths to get overnight clearance on her visa!''

''Ms. Peris?''

Hearing her name brought Gaby up short. She'd let her temper get away from her again. It was humiliating.

''Sorry. I sort of got wound up.''

''That's completely understandable. But for the record, Anatoly Kuzmina has never been engaged.''

What? ''How do you know that?'' she fired back in shock. ''I've seen her picture.''

''He was born in New York. Later on he moved

from Brighton Beach to work with the Russian mafia.''

Her eyes widened. ''New York?''

''That's right.''

''You mean, all that stuff he told me about living with his grandfather in Moscow was a bunch of baloney?''

He nodded.

Gaby jumped to her feet. ''But I found both their names in the INS immigration data bank!''

''Kuzmina has connections everywhere. It was a simple enough matter to enter bogus profiles.''

''He had me do all that work for nothing?'' she practically shrieked.

''He's an American citizen.''

Will you come and watch me take the oath of citizenship? We will celebrate after. Yes?

''There's more. He operates under other names as need be.''

''Like what?''

''Since you've been so involved with him, you're entitled to know what we know. He comes from Russian and Irish ancestry. Sometimes he uses the name Max Calder.''

''Max— You've got to be kidding! That was the name of my basset hound before he died of old age. My dad used to call him Mad Max.''

''An apt description I'd say.'' He got to his feet. ''Ms. Peris? Because of what we've learned today, we're going to put you on a flight to Atlantic City tonight. It's for your protection. While I make all the arrangements, I'll ask you to wait here. There's a federal agent who's been working undercover on this case from the very beginning. He'll be arriving any minute to talk to you. He's my best friend. We go way back to our days as rookie cops in the NYPD.

"Because of you and the testimony we have on tape from Irina, this case has been cracked wide open. Arrests are forthcoming. He wants to thank you personally for all your help. Without it, we might have been forced to wait another year or longer before we got names of the mafia bosses. More feds and police officers working undercover might have been killed. I wouldn't be at all surprised if you're recommended for a civilian medal of honor for such unprecedented courage and bravery."

Poletti rose to his feet. "You've got guts, Ms. Peris. It's a pleasure to know you."

He shook her hand, then left the room with the tape recorder.

Gaby appreciated all his kind words, but now that she knew she was out of immediate danger, her body bristled with anger, pain, incredulity.

She must have sat there for half an hour going over everything. Damned if her mind didn't replay every second of the time she'd spent with Anatoly. Damned if her body didn't remember the way it felt to lie in his arms and be kissed like she'd never imagined.

Gaby got up and started pacing. How much longer was she going to have to wait here, a victim of memories that would haunt her for the rest of her life?

She had a writer friend who said it was cathartic to get your feelings down on paper. Maybe that's what she'd do. Write a novel to exorcise Anatoly from her consciousness.

One Week in the Life of Gaby Peris, Number One Sucker.

She frowned. That was a lousy title.

Ten Ways to Tell When You're Being Conned Big Time!

Not bad.

Beware of Russians Bringing Flowers!

It was coming....

Beware of Tragic Russians Bearing Roses.

She almost had it.

Pink!

That was what was missing.

Beware of Tragic Russians Bearing Pink Roses.

Suddenly the door opened. "Gabriella? I'm sorry. I had to do it. I hope you can understand and forgive me. I've brought you these."

Pink roses...

CHAPTER FOURTEEN

GABY'S GAZE traveled from the two dozen, long-stemmed pink roses without thorns to the official ID clipped to the pocket of the man's dark gray suit jacket.

There it was in black and white.

A photograph of the living, breathing male standing in front of her. Special Agent Max Calder, decked out in his FBI attire. Conservative suit, white shirt, dark tie.

She couldn't lift her eyes any farther.

"Your friend has already told me everything I need to know."

"I asked him to prepare you."

"He did a good job. Just tell me one thing. Then I'm out of here."

"Gabriella..." He said her name on a ragged whisper.

That didn't wash anymore.

"Why didn't you leave me alone after the crash?"

His chest heaved. "Because I thought the mafia was worried I'd infiltrated their organization. I figured they hired you to either eliminate me or seduce me. So I was forced to check you out."

That brought her head up to his handsome face.

His handsome *deceitful* face. "Well, I certainly made that easy for you to accomplish, didn't I." Her fury was building. "You actually thought I ran into you on purpose?"

Not a muscle in his face twitched. He was cool as ice. "It's not uncommon for the mafia to send a woman. The right one could make a man lose his head and tell things he shouldn't."

"But you didn't lose yours, did you, Mr. Calder. How do you keep your roles straight?"

He put the food and roses on the table. "I know this has come a tremendous sho—"

"Don't."

His face darkened. "We have to talk."

Her chin lifted in defiance. "I don't have to do anything. According to your buddy, the department's grateful to me for what I did. *Sleeping with the Enemy.* I saw the movie. You and I didn't get quite that far, but it was just a breathless moment away from happening."

His jaw hardened.

"No doubt the bugs you planted in every conceivable place have provided free, week-long entertainment for the department's delectation." Ignoring his grim countenance, she charged on. "From their viewpoint, and the world's in general, you're a hero. What you do to fight crime, no man should have to do. From one American citizen to another—" her eyes flashed sparks "—I salute you. But speaking as a widow who's been working her way through the stages of grief and who had finally reached a plateau that was neither pleasure or pain, I damn you for making me feel things again. I won't thank you for that."

"Gabriella—"

"You're very good at what you do. At least, Anatoly Kuzmina was very good at it. He actually made me feel cherished. Ironic, isn't it, considering he's an underworld criminal. That's a feat a lot of men ought to try and emulate if they want the undying love and gratitude of their girlfriends and wives. But most of them don't know how. But my tragic Russian did. He performed everything perfectly, right down to his inability to make English contractions. I found that one of his most endearing traits. Especially the 'r' he emphasized on occasion to remind me of his Russian roots. I doubt even a Shakespearean actor could have carried that off without ever making one tiny mistake. Like I said, he was the best. I'm going to miss him."

"You don't have to miss him, Gabriella. He's right here."

"No. Max Calder is a stranger to me. I don't know him. I don't *want* to know him. I'm sure he's a nice guy, but he has a mistress more possessive and demanding than any woman I've ever met.

"I'm going back home to my family. After Paul died, I thought I can't run to my mother and expect her to make everything fine for me. I told myself, Gaby? You're a big girl now. You've got to grow up and face life the way it is. So I settled here and met Hallie. She was about the greatest thing that ever happened to me."

Gaby fought to hang on to her control. "Yesterday she moved on with her life. Today I'm moving on with mine. I'm a New Jersey girl at heart. Unlike Hallie, I have a big family at home waiting for me. None of them were happy when I told them I was going to live in San Diego. Only Dr. Karsh supported me. He said I should get in touch with myself again, but I wouldn't do that if I returned to old haunts and my comfort zone. Well, those were prophetic words. Thanks to one Anatoly Kuzmina, I got in touch with myself all right. But he was a fantasy. So I'm headed back to my roots where things are as they seem. Good luck winding up this case.''

He stood there without moving.

Her hands knotted into fists. ''You came to say what you had to say to me, Mr. Calder. Now I would appreciate it if you would leave. I gave Detective Poletti my statement.''

''I'm not going anywhere, Gabriella. You've said what you wanted to say. Now it's my turn.''

''I don't want to hear it. If you were a normal man, we would never have crossed each other's paths after the accident.''

''I'm a *very* normal man,'' he fired back. ''The minute you and I made eye contact at your car, the chemistry hit, so don't bother to deny it. In fact, it scared the hell out of me.''

''Oh, Antato—''

Too late she caught herself. If she listened to much more, he'd get to her again. She knew he would. He could talk faster and sweeter than a man had a right to talk.

Before she could think, he was leaning over her with both hands on the armrests. Trapped in the chair, she had no place to go as his mouth descended and he started kissing the daylights out of her.

"No!" she cried when he finally let her up for air.

He straightened, but his breathing was shallow. "*That's* what I wanted to do to you the first time I saw you. Have you any idea what it's like to come face-to-face with a woman you want to make love to when you believe she'll put a knife in your back at the first opportunity?" His eyes blazed. "Don't you know I would have given anything to have met you under different circumstances?"

"It wouldn't have mattered. You would simply have been using one of your other names. Your friend told me you have a number of them in your repertoire."

A bleakness entered his eyes. "You're not going to give me a chance to explain, are you."

"Explain what? I may have been naïve, but I'm not a complete imbecile. You have a job to do. It's not for everybody, but it has to be done. You're the best person I know to do it. I'm living proof of that. So get on with your life, Agent Calder, and let me get on with mine. Don't forget to take the food with you."

He ground his teeth. "I'm not interested."

"You see?" She flashed him a brittle smile. "You're nothing like Anatoly. He loved food. He relished life. He was too good to be true."

The face of the man standing in front of her darkened as if the sun had slipped behind a cloud. Then he was gone.

"GABRIELLA? DARLING?" Her mother poked her head into the bedroom. "Come downstairs and have some lunch. I've made a chicken salad. Come on. You didn't eat breakfast. You should be putting on a few pounds, not losing them."

"I-I'll come down in a little while, Mom. Thank you for being so wonderful to me. I'm sorry I'm such a disaster."

"You've been here three weeks. A vacation is supposed to be relaxing, fun. Maybe it wasn't such a good thing for you to come home, after all. The memories of Paul are still too strong." She turned away. "All right, darling. Come down when you're ready."

Gaby hated deceiving her parents and family. They thought she was still grieving for her husband. But after she'd arrived, she'd gone straight to her uncle's. First he'd put his arms around her. That had produced one of her better sob sessions. Then she'd told him everything. He was an excellent listener. When she finished, he'd told her she would be wise to keep the business about Anatoly to herself.

Dear God. He would always be Anatoly to her.

But there *was* no Anatoly!

Realizing she couldn't go on in this condition, she reached for the phone and called Dr. Karsh. By some miracle he was between patients and could talk to her.

"Gaby, there must be new developments. What can I do for you?"

She started to say something, but another sob welled up in her throat. "I'm sorry, Dr. Karsh." She fought to gain control of her emotions. "This is wasting your time. If I'd known I was going to do this, I wouldn't have called.''

''Sometimes my patients pay me to watch them cry the entire session. We are still talking about the same man, aren't we?''

''Yes,'' she croaked. ''It turns out he's an FBI agent who's been working undercover.''

After a silence, ''I have to tell you I'm relieved.''

''Naturally I am, too. But he's a person who does whatever he has to do to get the job done. That makes him amoral rather than immoral.''

''Gaby, the issue you must face has little to do with morality, and everything to do with the fear of loss and rejection.''

''Rejection?'' She plumped the pillow she'd been lying on.

''You and your husband shared a reciprocal love before he died. You and your Russian also shared a bond. But it turns out he was a fantasy you have to put away because a third man has emerged. Not only does he represent the unknown, he's in a high-risk career. For all of those reasons, you're frightened.''

How Dr. Karsh did it, she would never know. Not in a thousand years.

''What I'd like you to do is review what we talked about before you moved to San Diego. This time you have more to go on.''

''What do you mean?''

''You survived! I remember when you first came to me, you were sure you wouldn't.''

As usual, he helped her push the demons out of the way so she could see her path a little more clearly.

"I'd forgotten that. Thanks for reminding me, Dr. Karsh."

"Anytime."

THE NEWS THAT Yevgeny Babichenko, the man at the head of the Southern California branch of the Russian mafia, had been indicted on numerous counts of mail and insurance fraud had come out in the morning news. By evening, headquarters had turned into one big rocking bash.

Gideon pushed himself away from the desk. "I'm going to grab us some more calzones and Cokes."

Max nodded. "Sounds good."

There had to be at least forty agents and a dozen cops congregated in Karl's office for the celebration. And everyone knew that without the unexpected help from Gabriella and Irina, this party might not have taken place for another year or longer.

No one could be happier over the outcome than Max. Sixteen underbosses, ten cappers and twenty-five drivers had been indicted and would be going to prison with Yevgeny.

For all intents and purposes, the auto-accident ring run by Babichenko no longer existed.

Other men would spring up in his place. But for the moment, every federal agent, insurance agent and cop could take pleasure in a job well done.

Last week the guys had nabbed Nikolai on his way out of Galena's apartment. That gave Max and his backup team the chance to rescue the battered woman. Gideon helped to arrange a reunion between mother and daughter. It was a touching moment neither Max nor his friend would ever forget.

Between their two testimonies, the feds had an airtight case none of the mafia attorneys could beat. The Pedrovas were now in the witness protection program, living in another part of the country. Most of the loose ends had been tied up.

Except that Max was in hell.

"Whew! It's a madhouse in here." Gideon snagged a chair and sat down next to Max again.

"There's talk about a special presentation for Gabriella and the board from Girls' Village for meritorious service to the community."

"That ought to be interesting. They'll have to find her first," Max growled.

"You know where she is."

"If you're trying to tell me there's been some secret ballot nominating me to go get her, you can forget that. The woman wants no part of me."

"Sure she does. But she fell in love with Anatoly. She needs a little time to figure out that he's inside you anytime she wants him to come out."

Max shook his head. "The last few minutes in that room, it was like déjà vu."

"You mean with Lauren."

"Yup."

"Wait a minute. There's a huge difference here. Lauren hated what you did for a living."

"So does Gabriella."

"Are you kidding? She's your counterpart. Could you see Lauren disguising herself as a nun and confronting a mafia gang leader? Just to find out if Galena was still alive?''

Max's eyes closed tightly. ''If I'd known it was Gabriella…''

''It's just as well you didn't. I'm not sure even you could have kept your composure in front of Nikolai.''

''You're right. Lord, Gideon. Gabriella's the most—''

''She's one of a kind. You know in your gut you two were made for each other.''

''I wish she knew that. It's been a month. I've got this awful premonition that she's already practicing law in Atlantic City.''

''Why don't you send her some flowers to test the waters?''

''The way she feels about me, she'd kill the delivery guy.''

''Since Karl's put you on official vacation for a month, I could round up a couple of the guys who are due for some time off. We could kidnap her on the pretext that she isn't safe. You keep her somewhere and do your Anatoly act until she breaks.''

Max liked the sound of that. ''There's just one problem. Uncle Frank.''

Gideon drained his drink. ''You could ask Karl to assign you to a new case in New Jersey. That way you'd be in range.''

''Not if she doesn't want to see me. I'm better off staying at the apartment house and doing deliveries for Karin.''

''Max, I told you I can take my vacation any time

now. We could fly up to Alaska and do some salmon fishing.''

"I wish that sounded good to me, but it doesn't.''

"Then what do you want to do?''

"I want to go over to Gabriella's apartment and start all over again.''

"GABRIELLA?''

"Hi, Uncle Frank.''

"Come on in and shut the door.'

She loved visiting him at his office, but right now her heart was giving her a workout because she'd asked her uncle to see if he could find out any information on Max Calder.

"Sit down, honey. There's not a lot in his file. He was an excellent New York City cop for a couple of years. But as to your question why he left, this newspaper clipping will explain it.''

He handed it to her. As she read the text, her heart plunged to her feet.

Two officers had been suspended pending an investigation of police brutality. Even though the jury came in with a not-guilty verdict, they didn't go back on the beat. Four fellow officers had been called to testify in the case. Two names stood out. Max Calder and Gideon Poletti. Neither of them went back on the NYPD, either. According to the article, several divorces resulted. Max's marriage was one of the casualties.

He'd been married. But it was a long time ago.

"How tragic.''

Her uncle nodded. "It's one of the hazards of the

job. The worst part, I think. But to their credit, they relocated and got on with their lives. This man you love is a hero, honey."

She nodded and kissed his cheek. "Thank you more than you know. I love you, Uncle Frank."

"You sound like you're saying goodbye."

"I am. I'm going back to San Diego."

"Good for you. If all works out, bring him home for Thanksgiving."

"There's nothing I'd like to do more, but I hurt him a lot."

"He'll get over it. Men do."

"That's what I needed to hear. Well, I'd better get going. Daddy's meeting me for lunch before he drives me to the airport. But I had to drop by here first. Take care."

"You, too, honey."

MAX TAPPED KARIN on the shoulder. "What do you want me to do now?"

Her blue eyes widened. "You mean you finished cleaning the back room already?"

"Yes. I like to stay busy."

"I'm worried about you. You haven't heard from Ms. Peris yet?"

"No. After I told her I was working undercover for the FBI, she left California. I think she's moved away for good. When I went by her office, someone else was working there and they did not know anything about her plans."

"I'm sorry, Anatoly. I can't believe this has happened. I had such a strong feeling about the two of you.''

"So did I. I guess we were both wrong.''

"Well, go ahead and start on the afternoon deliveries. You keep the van at the apartment house tonight.''

"Thank you, Karin.''

"Thank *you*. The back room hasn't been cleaned in a year. You couldn't have given me a better present.''

It felt like a year since Gabriella had been gone. Maybe Sandra and Juanita had heard from her. After he'd made his deliveries, he'd go back to the apartment and give them a call. Even though the doctor had expected Sandra to have her baby early, she still hadn't gone into labor.

Gideon kept pressing Max to take a brief vacation, but he had a feeling the girls liked the attention. He couldn't leave San Diego right now. Always in the back of his mind was the hope Gabriella might phone him.

Max had come to the conclusion that a vacation was the last thing he needed right now. Tomorrow he'd drop by Karl's office and ask to be assigned to a new case.

"THAT'S MY CAR?''

"Yes, ma'am. Looks like new, doesn't it?''

"It does!''

Gaby's Sentra had sustained a couple of little knicks and dings before the accident. But with new parts, it looked great. She went over to the desk to pay the initial two hundred dollars, then she got behind the wheel and took off.

It felt good to get in her car again, to have her own wheels. Tomorrow she'd go to work and talk everything over with Anita before checking in with the attorneys working on her cases.

But right now all that could wait.

Finding Max couldn't.

After making a phone call, Gaby discovered the landlady of Max's apartment house hadn't rented Gaby's apartment yet. It was some sort of miracle. According to Mrs. Bills, Anatoly had insisted Gaby was only away on vacation and would be back.

No news could have thrilled her more. At least Gaby chose to look at that good news in a positive light. She didn't feel she deserved a second chance. After the way she'd cut him dead, that would be a tall order. But she'd finally come to her senses and was desperate for him to know she was ready to talk.

When she caught sight of the florist shop, her pulse rate tripled. Maybe Max was inside, but she saw no sign of the van as she pulled into the parking area on the side of the building. The excitement of seeing him made it difficult to breathe.

"Hello. Can I help you?" a salesgirl called out as soon as Gaby stepped inside.

"I hope so. Is Anatoly here?"

"No. I think he's out on delive—"

"Someone wants Anatoly?" a voice resounded from a room behind the counter of the shop. Gaby looked beyond the girl's shoulder to see a buxom woman with pink cheeks and blue eyes come hurrying through the door carrying some exquisite azaleas. She handed them to the girl.

"Good afternoon. I'm Karin Vriend. You must be Gabriella."

"Yes." Gaby smiled. So this was the woman Max was so fond of. "How did you know?"

"I recognized your voice from your phone calls. After the accident, you rang here to see if Anatoly was all right. You called another time, too."

"I'm amazed you remember."

"I have a knack for voices. Did you just get back into town?"

"Yes."

"I thought so. Anatoly's going to be so excited. Ever since you left, he hasn't been his usual self."

The woman's words were music to Gaby's ears.

"As long as he's not here, I'd like to get some flowers."

"Of course. What is the occasion?"

"I want to give them to Anatoly."

The older woman's face broke out in a ray of sunshine. "Now I know why he's been so sad. A woman who would give flowers to a man is very special."

"He once told me he loves growing things. He loves working for you," Gaby confided. "Is he partial to any particular flowers?"

"Oh, yes. Roses are his favorite. When the shipments arrive from South America, he likes to examine them. One time I heard the sound he made when he opened the box of deep-yellow roses for the first time. He turned to me. 'Karin?' he said. 'These are for a man who knows he is loved beyond all others. If a woman ever loved me that much, I would want her to give me roses just like these.' ''

Still smiling, she added, ''Anatoly has very definite ideas about things. White for new mothers. Pink for sweethearts. Red for brides.''

''What about wives?''

Karin's eyes twinkled. ''The pink and yellow hybrids. To represent the blending of two hearts.''

That sounded just like Max. How she loved him!

''Do you have the deep-yellow roses in stock?''

''Oh, yes.''

''Do you have two dozen?''

''I'll check.''

As the salesgirl moved about the showroom arranging azaleas, she kept darting Gaby glances. ''I'm Sylvia. I'm the one Anatoly asked to get some pink roses made up for you last month.''

Oh, dear. The last time Gaby had seen Max, she'd rejected everything he had to offer. What a fool she'd been. So much time wasted.

''They were beautiful.''

''He told me they were for a very special occasion. He said to wish him luck because he was going to need it.''

Don't say any more. You're rubbing salt in my gaping wound. That was the day I found out how much I loved him. And the day I left him.

''Here you are!''

Karin came through the opening with the long floral box. Like the roses Max had given her before, the heads were enormous, their color a breathtaking yellow.

"They're perfect. I can't wait to give these to him. Do me a favor and don't tell him I'm back? I want to surprise him."

"We won't say a word, will we, Sylvia." She put the lid on the box and wrapped a yellow ribbon around it.

Gaby started to get some money out of her wallet, but Karin shook her head.

"You're back. I'm so happy for Anatoly, let this be my treat."

The woman loved him almost as much as Gaby did.

"Thank you, Karin. One day I'll find a way to repay you." She turned to the girl. "It was nice talking to you, Sylvia. See you both again soon."

"Don't be a stranger!" Karin called to her as she left the store.

RECOGNIZING HE WAS in a depression, Max decided that after he'd showered and changed, he'd drive over to Gideon's for a talk. Something had to change.

No matter how bad things were after his world had crashed years ago, with no job, no wife, he still hadn't reached the point where he couldn't face another day.

This was different.

A cold sweat broke out on his body. He pressed on the accelerator and headed for the apartment house using every shortcut he could think of. When he walked inside, he was greeted by Mrs. Bills.

"Good evening, Anatoly."

"How are you, Mrs. Bills?" he responded as he passed the lounge on the way to his room.

"I can't complain."

"That's good."

Polite chitchat was impossible for him at the moment. When he reached his room, he started for the bathroom to take a shower. That's when he heard a knock.

Not now, Mrs. Bills.

The knocking persisted. "Delivery!"

His first thought was that Gideon had said something to Karl. His boss had probably assigned him to a new case and these were his orders.

"Just a minute."

He reached for the wallet he'd thrown on the dresser. After pulling out a couple of dollars, he opened the door.

A beautiful woman in a knockout black dress stood before him. Her shining eyes reflected the rich brown of her hair, which fell in a curve to her shoulders. She wore high heels, so he didn't have to look down as far to see those seductive lips, which could give and give, bringing him mindless rapture.

The little witch had disguised her voice. He didn't notice the money slip from his fingers.

Gabriella.

His heart slammed into his ribs.

"Do you remember me? One fine morning I crashed into your car. It was an accident. You brought me flowers. I told you that I should've been the one to bring them to you. And—"

"And I said, maybe one day you bring some to me, yes?"

Only then did he realize she held a florist's box

from Every Bloomin' Thing in her arms. Karin had
to be out of her mind with joy.

She wasn't the only one.

"These are for you."

"Come in."

He breathed in the scent of strawberries from her
shampoo as she moved past him. Some instinct
warned him not to touch yet. If he did, it might
ruin the moment. Max had a feeling that if he blew
this now, there would be no more miracles.

He closed the door while he watched her set the
box on the bed. His heart missed a beat as she lifted
the flowers from the tissue.

Yellow roses.

Like a woman approaching the wedding altar, she
walked toward him carrying the flowers in a sheaf
over her arm.

She drew closer. He could feel the warmth radiat-
ing from her. "The man who thrust pink roses in my
arms didn't give me a card. It wasn't necessary. I
knew what was written in my Russian's romantic
soul.

"Tonight *I* don't have a card. My heart's too full
to begin to find words." She thrust the flowers in his
arms. "For you, darling, with love."

CHAPTER FIFTEEN

GABRIELLA HAD JUST told him what he needed to hear so he could go on living. She was prepared to love *him*, Max Calder.

He lowered his face in the roses to breathe their delicious perfume. When he lifted his head, he found her lovely face close to his. Those velvety brown eyes were watching, searching. A slight trace of anxiety still lingered. He had plans to fix that.

"Do you want me to call you Gaby?"

"No!" she cried. "The first time you said my name, Gabriella, my bones turned to mush."

Max felt giddy. But before he did what his body was screaming to do, there were things that needed to be said. Maybe it was better not to let go of the roses yet.

"I always had the unfair advantage with you, Gabriella. I knew your every move except the one that brought you to Galena's apartment in the nun's habit. When I heard your voice, I thought I must be hallucinating."

"You were in there?" She was clearly shocked.

"Yes. It's a good thing that for once I didn't know you'd given my backup the slip. But the point is, I probably know more about you than you do. Unfortunately you don't have a clue about me."

"Yes, I do!" she came right back. "At least the important things."

"You mean that I'm an FBI agent."

"No."

He swallowed hard. Oh, hell. "What did Gideon tell you?"

"Only that you were best friends and had worked on the NYPD together. After I flew to New Jersey and calmed down, I asked my uncle Frank to do a little research because I kept wondering why you left New York to come to California. Most guys who root for the Bronx Knights prefer to stay there and watch them win year after year.

"My uncle handed me an article. I learned about the awful police-brutality charge that didn't hold up in court. About the fact that you and Gideon resigned after being forced to testify against those officers.

"An experience that traumatic would be hard on a marriage, especially for a very young couple just starting out in life."

Maybe Max was having a fantastic dream. With every word that fell from her lips, one of his greatest fears was dissolving.

"After Paul died, I learned about the fear of loss. Maybe if your wife had found a psychiatrist as good as mine, you'd still be together today."

Her call to Dr. Karsh. It was all making a wonderful kind of sense.

"Lauren's married to a surgeon from Vermont now."

"You see?" Gabriella's heart shone out of her eyes. "She chose the safer road. Being married to you is a scary proposition, Calder. You're a high-risk guy. Here today. Gone tomorrow."

Gabriella...

"That's the reality I've been dealing with. That's why it took me a whole month to figure it out. But I've got my head on straight now. You know what?"

"What?" he demanded, out of breath with anticipation.

"I like what you do for a living."

With that comment, he reached a state of euphoria.

"I like it a lot. When we're together, it's magic. So here's what we're going to do. We'll make every second count. Enjoy every moment to the fullest. Living on the edge with Anatoly was the most exciting experience I've ever known. I think that's why I got so upset when it all came to a stop at the police station.'

Max had felt exactly the same way. Deep laughter rumbled out of him.

"Tell me about it, sweetheart. I had the time of my life investigating you. The first thing I did was search your apartment before you got home from the hospital after the accident."

Her lips twitched. "The possibility of that occurred to me on the plane back to Atlantic City. Where did you hide the bug?"

"Inside the lampshade."

He could see those incredible wheels turning. A lot of activities went on in her living room. Verbal and physical. Color filled her cheeks.

"I know what brand of toothpaste you use, the difficulty level of your crossword puzzles. I know what day you went to Sea World. I saw the unpaid parking violation you got at Chicano Park. Some day we'll talk about *Brill's Content* together. Your subscription to *AGO* surprised me, because I never found a gun or a concealed-weapons permit."

Her eyes were smiling now. "I hate guns."

He should have known. "I noticed a bunch of oversize T-shirts in your drawer. If you've been sleeping in them, you can forget that."

"I figured since I was moving in here with you, I'd better get a new wardrobe to impress you. So I tossed out most of the clothes I had shipped back to New Jersey. Of course, I did save one of the shirts. In case of an emergency."

Max put the roses on the bed and pulled her into his arms. "What kind would that be?" he whispered, kissing her throat before he worked his way up.

"In case we have an argument."

"I don't follow your logic."

"If I have it on when you come to bed, you'll know we have to talk first."

He was trying to get down to some serious love-making. Maybe if she stopped talking...

"The answer is yes, if you're working up to a marriage proposal. You might as well know now, I don't sleep with men I'm not married to."

His groan resounded in the room.

"If you're going to be angry, blame my mother."

"I'm not angry," he said. "I'm happy. In fact, you've made me the happiest man on the planet."

"That's good, because I have to ask you a question."

"Anything."

Then he stopped her with a kiss. They made magic together. There was no doubt about it.

"This is important," she gasped a few minutes

later. "I know Anatoly didn't go to church. What about Max Calder?"

"Are the Irish Catholic?"

For that he was rewarded with such a passionate response he was willing to answer her questions all night. No sooner did they make it to the bed than his cell phone rang.

"Don't answer it," she begged. "You're still on vacation."

"You think I want to do anything but get you in my arms? But I'm afraid it might be Girls' Village. I promised Sandra she could call me if she needed anything."

"That's one of the reasons I love you so much." She slid her hand in his pocket and handed the phone to him. He clicked on and said hello.

"Mr. Calder? This is the maternity floor at St. Anne's. We have a patient named Sandra from Girls' Village. She's going to be delivering soon and asked if you could come."

"We'll be right there. Thank you for calling."

Gaby had already leaped off the bed. "We'll go in my car. It'll be faster than the van."

He kissed her again before they left the apartment.

"Good night, Anatoly," Mrs. Bills called out as they hurried toward the foyer.

He caught Gabriella around the waist to stop her.

"My fiancée and I want you to be the first to know that we are getting married as soon as possible."

Mrs. Bills's face became wreathed with smiles. "Congratulations."

Gabriella kissed his cheek.

He turned to his landlady. "For the next month we

will stay in both rooms. After that, we are going to move into our dream house on the beach.''

"You've got one of those?" Gabriella asked as they hurried out to her car.

"And a Porsche 911 cabriolet."

"Is all that part of another con?"

"After you become Mrs. Max Calder, I'll tell you everything."

"Let's get married in Las Vegas tonight."

"If we do that, then I'll never know if you married me for my money."

"It's tonight or nothing."

"You drive a hard bargain. Karin's going to be disappointed."

"We both had the wedding of our dreams the first time around. They were a big pain."

Max burst into laughter. Life with Gabriella was going to be something else.

"The thing is, my mother will be a lot more disappointed if I can't tell her I've been a good girl. You've got to help me out here, Calder.

"The way I feel about you, I can just about hold out long enough to see Sandra through her delivery. But I don't know about the trip to Las Vegas." She frowned. "It's a good thing one of us has to drive."

He gave her a long, hungry kiss. "You're right about that, darling."

"I filled the tank with gas. I brought some Dreher's beer with me from Atlantic City. It's on ice in the trunk. And there's chips and dip and Cracker Jack. That ought to help keep us occupied if we start feeling desperate."

If Max felt any more desperate—with love for this woman, that is—he'd probably go up in smoke.

WHILE GABY WAS WIPING Sandra's face with a cold damp cloth, the resident popped into the labor room. He glanced at her and Max. "It's time to take Sandra to the delivery room."

She grabbed Gaby's hand so hard, her nails bit into the palm. "I'm scared."

"Don't be, honey. We're right here. You've got the best doctors in the best hospital."

Her head rolled from side to side. "I don't mean that. What if the wrong people adopt my baby?" Tears gushed out of her eyes. "I don't want it to grow up like I did."

"It won't, honey. Remember what your counselor said? There's a wonderful couple just waiting for your baby."

Max's arm tightened around her shoulders. Ecstasy to agony, she thought. That was how this night was going.

"I know, but I don't know them. I wish you and Max were going to be its parents." Her whole soul implored them with her eyes.

Gaby couldn't talk.

"Remember when we went to the beach?" The orderlies started to move her out of the room on the gurney. "You said you were getting so old you'd probably never have a baby. And then you cried? If you'd met Max sooner, you could have had my baby. Maybe it's still not too late!"

The room echoed with those words as she was wheeled away.

"Oh, Max…"

Gabriella twisted in his arms and began to sob. She tried to stop the flow of tears, but it was impossible. He wrapped her tightly in his arms and rocked her.

"Go ahead and cry it out, Gabriella darling. This has been a long time in coming. You've been Sandra and Juanita's world for months."

"I know. It's the part about volunteering that's so hard."

"It happens in my work, too. You form attachments."

"Sandra doesn't know it, but months ago I met the couple the agency has picked out for her baby. They seem like terrific people. They're in their early thirties. Very stable and financially well off. The adoptive mother couldn't have another baby after her first one. They don't want it to grow up an only child."

"I'm sure it's all going to work out. You've helped her through the worst part. Now the best is going to come."

She sniffed. He handed her some tissues. "You're right. Under the circumstances, I don't dare look at the baby after they take it to the nursery. If I'm going to support Sandra, then I don't need to form another emotional attachment."

"I think that's wise," he murmured into her hair. "It will make it all too real otherwise."

"We'll wait till Juanita's is born. She's decided to keep hers. Then we can h-hold it," she stammered before the tears started gushing again. "I'm sorry, darling. This is no good. I've made a mess of your shirt. Excuse me for a minute while I run to the rest room down the hall. I need to get myself together. Sandra will be looking for us when they wheel her into recovery. I'll be right back."

He kissed her cheek. "I'll walk with you."

When she looked in the bathroom mirror, all she

saw was a blotchy, puffy face. After splashing it with cool water, she applied fresh lipstick, then hurried out to Max.

They walked down to the lounge, but didn't have to wait long to hear the news. Sandra had given birth to a baby girl. Both mother and daughter were doing well. But Sandra had been given a hypodermic for pain.

The nurse told Gaby she could go in to see Sandra for just a minute, then they wanted her to sleep.

"I'll wait here for you. Give her my love." Max's kiss sustained her as she hurried into the recovery room.

As soon as she disappeared, Max pulled out his cell phone.

A groggy voice answered on the fifth ring. "Max? Do you know it's the middle of the night? What's up? If you need to talk, just drive over. I'll go back to sleep till you get here."

"You're off the hook, Gideon. I've got someone else to talk to now."

There was a pause. "Then why...? You mean..."

"Yup. Gabriella. She's come home to me. We're leaving for Las Vegas in a few minutes to get married."

"Whoa."

Max smiled. "It's her idea. She wants to wait until we say our 'I do's,' so she thought we'd better get hitched tonight."

"That's got to be the best news I've heard in a decade. The guys are going to love it. Have you told Karl?"

"No. I'll leave that up to you."

"Where are you right now?"

"St. Anne's. Sandra just had a baby girl. As you know, she's giving her up for adoption. Gabriella's in the recovery room with her now to comfort her."

"That couldn't be easy."

"No. Not when Gabriella's dying to hold the baby and doesn't dare."

After a brief silence, "Are you saying what I think you're saying?"

"Yes. It's more than evident she wants a baby."

"Now isn't that nice, since you wanted to try fatherhood the first time around."

"I can't wait, Gideon! It means I'm going to resign from the bureau."

"Good. This undercover stuff isn't all it's cracked up to be. You can come back to being a San Diego cop with me."

"I like the sound of that. Uh-oh. Here she is. I'll feel her out this weekend."

Gideon chuckled. "I have no doubt of that."

"Cut the bull." But Max was grinning.

"You sound happy, Max. It's about time."

"I NOW PRONOUNCE you husband and wife. You may kiss the bride."

Gaby raised her mouth to her new husband. "Make this fast, darling," she whispered.

His pupils flared in surprise, but he carried out her wishes with dispatch.

As soon as they left the little wedding chapel and reached her car, he pulled her close. The desert sun shone in their eyes.

"What was that all about?"

"I don't like this place."

"It served its purpose. You're my wife now." His deep voice shook with emotion.

She threw her arms around his neck. They kissed long and hard. When he finally let her go, she said, "I don't think I've told you something important yet."

A puzzled look crept over his handsome face.

"What?"

"That I love you!" she cried from the depths of her soul. "You've transformed my life."

He grasped her hand where a new gold wedding band gleamed in the light. "You see?" Suddenly he'd become Anatoly for a moment.

"I told you we were compatible. I love you, Gabriella. You are the most exciting woman I've ever known. Now we are going to be lovers. If you want my baby right away, I will do my best. He will grow up to speak English without a Russian accent."

"He? Don't you mean she?"

"Yes. That is what I meant."

* * * * *

In August, watch for
MY PRIVATE DETECTIVE,
Gideon Poletti's story!

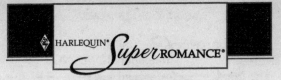

RETURN TO EAST TEXAS

After twenty years, they all come back—
Jed and Emmy and Will—to find the solution to
a long-buried mystery: *Why did their foster
mother, Frannie Granger, die? Who killed her?*
After twenty years, they're looking
for answers...and for love.

Join them in the town of Uncertain, Texas!

Enjoy this captivating trilogy

The Millionaire Horseman by **K.N. Casper,**
on sale in April 2001

Who Is Emerald Monday? by **Roz Denny Fox,**
on sale in May 2001

A Man of His Word by **Eve Gaddy,**
on sale in June 2001

Available wherever Harlequin books are sold.

HARLEQUIN®
Makes any time special ®

HSRRET